THE
MISSING

THE
MISSING

A THRILLER

CHRIS MOONEY

ATRIA BOOKS
New York • London • Toronto • Sydney

ATRIA BOOKS
1230 Avenue of the Americas
New York, NY 10020

ISBN-13: 978-0-7434-6380-5
ISBN-10: 0-7434-6380-3

ATRIA BOOKS is a trademark of Simon & Schuster, Inc.

Manufactured in the United States of America

For Jen,

who showed me how,

and

for Jackson,

who showed me why

Man has places in his heart which do not yet exist, and into them enters suffering in order that they may have existence.

—LEON BLOY

Genuine tragedies are not conflicts between right and wrong. They are conflicts between two rights.

—G. W. F. HEGEL

I

—

THE MAN
FROM THE WOODS
(1984)

CHAPTER 1

Darby McCormick grabbed Melanie by the arm and pulled her into the woods with no trails. Nobody came out this way. The real attraction was behind them, across Route 86, the biking and hiking trails along Salmon Brook Pond.

"Why are you taking me out here?" Melanie asked.

"I told you," Darby said. "It's a surprise."

"Don't worry," Stacey Stephens said. "We'll have you back at the convent in no time."

Twenty minutes later, Darby dropped her backpack on the spot where she and Stacey often came to hang out and smoke—a sloping wall of dirt littered with empty beer cans and cigarette butts.

Not wanting to ruin her new pair of Calvin Klein jeans, Darby tested the ground to make sure it was dry before sitting down. Stacey, of course, just plunked her butt right down in the dirt. There was something inherently grubby about Stacey, with her heavy mascara, hand-me-down jeans and T-shirts always worn a size too tight—nothing was ever quite able to mask the sense of desperation that hovered around her like Pig-Pen's dirt cloud.

Darby had known Melanie since, well, since forever, really, the two of them having grown up on the same street. And while Darby could recall all the events and stories she had shared with Mel, she couldn't for the life of her remember how she had met Stacey, or how the three of them had become such good friends. It was as if Stacey had suddenly appeared one day. She was with them all the time during study hall, at football games and parties. Stacey was fun. She told dirty jokes and knew the popular kids and had gone as far as third base, whereas Mel was a lot like the Hummel figurines Darby's mother collected—precious, fragile things that needed to be stored in a safe place.

Darby unzipped her backpack and handed out the beers.

"What are you doing?" Mel asked.

"Introducing you to Mr. Budweiser," Darby said.

Mel fumbled with the charms on her bracelet. She always did that when she was nervous or scared.

"Come on, Mel, take it. He won't bite."

"No, I mean, why are you doing this?"

"To celebrate your birthday, dumbass," Stacey said, cracking open her beer.

"And for getting your license," Darby said. "Now we have someone to take us to the mall."

"Won't your dad notice these cans are missing?" Mel asked Stacey.

"He has six cases in the downstairs fridge, he won't miss six lousy beers." Stacey lit a cigarette and tossed the pack to Darby. "But if he and my mom came home and caught us drinking, I wouldn't be able to sit or see straight for a week."

Darby held up her can. "Happy Birthday, Mel—and congratulations."

Stacey drained half her beer. Darby took a long sip. Melanie sniffed her beer first. She always smelled anything new before tasting it.

"It tastes like soggy toast," Mel said.

"Keep drinking, it will taste better—and you'll feel better too."

Stacey pointed to what looked like a Mercedes snaking its way up Route 86. "I'm going to be driving one of those someday," she said.

"I can totally see you as a chauffeur," Darby said.

Stacey shot Darby the finger. "No, shitbird, somebody's going to be driving *me* around in one of those 'cause I'm going to marry a rich guy."

"I hate to be the one to break this to you," Darby said, "but there are no rich guys in Belham."

"That's why I'm going to New York City. And the man I marry is not only going to be drop-dead gorgeous, he's going to treat me right. I'm talking dinners at nice restaurants, nice clothes, any kind of car I want—he's even going to have his own plane to fly us to our fabulous beach house in the Caribbean. What about you, Mel? What kind of guy are you going to marry? Or is your heart still set on being a nun?"

"I'm not going to become a nun," Mel said and, as if to prove her point, took a long sip.

"Does that mean you finally gave up the goods to Michael Anka?"

Darby nearly choked on her beer. "You've been making out with *Booger Boy*?"

"He stopped that back in the third grade," Mel said. "He doesn't, you know, pick it anymore."

"Lucky for you," Darby said, and Stacey howled with laughter.

"Come on," Mel said. "He's nice."

"Of course he's nice," Stacey said. "Every guy acts nice in the beginning. Once he gets what he wants from you, he'll treat you like yesterday's garbage."

"That's not true," Darby said, thinking about her father—Big

Red, they used to call him, just like the gum. When her father was alive, he always held open the door for her mother. On Friday nights, her parents would come home from dinner and Big Red would put on one of his Frank Sinatra records and sometimes dance with her mother, check to cheek, as he sang about how those were the days.

"Trust me, Mel, it's all an act," Stacey said. "That's why you've got to stop being so mousy. You keep acting that way, they'll take advantage of you every time, trust me."

Then Stacey started in on another one of her lectures about boys and all the sneaky things they did to trick you into giving them what they wanted. Darby rolled her eyes, leaned back against a tree and looked off in the distance at the big, glowing neon cross overlooking Route 1.

As Darby drank her beer, she watched the traffic zipping across both lanes of Route 1 and thought about the people inside those cars, interesting people with interesting lives off to do interesting things in interesting places. How did you become interesting? Was it something you were born with, like your hair color or your height? Or did God decide for you? Maybe God chose who was interesting and who wasn't, and you just had to learn to live with whatever you were handed.

But the more Darby drank, the stronger and clearer that inner voice of hers grew, the one that told her, with some sense of authority, that she, Darby Alexandra McCormick, was destined for bigger things—maybe not the life of a movie star but something definitely better and a whole lot bigger than her mother's Palmolive world of cleaning, cooking and cutting coupons. Sheila McCormick's biggest thrill was the greedy hunt for bargains on the clearance racks.

"You hear that?" Stacey whispered.

Snap-snap-snap—the sound of dry twigs and branches being crunched by footsteps.

"It's probably a raccoon or something," Darby whispered.

"Not the branches," Stacey said. "The *crying*."

Darby put her beer down and poked her head up over the slope. The sun had gone down a while ago; she saw nothing but the faint outline of tree trunks. The dry, snapping sound grew louder. Was someone really out there?

The snapping and cracking sounds stopped, and then they all heard the woman's voice, faint but clear:

"Please let me go, I swear to God I won't tell anyone what you did."

CHAPTER 2

"Take my purse," the woman in the woods said. "There's three hundred dollars in there. I can get you more money, if that's what you want."

Darby grabbed Stacey by the arm and pulled her back behind the slope. Melanie huddled up against them.

"This is probably just a mugging, but he might have a knife, maybe even a gun," Darby whispered. "She'll hand over her purse, and then he'll run away and it will be over. So let's just keep quiet."

Both Mel and Stacey nodded.

"You don't have to do this," the woman said.

As scary as it was, Darby knew she had to look over the slope again. When the police came with their questions, she wanted to be able to recall everything she saw—every word, every sound.

Heart beating faster, she poked her head back over the slope and looked around the dark woods. Blades of grass and dead leaves brushed against the tip of her nose.

The woman started crying. "Please. Please don't."

The mugger whispered something Darby couldn't hear. *They're so close,* she thought.

Stacey had decided to take a look, too. She moved closer to Darby.

"What's going on?" Stacey whispered.

"I don't know," Darby said.

A car was heading up Route 86. The headlights formed a pair of eerie white circles that were now sliding and bouncing across the tree trunks and the sloping ground full of rocks, leaves, and downed tree limbs and branches. Darby heard music—Van Halen's "Jump," David Lee Roth's voice growing louder along with the worrisome voice in her head telling her to look away, look away *now*. God knows she wanted to, but some other part of her brain had taken control, and Darby didn't look away as the head-lights washed over her, David Lee Roth's booming voice singing to go ahead and jump, and she saw a woman dressed in jeans and a gray T-shirt kneeling by a tree, her face a deep, dark red, eyes wide and fingers desperately clawing at the rope tied around her throat.

Stacey jumped to her feet and knocked Darby backward against the dirt. A rock smacked the side of her head hard enough that she saw stars. Darby heard Stacey pushing her way past branches, and when she rolled onto her side, she saw Mel running away.

Next came the dry crack of branches and twigs snapping—the mugger was coming toward them. Darby scrambled to her feet and ran.

Darby caught up with Stacey and Mel at the corner of East Dun-stable. The closest pay phones were the ones around the corner from Buzzy's, the town's popular convenience store, pizzeria and sub shop. They ran the rest of the way without talking.

It seemed to take forever to get there. Sweating and out of breath, Darby picked up the phone to dial 911 when Stacey slammed down the receiver.

"We can't call," Stacey said.

"Have you lost your goddamn mind?" Darby shot back. Behind her fear was a severe and growing anger directed at Stacey. It shouldn't have come as a shock that Stacey had pushed her aside and run off. Stacey always put herself first—like last month, when the three of them made plans to go to the movies only to have Stacey cancel at the last minute because Christina Patrick called and invited her to some party. Stacey was *always* doing stuff like that.

"We were drinking, Darby."

"So we won't tell them."

"They'll smell the beer on our breath—and you can forget about chewing mint gum or brushing your teeth or gargling with mouthwash, because none of that works."

"I'll risk it," Darby said, and tried to yank Stacey's hand away from the receiver.

Stacey wouldn't let go. "The woman's dead, Darby."

"You don't know that."

"I saw the same thing you did—"

"No, you didn't, Stacey, you couldn't have seen the same thing I did because you ran away. You pushed me aside, remember?"

"It was an accident. I swear I didn't mean—"

"Right. As usual, Stacey, the only person you care about is yourself." Darby ripped Stacey's hand away and dialed 911.

"All you're going to get is punished, Darby. Maybe you won't get to go down the Cape with Mel, but your father won't—" Stacey stopped herself. She was crying now. "You don't know what goes in my house. None of you do."

The operator came on the line: "Nine-one-one, what is the nature of your emergency?"

Darby gave the operator her name and described what had

happened. Stacey ran behind one of the Dumpsters. Mel stared down at the hill where they used to go sledding as kids, her fingers touching each of the charms on her bracelet.

An hour later, Darby was walking back through the woods with a detective.

His name was Paul Riggers. She had met him at her father's funeral. Riggers had big white teeth and reminded Darby of Larry, the slimy next-door neighbor from *Three's Company*.

"There's nothing here," Riggers said. "You kids probably scared him off."

He stopped walking and shined his flashlight on a blue L.L. Bean backpack. It was unzipped all the way and she could see the three Budweiser cans lying inside the bottom.

"I take it that's yours."

Darby nodded as her stomach flipped and squeezed and flipped again, as if it were trying to tear itself away to find a place to hide.

Her wallet had been removed from her backpack. It was now lying on the ground, along with her library card. The money was gone, and her learner's permit, printed with her name and address, was missing.

CHAPTER 3

Darby's mother was waiting for her at the police station. After Darby finished giving her statement to the police, Sheila had a private talk with Detective Riggers for about half an hour and then drove Darby home.

Her mother didn't talk. Darby didn't get the sense Sheila was mad, though. When her mother got this quiet, generally she was just deep in thought. Or maybe she was just tired, having to pull double shifts at the hospital since Big Red died last year.

"Detective Riggers told me what happened," Sheila said, her voice dry and raspy. "Calling nine-one-one—that was the right thing to do."

"I'm sorry they had to call you at work," Darby said. "And I'm sorry for the drinking."

Sheila put her hand on Darby's leg and gave it a squeeze—her mother's signal to let Darby know everything was okay between them.

"Can I give you a piece of advice about Stacey?"

"Sure," Darby said. She had an idea what her mother was going to say.

"People like Stacey don't make good friends. And if you hang out with them long enough, at some point they'll end up dragging you down with them."

Her mother was right. Stacey wasn't a friend; she was dead weight. Darby had learned the lesson the hard way, but the lesson was learned. As far as Stacey was concerned, good riddance.

"Mom, the woman I saw . . . Do you think she got up and ran away?"

"That's what Detective Riggers thinks."

Please God, please let him be right, Darby said to herself.

"I'm glad you're okay." Sheila squeezed Darby's leg again, only this time it felt harder, the way you grip something to keep from falling.

Two days later, on a Monday afternoon, Darby came home from school and found a black sedan with tinted windows parked in her driveway.

The door opened and out stepped a tall man wearing a black suit and a stylish red tie. Darby spotted the slight bulge of a sidearm under his suit jacket.

"You must be Darby. My name is Evan Manning. I'm a special agent with the Federal Bureau of Investigation." He showed his badge. He was tanned and handsome, like a TV cop. "Detective Riggers told me about what you and your friends saw in the woods."

Darby could barely get the words out. "You found the woman?"

"No, not yet. We still don't know who she is. That's part of the reason why I'm here. I'm hoping you can help me identify her. Would you mind taking a look at some pictures?"

She took the folder and, with a sense of falling, opened it to the first page.

The word MISSING ran across the top sheet. Darby looked at a Xeroxed picture of a woman wearing a nice string of pearls over a pink cardigan sweater. Her name was Tara Hardy. She lived in Peabody. According to the information printed under her picture, she was last seen leaving a Boston nightclub on the night of February 25.

The woman in the second picture, Samantha Kent, was from Chelsea. She had failed to report to her shift at the Route 1 IHOP on March 15. Samantha Kent had a painfully toothy smile and was the same age as Tara Hardy. Only Samantha was heavily into tattoos. She had six of them, and while Darby couldn't see any of them in the picture, the description and location of each of the tattoos were listed.

Both women, Darby sensed, carried the same desperate quality as Stacey. You could see it in their eyes, that bottomless need for attention and love. Both women had blond hair—just like the woman from the woods.

"It might be Samantha Kent," Darby said. "No, wait, it can't be her."

"Why not?"

"Because it says here she's been missing for over a month."

"Look at her face."

Darby studied the picture for a moment. "The woman I saw, her face was thin and her hair was real long," she said. "Samantha Kent's face is round and she has short hair."

"But it looks like her."

"Kind of." Darby handed the folder back and rubbed her hands on her jeans. "What happened to her?"

"We don't know." Manning gave her a business card. "If you remember anything else, even the smallest detail, you can call me at this number," he said. "It was nice meeting you, Darby."

Her nightmares didn't stop until about a month later. During the day, Darby rarely thought about what happened in the woods unless she happened to bump into Stacey. Avoiding her was easy enough—too easy, really. It just went to prove how they'd never really been true friends.

"Stacey said she was sorry," Mel said. "Why can't we go back to being friends?"

Darby shut her locker. "You want to be friends with her, that's your business. But I'm done with her."

One thing Darby had in common with her mother was a love of reading. Sometimes on Saturday mornings she'd join Sheila on her yard sale trips, and while her mother was busy haggling over the price of another stupid knickknack, Darby would be on the prowl for cheapo paperbacks.

Her latest find was a book called *Carrie*. It was the cover that had grabbed her attention: a girl's head floating above a town in flames. How cool was that? Darby lay on her bed, deep in the part where Carrie was going to the prom (only the popular kids were going to play a sick, cruel joke on her) when the living room stereo kicked on and Frank Sinatra's booming voice started singing "Come Fly with Me." Sheila was home.

Darby glanced over at the clock on her nightstand. It was almost eight-thirty. Her mother wasn't supposed to be home until eleven or so. Sheila must have knocked off work early.

What if it isn't your mother? Darby thought. *What if the man from the woods is downstairs?*

No. This was the writer's fault; that stupid Stephen King had gotten her imagination all worked up. Her mother was downstairs, not the man from the woods, and Darby could prove it by simply taking a walk down the hallway to her mother's bedroom and looking out the windows at the driveway where Sheila's car would be parked.

Darby dog-eared her page and walked into the hallway. She leaned over the banister and looked into the foyer.

One dim light was on, and it was coming from the living room—probably the banker's lamp on the table next to the stereo. The kitchen lights were off. Had she turned them off on her return trip upstairs? Darby couldn't remember. Sheila had this thing about leaving lights on in empty rooms, always made it a point to say she wasn't working all these extra hours to put Lester Lightbulb through college—

A black-gloved hand gripped the downstairs banister.

CHAPTER 4

Darby jerked away from the railing, her heart hammering so hard and fast she felt dizzy.

Instinct took over, and with it came an idea. Her boom box radio was set on top of her bureau, right next to the door. She turned it on, clicked her bedroom door shut and slipped inside the spare bedroom across the hall as a shadow on the stairwell grew larger.

The man from the woods was coming up the stairs.

Darby wiggled underneath the bed, over boxes of shoes and stacks of old decorating magazines. Through the three-inch gap between the dust ruffle and the carpet she saw a pair of work boots come to a stop outside her bedroom door.

Please God, let him think I'm in there listening to my music. If he went in there, she could make a run for the stairs—no, not the stairs, her mother's bedroom. The nearest phone was in her mother's bedroom. She could lock the door and call the police.

The man from the woods stood in the hallway, deciding what to do.

Come on, go into my bedroom.

The man from the woods stepped inside the spare bedroom. Darby watched in horror as the boots came closer . . . closer . . . oh

Jesus no, he was standing only a few inches from her face, the boots so close she could see and smell the grease stains.

Darby started to tremble. *He knows. He knows I'm hiding under the bed—*

A crude mask of stitched-together, flesh-colored strips of Ace bandages fell to the floor.

The man from the woods picked up the mask. A moment later, he walked out of the bedroom and back into the hallway. Her bedroom door burst open to bright light and dance music.

Darby scrambled from underneath the bed and ran into the hallway. The man from the woods was standing in her room, looking for her. She ran into her mother's bedroom and swung the bedroom door shut, catching a glimpse of the man chasing after her, a real-life Michael Myers dressed in greasy blue coveralls, his face covered by the mask of Ace bandages, his eyes and mouth hidden behind strips of black cloth.

She locked the door and then grabbed the phone from the nightstand. The man from the woods kicked the door, rattling it against the frame. Her hand was shaking as she dialed 911.

There was no dial tone.

Thump as he kicked the door. Darby tried the phone again. Still nothing.

Thump. The phone *had* to work, there was no reason why it shouldn't work. *Thump.* She flipped over the phone, and in the dull white light coming from the outside street lamps Darby saw the plug, nice and snug, in the back of the phone. *Thump.*

Darby jammed her finger on the receiver again and again and still no dial tone and *THUMP* and *CRACK* as the one of the door panels split open.

A jagged line ran down the panel, a foot or so above the doorknob. *THUMP* and *CRACK* and the wood split wider as a black-gloved hand reached through the hole in the door.

Sheila's blue plastic toolbox, the one she used for her small projects around the house, sat on the edge of the TV stand. Inside the toolbox full of old plastic medicine bottles holding tacks, small nails and hooks, Darby found her father's hammer, the big Stanley he had used around the house.

The hand was on the doorknob. Darby swung the hammer and hit him on the arm.

The man from the woods screamed—an ungodly howl of pain Darby had never heard another human being make. She went to hit him again and missed. He yanked his hand back through the hole.

The doorbell rang.

She dropped the hammer and opened the window. The storm window was still down. As she worked on opening it, she remembered her mother's words about what to do when you were in trouble: Never yell for help. Nobody comes running when someone yells for help, but everyone comes when someone yells fire.

Screaming coming from inside the house. The song ended and Darby heard a woman crying hysterically.

"DARBY!"

Melanie's voice, coming from the foyer.

Darby stared at the hole in the door, sweat running into her eyes as Frank Sinatra sang "Luck Be a Lady Tonight."

"He just wants to talk," Melanie said. "If you come downstairs, he promised to let me go."

Darby didn't move.

"I want to go home," Melanie said. "I want to see my mother."

Darby couldn't turn the doorknob.

Mel was sobbing. "Please. He has a knife."

Slowly, Darby opened the door and, crouching low, looked through the banister and into the foyer.

A knife was pressed against Melanie's cheek. Darby couldn't see the man from the woods; he was hiding around the corner, against the wall. She saw Mel's terrified face and the way her body shook as she sobbed and struggled to breathe around the arm clutched tightly around her throat.

The man from the woods moved Mel closer to the bottom steps. He whispered something in her ear.

"He just wants to talk." Black tears from Melanie's mascara ran down her cheeks. "Come down here and talk to him and he won't hurt me."

Darby didn't move, couldn't move.

The man from the woods cut Mel's cheek. She screamed. Darby moved down the steps.

Drops of blood, bright and red, ran down the wall near the kitchen. Darby froze.

Melanie screamed, *"He's cutting me!"*

Darby took another step, her eyes on the wall, and saw Stacey Stephens lying on the kitchen floor, blood spurting between the fingers clutched against her throat.

Darby ran back up the stairs. Melanie screamed again as the man from the woods cut her.

Darby slammed the bedroom door shut and opened the window facing the driveway. The branches from the hedges tore up her bare legs and the soles of her feet something awful. She limped her way to her next-door neighbor's house. When Mrs. Oberman finally answered the door, she took one look at Darby and immediately ran to her kitchen to call the police.

⋆   ⋆   ⋆

Darby had overheard two things: the phone lines to the house had been cut, and the spare key her mother kept under the rock in the garden was missing. The key had been there a little over two weeks ago. She had last used it after locking herself out of the house and definitely remembered putting it back.

To know about the hidden key, the man from the woods must have been casing the house for some time. Nobody would come right out and say it, but Darby knew it was true.

She sat in the back of the ambulance parked in Mrs. Oberman's driveway. The back doors were open, and she could see the shocked and curious faces of her neighbors in the revolving blue and white lights from the police cruisers. Policemen armed with flashlights were searching her backyard and the wooded area separating Richardson Road from the nicer homes on Boynton Avenue.

All the lights in her house were on. Through the downstairs windows Darby could see part of the foyer, the blood on the pale yellow walls. Stacey's blood. Stacey was still lying inside the house because she was dead. Police were taking pictures of her body. Stacey Stephens was dead and Melanie was missing.

"Don't worry, Darbs, your mom will be here any minute." The deep but calming voice belonged to the patrolman standing next to the ambulance door. This huge intimidating bear of a man was a close friend of her father's named George Dazkevich. Everyone called him Buster. Buster had helped out around the house after her father died, taking her to movies and to the mall. His presence helped calm her.

"Have you found Mel yet?"

"We're working on it, kiddo. Now try to relax, okay? Can I bring you something? Some water? A Coke?"

Darby shook her head and looked at the car parked against the curb, a beat-up Plymouth Valiant. Melanie's car.

Melanie's going to be okay. The man from the woods was in a lot of pain. I'm pretty sure I broke his hand. Melanie would have figured that out and would have fought back and escaped. She's probably hiding someplace in the woods. They're going to find her.

Sheila arrived just as the EMT finished stitching up a particularly nasty gash on the inside of Darby's thigh. The blood drained from her mother's face as she stared down at the Frankenstein mess of stitches on Darby's legs and feet.

"Tell me what happened."

Darby fought the urge to cry. She needed to say strong. Brave. She sucked in air and then broke down in tears, hating herself for it, for being small and scared and weak.

CHAPTER 5

The next morning, Melanie was still missing.

With the house now a crime scene, the police moved Darby and Sheila to the Sunset Motel on Route 1 in Saugus. The room Darby shared with her mother had shag carpeting and a hard mattress with coarse sheets. Everything smelled of cigarette smoke and desperation.

For the next week, Darby looked through binders packed with mug shots. The police were hoping a face might spark something. It never did. They tried hypnosis more than once and finally gave up when detectives were told she wasn't a "willing subject."

Darby went to bed each night with her head stuffed with mug-shot faces and unanswered questions. The police wouldn't tell her anything beyond variations of "everyone's working real hard."

Both the newspapers and TV had talked about the vicious stabbing of Stacey Stephens and the frantic search efforts for Melanie Cruz, who had been abducted from the house of a friend. The friend was a minor and her name couldn't be released, but an "unnamed source close to the investigation" stated this "friend" was believed to be the intended target. The only piece of evidence ever mentioned was a chloroform-soaked rag the police found in the woods behind the house.

By the end of the week, with no new information coming in on the case, reporters started focusing on Stacey's and Melanie's parents. Darby found she couldn't read their tearful pleas, couldn't face the anguished looks captured in the pictures and video footage.

One evening, after Sheila had left for work, the FBI agent, Evan Manning, stopped by with a pizza and two cans of Coke. They ate on a rickety table near the pool. They had a lovely view of the liquor store and trailer park.

"How are you holding up?" he asked.

Darby shrugged. The droning sound of traffic and the smell of exhaust filled the warm air.

"If you don't want to talk, that's fine," Manning said. "I'm not here to pump you with questions."

Darby thought about telling him about school, how everyone, including most of her teachers, stared at her as though she had stepped off a UFO. Even her friends were treating her differently, talking to her in cautious tones, the way you'd speak to someone afflicted with some rare, terminal disease. Suddenly, she was interesting.

Only she didn't want to be interesting. She wanted to go back to being her old boring self, back to being a normal teenager looking forward to a long summer of reading books and pool parties and hanging out with Mel down at the Cape.

"I want to help find Mel," Darby said. The way she figured it, if she helped find Melanie, then all would be forgiven, and people would stop staring at her as though what had happened to Mel and Stacey were her fault.

Manning placed a hand on her arm, squeezing it. "I'll do everything in my power to help find Melanie. And I'm going to find the man who did this to you. That's a promise."

After Manning left, Darby headed to the vending machine for

another Coke. She saw the pay phone outside the office door. The words she had practiced saying over and over again this past week were now burning to get out.

She dropped a quarter into the pay phone.

"Hello?" Mrs. Cruz said.

I'm sorry for everything that's happened. I'm sorry for Mel and I'm sorry for what you're going through I'm sorry I'm sorry I'm sorry.

As hard as she tried, Darby couldn't get the words out. They were stuck in her throat, lodged in there like hot stones.

"Mel, is that you?" Mrs. Cruz said. "Are you okay? Tell me you're okay."

Mrs. Cruz's hope, bright and so alive, made Darby hang up and want to run someplace far away, someplace where nobody, not even her own mother, would ever find her.

Sheila couldn't afford the motel anymore. The house still hadn't been released by the police, and when it was, there would be cleanup and repairs. Darby was going to spend the summer at her aunt and uncle's beach house in Maine. Sheila was going to stay in town with a coworker. She would drive to Maine on her days off.

Darby went with her mother to a grocery store in Saugus to stock up on food for the long drive. Taped inside the grocery store window, right near the front door so no one would miss it, was a poster board holding a blown-up picture of Melanie. It was yellowed from the sun. The word MISSING was written in big, bold red letters above her smiling face. A reward for $25,000 was listed, along with a toll-free phone number.

Sheila was rummaging through her coupon folder when Darby turned the corner near the cash registers and spotted Mrs.

Cruz talking to the store owner. He took the rolled-up poster board from Melanie's mother and walked toward the front window.

Mrs. Cruz saw her. Their eyes locked, and Darby felt the full weight of Helena Cruz's stare, only this stare carried something that made Darby want to duck and run: hatred, cold and hard and fixed on her. If given the chance, she was sure Mrs. Cruz would, without a moment's hesitation, trade Darby's life for Melanie's.

Sheila slipped her hand around her daughter's shoulder, and Mrs. Cruz's stare withered and died.

The store owner handed Mrs. Cruz the old poster board with the sun-faded picture of her daughter. Melanie's mother walked away, taking small, deliberate steps as though the floor were a thin sheet of ice that might break. Darby recognized that walk. Her mother had moved the same way when she had walked to Big Red's casket that final time to say good-bye.

Maybe there was still time. Maybe Evan Manning would still find Melanie alive. Maybe he would find the man from the woods and kill him. At the end of the movie, the hero always killed the monster. If Special Agent Manning found Mel and brought her home, life would be okay—definitely not the way it was before the monster had arrived, and certainly not back to being normal, but okay.

On Saturday morning, the start of Labor Day weekend, Darby woke up early to help her uncle dig the fire pit for the annual lobster bake. By noon, they were sweating. Uncle Ron put his shovel in the sand and said he was heading up to the house to grab a couple of sodas.

Darby kept digging. As she breathed in the cool, salty air blowing off the water, she kept thinking of Melanie, wondering about the kind of air she was breathing right now, if she was still breathing at all.

Three more women had disappeared back home. Darby had found out two weeks ago when Uncle Ron and Aunt Barb had taken her to breakfast. While they were waiting for a table, Darby had spotted a copy of the *Boston Globe* lying on a table. The phrase "Summer of Fear" was stretched across the top page above the smiling faces of five women and a teenage girl in braces.

Darby recognized Melanie's picture right away, along with the pictures of the first two women, Tara Hardy and Samantha Kent. Darby had held the exact same photographs in her own hands.

The information on Hardy and Kent was pretty much a rehash of everything she already knew. The article's main focus seemed to be on the three women who had disappeared *after* Melanie— Pamela Driscol, twenty-three, from Charlestown, going to school nights for her nursing degree and last seen walking through a campus parking lot; Lucinda Billingham, twenty-one, from Lynn, a single mother who went out for cigarettes and was never seen again; and Debbie Kessler, also twenty-one, a Boston secretary who went out for drinks one night after work and never made it home.

The police handling each of these investigations wouldn't comment on what evidence linked these women together, but they did confirm that a task force had been established headed up by a special agent who belonged to the FBI's newly formed unit called Behavioral Science. The agents who worked in this group, the article said, were specialists in studying the criminal mind, especially those who were serial murderers.

"Hello, Darby."

Not Uncle Ron but Evan Manning, holding out a can of Coke.

She caught the sad, almost empty look in his eyes and knew, right then, what he was here to say.

She dropped the shovel and ran.

"Darby."

She kept running. If she didn't hear him say the words, then they couldn't come true.

Manning caught up with her near the water. The first time she broke free of him. The second time he grabbed her by the arm and spun her around, hard.

"We caught him, Darby. It's over. He can't hurt you."

"Where's Melanie?"

"Let's go back to the house."

"Tell me what happened!" Darby was shocked by the sudden anger in her voice. She tried to pull it back, but the fear was already humming through her limbs, telling her to go ahead and scream it out. *"I don't want to wait anymore, I'm sick of waiting."*

"The man's name was Victor Grady," Manning said. "He was an auto mechanic and he abducted women."

"Why?"

"I don't know. Grady died before we got a chance to speak with him."

"You killed him?"

"He killed himself. I don't know what happened to Mel or any of the other women. Chances are, we'll never know. I wish I had a better answer for you. I'm sorry."

Darby opened her mouth to speak, but no sound came out.

"Come on," Evan Manning said. "Let's go back to the house."

"She wanted to be a singer," Darby said. "For her birthday, her grandfather bought her a tape recorder and one day Mel came to me in tears 'cause she had never heard her voice on tape and thought she sounded ugly. She came to me because I knew she wanted to be a singer. Nobody knew it but me. We had a lot of secrets like that."

The FBI agent nodded, urging her along in that quiet, confident way he had.

"She loved Froot Loops but hated the lemon ones and always picked them out. She was always this real picky eater—she couldn't have her food touching, thought it was gross. She had this really great sense of humor. She was really quiet, but she could—there were all these times when she'd say something, and it would get me laughing so hard my stomach would hurt. She was . . . Mel was just a really great person."

Darby wanted to keep talking, wanted to find a way to use her words to build a bridge that would take Special Agent Manning back through time and show him how Melanie was more than chunks of newsprint and two-minute sound bites. She wanted to keep talking until Melanie's name carried the same weight in the air as it did in her heart.

"I shouldn't have left her there all alone," Darby said, and the tears came again, harder this time, and she wished her father was standing here with her right now—wished he hadn't stopped to help that driver, a schizophrenic man who was on early probation after serving a three-year jail sentence for trying to kill a cop. She wished she could have her father back with her for one minute, just one lousy minute, so she could say how much she still missed him and loved him. If her father were here, Darby could tell him everything she was thinking and feeling. Her father would understand. And maybe, just maybe, he would carry her words back with him and share them with Stacey and Melanie, wherever they were now.

II

—

LITTLE GIRL LOST

(2007)

CHAPTER 6

Carol Cranmore lay back on her bed, panting, as Tony collapsed on top of her.

"Jesus," he said.

"I know."

She ran her hands up and down the small of his back. His sweat smelled of cologne and beer and the faint but sweet and pleasant odor of the marijuana they had smoked out on the back porch. Tony was right. Making love when you were high was *unbelievable*. She started giggling.

Tony popped his head up. "What?"

"Nothing. I love you."

He kissed her cheek, about to push himself up when she wrapped her legs around the small of the back. "No, not yet," she said. "I just want to lie like this for awhile, okay?"

"Okay."

Tony kissed her again, harder this time, and lay back on top of her. Carol's mind ran to those ridiculously sappy love songs she heard on *American Idol*. Maybe those lame-o songs were about this feeling she had with Tony, this perfect feeling of coming together and forming one person that could take on the world. Maybe all the crap and disappointment you went through on a daily basis—

especially if you lived here, in the armpit of the universe—Belham, Massachusetts—maybe it made moments like she had just shared with Tony all the more special.

Smiling, she listened to the rain drumming against the roof and drifted off to sleep.

Carol Cranmore woke up from a dream where she had been named prom queen—totally ridiculous because she had no interest in proms. Both she and Tony had boycotted this year's junior prom and went to dinner and the movies instead.

Still, there was one aspect of the dream she liked, the part where she felt accepted by everyone gathered around the front stage, clapping for her. And she might have stayed there, wrapped in that warm memory if it wasn't for the noise that sounded like a car backfiring. She reached across the dark for Tony.

The other side of the bed was warm but empty. Had he gone home?

Carol had told him he could stay over. Her mother was heading over to her new boyfriend's house in Walpole after her shift at the paper factory. Walpole was a closer ride to her job in Needham, so that meant Carol had the house to herself to do whatever she wanted, and what she wanted was for Tony to spend the night. He had called his mother and told her he was crashing at a friend's house.

The candles were still burning on her nightstand. Carol sat up. It was almost two a.m.

Tony's clothes were still on the floor. He was probably using the bathroom.

Carol had a case of the munchies from the pot. A bag of Fritos and a Mountain Dew would hit the spot.

She pulled back the sheet and stood naked, a tall girl for her age, her body long and lean, developing curves in the right places.

She didn't put any clothes on, didn't mind being naked around Tony, who kept telling her how beautiful she was. He couldn't keep his hands off her. She opened the bedroom door, the night-light from the bathroom cutting the darkness in the hallway.

"Tony, you mind making a run to the 7-Eleven?"

He didn't answer. She peeked inside the bathroom and saw that he wasn't in there.

Maybe he was using the downstairs bathroom for some privacy.

There were some Ritz crackers in the kitchen cabinet. She could snack on those until Tony was done in the bathroom.

A cold draft was coming from the hallway. She put on her underwear and Tony's white shirt. Walking made her feel dizzy. Several times she had to reach out and touch the wall.

The kitchen door was wide open, as was the door leading to the back porch. Tony hadn't left; his car keys and wallet were inside his Red Sox baseball hat sitting on top of the counter. *Probably went outside for a smoke,* she thought. Her mother didn't have many rules, but she was dead set against smoking in the house, hated the way it stunk up the furniture.

Carol poked her head out into the small hallway and saw the rain pounding the street, the sound hard and unrelenting, a steady throbbing hum in her ears. Parked in front of Tony's car was a black van that had seen better days. One of the van's back doors was wide open, swinging in the driving wind that was blowing curtains of rain across the street. She thought she heard the creak of the door's hinges, knowing she was imagining it. Good Lord, she was high.

The van probably belonged to her next-door neighbor's son, Peter Lombardo, who had a habit of disappearing for months at a stretch only to return home, miserable and broke, then staying long enough to save up enough money to disappear again. Peter must have forgotten to lock up, probably in a rush to get inside, out of the rain.

Carol was thinking about going outside and shutting the doors—there was a raincoat in the front door closet—when she heard Tony step up behind her. He grabbed her hard around the waist and lifted her up. Carol giggled as she turned to kiss him.

A hand came up and clamped a foul-smelling cloth over her mouth.

Carol turned away, clawing at the man's wrist as he tried to carry her back inside the kitchen. Her foot hit the wall and, using it as leverage, she kicked the man backward against the doorjamb. He let her go. She dropped to the floor.

Dizzy, she felt dizzy because there was something on the rag. She could barely move, but she saw the rag on the floor. The man reached into his pocket and came back with a small envelope and a plastic bottle.

He dropped a tiny piece of string or something on the floor, near the kitchen door, and then took the plastic bottle and squirted some cold red liquid onto her fingers. *It looks like blood,* she thought as he took her hand and used it to smear the red liquid across the hallway wall.

The man picked up the rag. Carol drew in a breath to scream, sucked in chloroform and heard a crack of thunder rumble and die.

CHAPTER 7

Darby McCormick stood on the back porch of the Cranmore home, running the beam of her flashlight over the door, a reinforced steel model with two deadbolts. The thunderstorm had stopped, but the rain hadn't tapered off, still coming down fast and strong.

Detective Mathew Banville of the Belham police had to yell over the noise, in a tone that left little doubt he was running thin on patience.

"The mother, Dianne Cranmore, came home around quarter of five because she forgot her checkbook and needed it for when she swung by the bank later today to pay the mortgage. When she pulled in, both doors were open and then she saw this—" Banville used his penlight to point to the bloody hand print on the hallway wall. "The mother didn't find her daughter, but she found her daughter's boyfriend, Tony Marceillo, slumped on the stairs and immediately called nine-one-one."

"Besides the mother, who else has been inside?"

"The first responding officer, Garrett, and the EMTs. They all went in through the front to get to the boyfriend. The mother gave Garrett the keys."

"Garrett didn't come in this way?"

"He didn't want to destroy any evidence so he sealed the place off. We've issued an Amber Alert, but so far nothing."

Darby glanced at her watch. It was coming up on six a.m. Carol Cranmore had been missing for several hours, enough time for her to be well out of Massachusetts.

On the gray carpet was a single tan fiber. Darby placed an evidence cone next to it.

"There's no sign of forced entry. Who else has keys to the house?"

"We're talking to the ex-husbands," Banville said.

"How many she have?"

"Two, and that's not including the biological father. They were married for about fifteen minutes back in ninety-one."

"And does this fine gentleman have a name?" Darby checked the kitchen floor, glad to see it was made of linoleum. It was an ideal surface for picking up footwear impressions.

"Mother called him 'the sperm donor.' Said he went back to Ireland right after he found out he was going to be a daddy. She hasn't heard from him since."

"And they say all the good ones are taken." Darby rummaged through her kit.

"The other two ex-husbands, one lives in Chicago, and the other lives here, in the wonderful city of Lynn," Banville said. "The dipshit from Lynn is the most interesting of the bunch. Street name is LBC, short for Little Baby Cool—don't ask me what that means. LBC's biological name is Trenton Andrews, did a five-year stretch in Walpole for the attempted rape of a minor—a fifteen-year-old girl. The Lynn police are looking for Mr. Andrews right now. We're looking for registered sex offenders who live in the area."

"I'm sure it will be quite a list."

"You need anything else or can I go?"

"Hold on a moment."

"Let's hurry it up."

Darby didn't take Banville's clipped tone personally; he spoke to everyone this way. She had worked with him on two previous crime scenes and found him to be a thorough investigator; but his personality was gruff, to say the least, and he generally avoided eye contact. He also made sure people didn't stand too close to him—like now, he was leaning against the porch railing, a good five feet away.

She grabbed another flashlight, the heavy-duty Mag-Lite, and laid it down on the kitchen floor, angling the light until she found what she was looking for—a series of wet latent footwear impressions.

"Sole pattern looks like a men's boot, around a size eleven," Darby said. "Looks like our man came in through here and left through here. You might want to check and see what LBC favors for footwear."

"Anything else?"

"You're free to go."

Banville bolted down the stairs. Darby went to work bracketing off the boot impressions with tape. When she finished, she placed evidence cones next to the best impressions, then grabbed her kit and umbrella and stepped into the rain.

Across the driveway, seated at a table behind the kitchen window at the next-door neighbor's house, was Carol's mother. Dianne Cranmore pressed a wadded-up tissue against her eyes as she talked to a detective writing in a notepad. Darby looked away from the mother's broken expression and hustled to the front door.

The busy street was lit up by flashing blue and white lights.

Police were standing out in the rain, directing traffic and keeping the crowds of reporters behind the sawhorses blocking off the street. The entire neighborhood was awake. People were standing out on their porches and watching from behind windows, wanting to know what was going on.

Darby slipped a pair of disposable booties over her shoes and stepped inside the foyer. Her partner, Jackson Cooper, who was known to everyone simply as Coop, was hunched over a well-muscled young male dressed in a tight pair of black bikini briefs. The body was slumped at an awkward angle against the wall on the carpeted landing between the two sets of stairs. Blood had pooled under him, soaking into the carpet. Darby counted three shots—one in the forehead, two in a tight pattern on the cougar tattooed above the heart.

Coop pointed to the tight shot pattern on the teenager's chest. "Double tap."

"I'd say our guy's a trained marksman," Darby said.

"If I had to guess, I'd say the boyfriend heard something and decided to come downstairs to investigate. He comes down these steps to check the front door, finds it locked, and on the way back up gets shot twice in the chest. Then he falls, lands here and gets one planted in the forehead to make sure he doesn't get back up."

"Which means our guy is used to shooting in the dark."

Coop nodded. "No scratches on his hands or arms. He didn't get a chance to fight."

"But his girlfriend did," Darby said, and told him about the bloody handprint.

"What's Banville's take on this?"

"He's starting with the ex-husband angle."

"Why add murder to kidnapping?"

"Who knows?"

"That doctorate in criminal psychology is really paying off for you," Coop said. "ID here?"

"Not yet." Darby told him about the footwear evidence in the kitchen. "I'm going to take a look around, and then we can do the preliminary walk-through."

Light gray carpeting covered the stairs and the tiny hallway leading to a spacious TV room with mint-green walls and a brown couch and a matching chair mended by strips of duct tape. The mother had tried to brighten the place up with decorative throw pillows, a good area rug and assorted knickknacks.

An archway separated the TV room from the dining room. On the table were several paperback romance novels by Nora Roberts and stacks of coupons. The two rooms had the stale, soiled-wrapper feel of too much fast food and the fading odor of dope.

Stretching across the upstairs wall were dozens of pictures of Carol and her achievements. Here was one of Carol as a toddler holding a paintbrush. In another one, Carol was wearing Mickey Mouse ears at Disney World. An expensive-looking frame held a certificate from Belham High School for the distinction of being a straight-A student. Then another framed certificate, this one for her leadership abilities on the student council. Here was a framed watercolor of the ocean, a ribbon pinned on it. Carol had won first place in an art contest.

Carol's mother had hung the most prestigious awards and certificates at eye level outside her daughter's bedroom. That way, when Carol walked outside her bedroom door every morning and returned each night, she would always be reminded of her extraordinary talents.

Car doors slammed. ID, the section of the lab that dealt exclusively with crime scene photography, had arrived. Darby grabbed her umbrella and headed out.

She told Mary Beth Pallis about the body and the footwear impressions in the kitchen. After Mary Beth left, Darby examined the porch steps.

The only interesting item she found was a discarded match-book at the bottom step. She placed an evidence cone next to it. She backed up and stared at the porch. It hung suspended above the ground by columns. Latticework, also painted white, covered the perimeter. To the left of the stairs was a small door. Inside were plastic garbage cans and recycling bins.

One of the garbage cans tipped over. A raccoon was in there, its eyes reflected in the flashlight—

"Oh my God."

Darby opened the small door. The woman underneath the porch started to scream.

CHAPTER 8

Darby dropped her flashlight. She didn't pick it up. She stood absolutely still, staring wide-eyed at the woman who was now pressing a garbage can against the doorway to prevent anyone from entering.

Patrolmen came running. One of them grabbed Darby roughly by the arm and yanked her away from the door. He reached inside to move the garbage can.

The woman's teeth, what few of them remained, sunk deep into exposed skin of his wrist. She twisted her head ferociously from side to side like a mongrel dog trying to rip free the last piece of meat from a bone.

"My hand! The goddamn bitch is biting my hand!"

Another patrolman moved in with a can of Mace. The woman saw it, let go of her bite and started knocking over the barrels and recycling containers as she screamed, scurrying back underneath the porch.

Darby pushed the patrolman away and slammed the porch door shut.

The patrolman holding the Mace said, "What the hell you doing?"

"We're going to give this woman some breathing room to calm

down," Darby said. The first patrolman, his eyes tearing, grabbed the dangling meat of his bleeding wrist with a shaking hand. "Go and help him."

"All due respect, hon, your job is to—"

"Move everyone out of the driveway—and while you're at it, make sure the ambulance doesn't pull in with its sirens blaring."

Darby turned and addressed the crowd of men who had gathered around her. "Back up, I want everyone to back up now."

No one moved.

"Do what she says." Banville's voice. He emerged from the crowd, his black hair flattened by the rain.

The patrolmen moved out of the driveway. Banville stepped up next to her. Darby explained what she had seen.

"She's probably a crack addict," Banville said. "There's an abandoned house down the road where they all hang out."

"Let me try and talk her out of there."

Banville stared at the porch door, water dripping over his lumpy face. With his hangdog expression, he bore a striking resemblance to the cartoon character Droopy Dog.

"Fine," he said. "But under no circumstances are you to go underneath the porch."

Darby put down her umbrella. Slowly, she opened the porch door. No screaming. She knelt in a cold puddle. The flashlight was still on and gave her enough light to see.

During a college history course, Darby had seen grainy black-and-white footage taken of prisoners inside Hitler's concentration camps. The woman underneath the porch had clearly been starved. Most of her hair had fallen out; what little remained was thin and stringy. Her face was incredibly gaunt, the cheeks sunken, the skin waxy and white. The only color came from the blood around her lips.

"I'm not going to hurt you," Darby said. "I just want to talk."

The woman didn't look at her so much as *through* her. *Vacant eyes,* Darby thought.

Then, incredibly, the vacant sign disappeared. The woman's eyes came into focus, narrowing first in recognition, then widening in surprise mixed with, what, relief? Was that it?

"Terry? Terry, is that you?"

Use it. Whatever it is, use it.

"It's me." Darby's mouth was dry. "I'm here to—"

"Lower your voice, he's watching." The woman pointed with her chin at the porch ceiling.

There was nothing on the ceiling but spiderwebs and the dried-out husk of an old hornet's nest.

"I'll shut off the flashlight," Darby said. "That way he won't see us."

"Okay, good. That's good. You were always smart, Terry."

Darby turned off the flashlight. The flashing blue and whites blinked through the spaces between the latticework. The woman was still holding on to the barrel, still using it as a barrier.

Ask her name? No. She already believes I know her. Darby didn't want to risk breaking the connection. Better off going along with the delusion.

"I thought you were dead," the woman said.

"Why did you think that?"

"You were screaming. You were screaming for me to come help you and I couldn't reach you in time." The woman's face crumbled. "You weren't moving, and you were bleeding. I tried to wake you up and you didn't move."

"I fooled him."

"I did, too. I fooled him real good this time, Terry." The woman grinned and Darby had to look away. "I knew what he was going to do when he put me in the van, and I was ready."

"What color was his van?"

"Black. He's still out there, Terry."

"Did you see a license plate?"

"He's looking for me—for us."

"Who's looking for us? What's his name?"

"We've got to hide until the screaming stops."

"I know a way out," Darby said. "Come on, I'll show you."

The woman didn't move, didn't answer. She continued her examination of the porch ceiling. She was crouched behind the other side of an overturned barrel, holding it in a way to keep anyone from getting close to her.

Two choices: She could go in there and see if she could somehow guide the woman out, or she could let the patrolmen take care of it.

Darby moved the barrel blocking the door. When the woman didn't scream, Darby slid underneath the porch.

CHAPTER 9

"I'm going to come closer so we can talk," Darby said. "Okay?"

Darby crawled across the muddy ground of spilled trash, soda cans and newspapers. The most atrocious body odor she had ever smelled hit her. She dry-heaved, coughed.

"You okay, Terry? Please tell me you're okay."

"I'm fine." Darby was breathing through her mouth now. She leaned her back against the wall. She sat less than two feet away, on the other side of the barrel. The woman wasn't wearing pants or shoes. Bones jutted out from underneath her skin.

"Did you see Jimmy?" the woman asked.

Darby had an idea. "I saw him, but I didn't recognize him at first."

"You've been gone away for a long time. I bet he's changed a lot."

"He has, but it's . . . I'm having trouble remembering things. Small things, like my last name."

"It's Mastrangelo. Terry Mastrangelo. Will you introduce me to Jimmy? After everything you've told me, I feel like I know him as much as you do."

"I'm sure he'd like that. But first, we have to get out of here."

"There's no way out, only places to hide."

"I found a way out."

"You've got to stop that foolish thinking. I tried, remember? We both did."

"I came back for you, didn't I?" Darby took off her wind-breaker and held it across the barrel. "Put this on. It will keep you warm."

The woman went to grab the jacket, then pulled her hand away.

"What's wrong?"

"I'm afraid you'll disappear again," the woman said. "I don't want you to disappear on me again."

"Go ahead and take it. I won't disappear, I promise."

It took several minutes of thinking, but finally, the woman touched the jacket. The terror, the pain and fear—all of it seemed to collapse. She hugged the jacket against her chest, burying her face in the fabric and rocking back and forth, back and forth.

The ambulance was here now. It had pulled up to the bottom of the driveway without the sirens or spinning red lights. *Thank God for small favors.*

"You really found a way out?" the woman asked.

"I did. And I'm going to take you out with me."

Every part of Darby's body screamed at her not to do it, but she ignored the warning and held out her hand.

The woman gripped it fiercely. Two of her fingers had been recently broken and had healed at sharp, painful angles. Splinters covered her arms.

The woman was watching the ceiling again.

"There's nothing to be afraid of anymore," Darby said. "You're going to hold my hand and we're going to walk out this door together. You're safe."

CHAPTER 10

Much to Darby's surprise (and her considerable relief), the woman didn't scream or put up a fight when she stepped out into the driveway of blinking lights. She squeezed Darby's hand.

"Nobody here is going to hurt you," Darby said, reaching for her umbrella. She didn't want to risk having the rain wash away any potential evidence. "Nobody here is going to hurt you, I promise."

The woman pressed the jacket against her face and started sobbing. Darby slipped an arm around the woman's waist. Her bones felt as frail and as delicate as a bird's.

Taking slow, careful steps, she guided the woman toward the waiting ambulance. Standing by the front doors were two EMTs. One of them was holding a syringe.

There was no way around this part. They had to sedate her. Best to do it out here, in the open, in case things turned nasty again. It would be harder to confine her inside the ambulance's tight space.

Both EMTs circled behind the woman. Cops were hovering close by, ready to intervene, if necessary.

"We're almost there," Darby whispered. "Just keep holding my hand, and everything will be fine."

The EMT sunk the needle into the woman's buttock. Darby tensed, bracing herself for the worst. The woman didn't flinch.

When the woman's eyes fluttered, the EMTs took over.

"Don't strap her in yet," Darby said. "I'm going to need her shirt and to take some pictures."

Coop was already standing outside with his kit. There wasn't much space to work in the ambulance. Darby, small and petite, got inside while Coop stood near the back doors. They wore masks to help with the odor. The woman's sick, raspy breathing could be heard over the rain pelting the ambulance roof.

Mary Beth handed Darby the camera. She took pictures of the woman lying on her back, then close-ups of the tear marks on the black T-shirt.

Using a pair of scissors, Darby cut a straight line up the T-shirt's neckline, and then made two more cuts, one to each armpit. She slid the T-shirt off the woman's body, exposing her chest. The pale skin, marred with thick scars and sores and cuts that hadn't healed, had sunken far below the ribs.

"It's a miracle she didn't die of heart arrhythmia," Mary Beth said.

Darby moved the woman onto her side. She folded the T-shirt and dropped it inside the evidence bag Coop was holding.

"Let's get fingernail scrapings," Darby said.

Darby did an oral swab on the insides of the woman's cheeks. Coop used a wooden toothpick under the woman's thumbnail. It tore in half and started to bleed.

"What the hell happened to her?" Coop asked.

I wish to God I knew. "Let's get her fingerprinted," Darby said.

CHAPTER 11

The Serology Lab is a long and airy rectangular room of black-slab countertops often referred to as benches. The high windows overlook some green hills, twin basketball courts and, directly below them, a concrete promenade with picnic tables where people ate lunch in the nice weather.

Leland Pratt, the lab director, was waiting for Darby by the door. He smelled of shampoo and some citrus-scented cologne—a welcome relief from the atrocious body odor that was still lining her nose and clothes.

"It's all over the news," he said as he followed her to the bench in the back corner where Erin Walsh, the head of the DNA unit, was set up. "Who's handling the investigation?"

"Mathew Banville."

"Then the girl's in good hands," Leland said. "What about the Jane Doe you found underneath the porch?"

"That made the news?"

"They're playing video footage of you helping her to the ambulance. They didn't mention her name."

"We don't know who she is—we don't know anything."

Darby handed Erin four marked envelopes. "Blood from the kitchen doorway. Buccal swab for Jane Doe. These last two envelopes are the comparison samples, Carol Cranmore's toothbrush and her comb. If you need me, I'll be across the hall."

"Keep me updated on everything," Leland said.

"I always do," Darby said and left Serology. She dropped off the envelope with the tan fiber to the Trace section and then went to assist Coop.

Because the shirt was biologically contaminated with blood and other bodily fluids, Darby suited up. Next she put on a mask, safety goggles and neoprene gloves.

The small, dark room was filled with the faint hum of the rain. The shirt had been placed inside a fume hood.

"Take a look at this," Coop said, stepping away from the illuminated light magnifier.

A white sliver marked by dry blood was caught in the fabric. Using a pair of tweezers, Darby freed the sliver and turned it over under the magnified light.

"Looks like a paint chip. This patch here is probably rust."

Coop nodded. "The T-shirt is a mess," he said. "We're going to be in here all day collecting samples."

Half an hour later, they had collected two more slivers.

The secretary's voice came over the speaker: "Darby, Mary Beth on line two."

Darby collected the glassine envelopes. "I'll run these down to Pappy."

Mary Beth was seated in front of her computer, working the keyboard and mouse. Her blond hair was now a dark red.

A black footwear impression was on the monitor. Darby could make out the grooves in the soles and the cuts and gouges from stepping on such things as tacks and nails and glass. All of these individual marks, along with gait characteristics, made a boot impression as unique as a person's fingerprint.

"When did you color your hair?" Darby asked as she sat down.

"Yesterday. I needed a change."

"This wouldn't have anything to do with Coop, would it?"

"Why would you ask me that?"

"Because you were eating lunch with us when he announced he had a thing for redheads."

"Bear with me for a moment. I'm almost done."

Darby leaned in closer. "Coop only dates women who can string no more than four words together at a time. It's a policy with him."

Mary Beth pointed to the monitor. Inside a circle were lines drawn to resemble a mountain top and, below it, what appeared to be the letter R.

"This is the manufacturer's stamp," Mary Beth said. "Some companies stamp their name and logo into the soles of their footwear. I'm pretty sure this is the company logo for Ryzer Footwear."

"I've never heard of them."

"But you have heard of Ryzer Gear."

"The ones that make those ridiculously expensive winter jackets?"

"They're the same company," Mary Beth said. "When Ryzer started out—this is going all the way back to the fifties, I think—they started out making boots for the military. Then they branched out into hiking boots. That's all they did for a number of years. You could only buy them through their catalogue. The boots were very upscale and highly overpriced. During the eighties they were swallowed up by some global corporation, and Ryzer Footwear became Ryzer Gear. They still make hiking boots, but they also sell stuff like weatherproof coats, wallets and belts—they even came out with a kids' line of clothing and accessories. They're like a very upscale Timberland for the high-society set."

"How do you know all of this? You own stock in the company?"

"During my teenage years, I was a big-time hiker. My parents gave me a pair of Ryzer boots one Christmas. The ones they make now are mass produced and are crap, but the originals? You take care of them, they'll last you a lifetime. I still have mine. They are, hands down, the most comfortable pair of boots I've ever owned. That's why I recognized the logo—it's their old logo. These boots we're looking at, they don't make them anymore."

"I'll see what I can do to track them down. Thanks, Mary Beth."

"You're wrong about Coop. He likes smart women. Like you, for example."

"We're just partners."

"Whatever you say," Mary Beth said. "By the way, you really need to take a shower. And a couple of breath mints wouldn't hurt, either."

CHAPTER 12

The lab's footwear database consisted of a collection of three-ring binders.

Darby spent the rest of the morning poring through lifted samples of men's boots gathered from Boston cases. The footwear impression Mary Beth recovered didn't match any local cases.

During her lunch hour, Darby went online and sifted through two forensic message boards devoted exclusively to footwear evidence. While hunting, she found the name of a former FBI agent whose specialty was identifying footwear impressions. He had been used as an expert in court on several high-profile criminal cases.

Head pounding from hunger—she had skipped breakfast—Darby rushed down to the cafeteria and came back with a tuna salad and Coke. She swung by Leland's office to give him an update. He wasn't in.

The message light on her office phone was on. It was a message from her mother. Sheila had seen the morning news and wanted to know if everything was okay.

Sturgis "Pappy" Papagotis popped his head into the office. "Got a moment?" he asked.

"Come on in."

Pappy pulled out Coop's chair. He had the curse of being the world's youngest-looking man. He was a breath over five feet and had the kind of boyish face that made bouncers take a serious look at his license.

"I ran your white flecks through FTIR," he said. "Aluminum and alkyd-melamine."

"Automobile paint," Darby said. "What about styrene?"

"No, this was a factory job. It wasn't done in an auto body shop. How familiar are you with automobile paint?"

"Melamine's a resin added to paint to improve durability."

"Correct. Acrylic-melamine and polyester-melamine are the main polymers that make up paint. Alkyd-melamine is one of the super alkyds enamels they started using in the sixties. A lot of the automakers today favor using a polyurethane clear-coat system. It has higher gloss retention, for one, but the biggest reason is cost. Polyurethane is a fast air-drying top coat while melamine top coats need to be baked. The paint chip you found, it's the original paint job."

"What about color?"

"That's where I hit a dead end," Pappy said. "I ran the chip through FTIR and it came up blank."

"But that doesn't mean anything."

"Yes, I know what you're going to say—Fourier Transform Infared Spectroscopy is only as good as our computer library, and my failure to identify it, all it means is that we couldn't connect the paint chip to a local case. So I tried the Paint Query Database system run by our Canadian friends. No dice. I'll send a sample to the feds. Their lab stores the lesser-known, harder-to-find paint samples on their National Automobile Paint File database."

"Have you used the feds before?"

"I've never had to go to them since PDQ generally does the

job. If we strike out there, we could try that Farfegnugen-thing run by the Germans. Supposedly, they have the largest known paint sample database in the world."

"You have any contacts at the federal lab?"

"I did take a paint course given by the head of the Elemental Analysis Lab, this guy named Bob Gray. I could give him a call."

"Tell him we have an abduction case and we need him to move this to the front burner."

"I can ask." Pappy was grinning.

"I know, don't hold my breath and wait by the phone," Darby said.

Leland still wasn't in his office so Darby headed down to the first floor.

Missing Persons was tucked at the end of a long hallway. Standing behind the counter was a slim woman in a dark gray charcoal suit. The name on her ID tag was Mabel Wantuck. Mabel wasn't smiling in the picture, and she wasn't smiling now.

"Good morning," Darby said. "I was wondering if you could help me."

The look on Mabel Wantuck's face said, *Don't bet on it.*

"I've come across some evidence which may be connected to a missing person's case," Darby said.

"You know I can't show you—"

"The actual case file, yes, I know, only a detective can see that. All I need to know is if the person is, in fact, missing."

Mabel Wantuck took a seat at a paper-filled desk cluttered with several small framed pictures of two chocolate Labrador retrievers. She pulled out the keyboard.

"What's the name?"

"I'm not sure of the spelling, so we may have to try a few variations. What are the search parameters?"

"Last name first."

"Last name is Mastrangelo," Darby said. "Let me try and spell that for you . . ."

CHAPTER 13

Coop rolled a ball of Play-Doh between his hands while Darby explained the results of the Missing Persons search. She was bringing him up to date on the evidence when the lab secretary popped her head inside their office.

"Leland wants to see you in his office, Darby."

Leland was on the phone. He saw Darby standing in the doorway and pointed to the single chair set up in front of his desk.

Behind him was a wall crammed full of pictures taken at exclusive black-tie fundraisers. Here was Leland, the proud Republican, standing arm-and-arm with both George Bush junior and senior. Here was Leland, the caring Republican, standing next to the governor as they handed out Thanksgiving Day turkeys to the poor. To prove he had a sense of humor beneath all that Brooks Brothers clothing, here was a picture of Leland, the funny Republican, holding a copy of *The Complete Cartoons of the New Yorker* given to him at a book party.

Darby was thinking about the pictures on Carol Cranmore's wall when Leland hung up.

"That was the commissioner calling for an update. He was a bit surprised when I told him I didn't have anything to tell him yet."

"I came by twice," Darby said. "You weren't here."

"That's what voice mail is for."

"I thought you'd want an update in person, in case you had any questions."

"You now have my full attention." Leland leaned back in his chair.

Darby told him about the paint chip first, then the footwear impression.

"It's a men's size eleven, and the logo's a perfect match for Ryzer footwear. The logo stamped on the sole of the footwear impression we found was their second and last logo before they were bought out in eighty-three and became Ryzer Gear. Based on my research, they only manufactured four models, which they sold through catalogues and specialty stores in the northeast. We're talking a select group of customers. I tried our cases and struck out."

"So submit a copy to the feds and have them run it through their footwear database."

"Even if we ask them to expedite it, it will be a minimum of a month before they get around to processing it."

"I can't change that."

"Maybe we can," Darby said. "This afternoon I talked with a man named Larry Emmerich. He used to work for the FBI lab. He's the go-to expert on footwear impressions. Emmerich's retired now, hires himself out as a consultant. Not only does he have all of Ryzer's old catalogues, he has vendor information and contacts. Plus, he'd be willing to look at it right away. If he can narrow down the make and model, all the feds would need to do is to run the boot impression through their footwear database. Emmerich has contacts at the lab. Running it through the database to see if it's connected to any nationwide case would take a day, tops."

"And his fee for this service?"

Darby told him the price.

Leland's eyes widened.

"What did Banville say?"

"I haven't talked to him yet," Darby said.

"Good luck selling him on that."

"If he won't pay for it, I say we pick up the tab. The person who abducted Carol Cranmore has done this sort of thing before—at least twice."

Leland was already shaking his head. "There's no way I'll be able to get a purchase authorization—"

"Let me explain. The woman under the porch, Jane Doe, she thought I was this woman named Terry Mastrangelo. I had Missing Persons run the name through their computer. Terry Mastrangelo is twenty-two, lived in New Brunswick, Connecticut. Her roommate said Terry went out for ice cream. She didn't take her car, she walked. She never made it home."

"How long has she been missing?"

"Over two years."

Leland sat up in his chair.

"Terry Mastrangelo also has a son named Jimmy," Darby said. "He's eight now, lives with his grandmother. That's all I know. I don't have access to the actual case file, so Banville will have to request it."

"It wouldn't hurt him to take a look at VICAP, see if there's anything mentioned in there, like your footwear impression."

Darby was sure Banville had already consulted the Violent Criminal Apprehension Program. "Here's a copy of Terry Mastrangelo's picture."

Leland studied the piece of paper.

"You definitely share a similar look," he said. "You both have fair skin and auburn hair." He placed the paper on his desk blotter. "The woman you found underneath the porch, do we have any news on her condition?"

"Not yet," Darby said. "As for her prints, they're still running through AFIS."

"So the person who abducted Carol Cranmore is most likely keeping her somewhere—probably the same place where Terry Mastrangelo and the porch woman were kept."

"Now you know why I'm in such a rush to identify the footwear impression we found."

"I talked with Erin," Leland said. "The blood you found on the wall is AB negative. Carol's blood is O positive. Erin also found dried blood on the tan fiber and several spots on the T-shirt. The blood on the fiber matches the blood on the wall."

Darby wasn't holding out hope for a match on CODIS. The Combined DNA Identification System, while state-of-the-art, was relatively new; only the most recent cases were stored in there. Because of a lack of funding—each DNA extraction test cost hundreds of dollars—the majority of rape kits and DNA evidence sat in evidence rooms across the country.

"Trace said the tan fiber is used in commercial rugs. That's all I have." Darby stood.

"Hold on, I want to talk to you about something."

Darby had an idea what was coming.

"Abduction cases are pressure cookers. Once the media finds the link between Carol Cranmore and Jane Doe—and you and I both know they will—they'll be camped out here, and we'll have people like Nancy Grace doing a countdown every night on TV until Carol Cranmore's body is found.

"I know you're living with your mother at the moment to help ease her through her . . . situation," Leland said. "A case like this is very demanding on someone's time. You may not be able to spend that much time with her. You have plenty of vacation time—and there's family leave."

"Do you have a problem with my job performance?"

"No."

"Then I guess you're having reservations because my former partner was convicted of planting evidence on the Nelson rape case."

Leland clasped his hands behind his head.

"Not only did I tell you—repeatedly—that I was innocent, the grand jury cleared me," Darby said. "I wasn't responsible for Steve Nelson being let go and raping another woman. And I wasn't responsible for the media coverage either."

"I'm aware of that."

"So why are we having this conversation again?"

"Because putting you on this case could bring us more media attention. You're already on TV. I'm worried that the media is going to resurrect the Nelson case and drag it back into the spotlight."

"This case is going to have media attention whether I'm on it or not."

Leland didn't say anything, leaving Darby with the sense—and not for the first time—that he had privately come to some sort of conclusion about her. Leland Pratt was the kind of man who preferred observing people when they weren't paying attention, recording their words and gestures and cataloguing them in that locked-up place where he held his true judgments of people. Darby, for better or for worse, often caught herself working twice as hard to impress him. She hoped she could impress him now.

"I can run this thing, Leland. But if you still have some lingering doubts, if you don't trust me, then put it on the table and talk about it. Stop denying me access to cases because you're afraid I'm going to embarrass the lab. It's not fair."

Leland stared at the framed certificates and diplomas hanging on the wall behind her. Finally, after a long moment, he turned his attention back to her.

"I want to be updated at every turn. If I'm not in my office, leave a message or call me on my cell phone."

"Not a problem," Darby said. "Anything else?"

"If Banville won't pick up the tab for the footwear specialist, let me know and I'll see what I can do."

Darby stepped into the office she shared with Coop. He was on the phone, flipping through a comic book. He had changed into jeans and a T-shirt with the slogan "Beer Is Proof That God Loves Us and Wants Us to Be Happy."

"I don't remember Wonder Woman having breast implants," Darby said after Coop hung up.

"This is the new improved Wonder Woman."

"Great. Now she looks like a stripper."

"I see you're not wearing your happy face. Would you like to play with the Play-Doh? I'm telling you, it's great for stress."

"Our boss has some serious doubts about my abilities."

"Let me guess: the Nelson case."

"Bingo." Darby gave him the condensed version of her conversation with Leland.

"Why are you grinning?" Darby asked.

"You remember that girl Angela I dated a few months back?"

"The lingerie model from *The Improper Bostonian*?"

"No, that was Brittney. Angela was the British girl, the one with the diamond belly button ring."

"It's amazing how you can keep them all straight."

"I know, I should belong to Mensa. Anyway, Angela and I were out for drinks one night, and I was telling her about work and mentioned Leland's name. Seems the word *prat* over in the U.K. means idiot or fool. Try to keep that in mind as we move forward."

CHAPTER 14

There was one stop Darby wanted to make before heading home.

Scrubbed clean, her hair still damp from the gym shower, Darby stepped into the main lobby of Mass General, Boston's largest hospital. She didn't need to stop by the information desk; she knew her way to the intensive care unit. She had been there once, to say good-bye to her father.

The sign posted outside ICU's double doors read TURN OFF ALL CELL PHONES AND ELECTRONIC DEVICES BEFORE ENTERING. Darby shut off her phone, showed her ID to the male nurse sipping coffee behind the reception desk and asked about the condition of a woman brought in last night from Belham. He didn't know—he had just come on shift—and pointed to the patrolman sitting in a chair outside a room at the end of a long corridor.

There is no privacy in ICU. Glass windows look into each room. Family members, faces shocked and scared, wait to take turns holding a loved one's hand or, in most cases, to say good-bye.

Memories of her father crowded Darby's thoughts, growing stronger when she passed the empty room where her father had died.

The old patrolman glanced up from his golfing magazine and examined her ID card. A web of broken blood vessels lined his nose.

"You missed all the excitement," he said, stretching. "Porch Lady attacked a nurse."

"What happened?"

"She stabbed a nurse with a pen. Doc's in there right now. I suggest breathing through your mouth."

The doctor was leaning over Jane Doe, listening to her heartbeat. Under the bright fluorescent light, Jane Doe appeared even more emaciated. She was on both an IV and a nasogastric tube. Her arms and legs were secured with restraints, and almost every inch of her gray-colored skin was covered with bandages or wrapped in gauze.

Darby moved closer to the bed and saw bright drops of blood on the sheets. The sick wheezing she had heard early this morning in the ambulance now seemed labored, painful.

Jane Doe's eyes fluttered beneath the paper-thin eyelids. *What are you dreaming about?*

"You're with the crime lab," the doctor said in a surprisingly soft voice. It didn't go along with her hard, plain face.

Darby introduced herself. The doctor's name was Tina Hathcock.

"I hope you didn't come here for the rape kit," Hathcock said. "Someone from the lab already picked it up."

"No, I just stopped by to see how she's doing."

"Aren't you the one who helped her out from underneath the stairs?"

"Yes, that's me."

"I thought so. I recognized your face. You're all over the news."

Wonderful, Darby thought. "I heard she attacked a nurse."

"About two hours ago," the doctor said. "The nurse was checking the IV line and was stabbed repeatedly with a pen. She's in surgery right now. Hopefully, they'll save her eye."

"Where did she get the pen?"

"We think she got it from the clipboard we post at the end of the bed. I understand she bit a police officer."

Darby nodded. "He reached inside to help her. She thought she was going to be attacked."

"Confusion and delirium are symptoms of sepsis—a blood infection caused by toxin-producing bacteria. In this case, it's *Staphylococcus aureus.* Several of the cuts and sores on her arm are infected with staph. We are treating her with a broad-spectrum IV antibiotic therapy, but staph has become particularly resistant to antibiotics over the past few years. Given her already weakened condition, and her compromised immune system, the prognosis doesn't look good."

"When she was conscious, did she say anything?"

"No. She ripped out her IV lines and then tried to escape. We had to sedate her again, which has been tricky, given her irregular heartbeat. I don't want to keep her sedated any more than I have to, but we can't afford another psychotic episode. Do you have any idea who she is?"

"We're still trying to find out."

The doctor turned her attention to the bed. "As you can see, she's emaciated. At this stage, what happens is vital organs shift into lower gear—the heart rate declines and becomes irregular. Most of her hair has fallen out from lack of protein. The grayish color on her skin is due to severe vitamin deficiencies. You see that fine, almost downy covering on her skin? Almost looks like body hair? That's lanugo. We generally see it during the late stages of anorexia. It's the body's way of reacting to loss of muscle and fat tissue—sort of a last-ditch effort to keep the body warm."

Darby stared down at the sickly, waiflike creature wheezing in the bed. She thought of the picture of Terry Mastrangelo and tried to see her the same way her abductor did—as an object, a means to an end. How long had she been missing? And what had she endured?

"Can I borrow your penlight?"

"Of course," the doctor said, reaching inside her pocket.

Darby pulled back the sick tent and examined the woman's left forearm.

Written in blue ink, in tiny letters on the exposed area of skin between the bandages, were a series of letters and numbers: 1 L S 2R L R 3R S 2R 3L.

And underneath it, three more lines:

2 R R S 2L S R R L 3R S

3 L 2R S S 2R L R 4 R

The fourth line was illegible.

The doctor leaned in. "What in God's name is that?"

"Directions would be my first guess—L for left, R for right."

"That last letter, or number, whatever it was, it looks like she was writing and then had to stop," the doctor said. "Maybe that was when the nurse came in."

Darby had been wondering the same thing. "Excuse me for a moment."

ID was gone for the day. Darby called Operations and crossed her fingers, hoping that Mary Beth was on call. She was.

It would be at least an hour before Mary Beth arrived with her equipment. Darby took pictures with her digital camera for her files.

Jane Doe was heavily sedated, so the doctor was willing to undo the restraints so Darby could take close-up pictures. She examined the rest of Jane Doe's body and didn't find any other writing.

"Someone from the lab is going to be here to take more photographs," Darby said after she finished. "You might have to undo the restraints again."

"As long as she's sedated. I meant to ask you this earlier: Do you know why she didn't attack you?"

"I think I reminded her of someone." Darby took out a business card and wrote down her home number. She handed the card to the doctor. "That's my home number. When she wakes up, I'd appreciate if you'd call me, even if it's late. I'll leave my cell on, too."

"When you find the person who did this to her," the doctor said, "I hope you all have the good sense to string the son of a bitch up by his balls."

CHAPTER 15

Darby did the documentation work for Mary Beth. When they stepped back outside the ICU, Darby turned on her phone and checked her messages. There was another one from Sheila, asking her to call. She was worried; Darby could tell by the tone of her mother's voice. The second message was from Banville.

Her cell phone battery was almost dead. Darby found a pay phone on the wall next to a pair of vending machines. Across the hall was the ICU waiting room, a small area with stiff plastic chairs and magazines wrinkled by sweat. A man with rosary beads stared at the floor while a woman cried in the corner underneath the TV playing a news report on the war in Iraq.

When Banville answered his phone, Darby brought him up to date on the day's events.

"I agree, the letters do sound like directions," Banville said after she finished. "I wonder how the numbers factor into it."

"It could be a shorthand of some sort."

"And the only person who can decipher it is still sedated."

"I asked the doctor to call me when she wakes up. I want to be there when you question her."

"I think that's a good idea. It might help keep her calm. Let's hope she wakes up soon."

"I hear I'm all over the news."

"Some reporter got footage of you climbing under the porch with Jane Doe," Banville said. "I bet our boy is getting real nervous."

"How's the mother holding up?"

"About the same as any mother would hold up in this situation," Banville said. "The Lynn police went to Little Baby Cool's last known address. He doesn't live there anymore and—imagine this—he forgot to notify his parole officer. I'll tell them about the footwear impression."

"I want to talk to you about that," Darby said, and launched into her reasons for hiring the footwear consultant.

"It's something to consider," Banville said.

"The last FedEx drop is at seven. Emmerich said he'd work on it first thing in the morning."

"That's a hell of a lot of money to gamble on something that might not pan out."

"What would Carol want you to do?"

"I didn't realize you were on a first-name basis with the vic," Banville said. "I'll be in touch."

Darby heard the sting of the dial tone. She hung up the phone, her face burning. Her attention drifted back over to the man holding the rosary beads.

In a flash she saw herself at fourteen, rosary beads in hand, pacing the worn-out carpet, waiting for her mother to come out of ICU where she was talking to the surgeon. Her father was going to be okay. Big Red had been in plenty of tough spots before; he was going to pull through this. God always protected the good.

Now, at thirty-seven, she knew better.

Darby thought about her mother wasting away at home and felt a cold, empty space hanging inside her chest as she walked toward the elevators.

CHAPTER 16

Daniel Boyle rubbed the rosary beads between his fingers as he watched the crime scene investigator, the attractive redhead who had helped Rachel Swanson out from underneath the porch, disappear around the corner. He had changed seats when she picked up the pay phone. He had listened to most of her conversation and was relieved to hear the police had found the footwear impressions he had left on the kitchen floor.

Once the blood from the hallway was processed through their CODIS system, they would get a hit for Earl Slavick. The FBI was looking for Slavick in connection with a string of missing women that started in Colorado.

The FBI didn't know Slavick was now a resident of Lewiston, New Hampshire. When Boyle decided to lead the police to Slavick's house, they would find a pair of Ryzer hiking boots, size eleven, in Slavick's office closet, along with some other valuable evidence connecting him to the disappearances of several New England women.

What was troubling Boyle was this business about the writing found on Rachel's arm. He had an idea what the numbers and letters meant, but it would be meaningless to the police unless Rachel woke up and started talking.

Boyle knew Rachel had already woken up once and attacked a nurse. If Rachel woke up again, if they could stabilize her long enough to pump her system with some antipsychotic medication, she might be able to tell the police about what had happened to her and the other women in the basement.

Boyle still couldn't figure out how Rachel had escaped. The two pairs of handcuffs were good and tight, the ball gag still wedged securely in her mouth, when he left to get Carol. And Rachel was sick. She wasn't going anywhere.

When he came back, the van's back doors were open. The ball gag and handcuffs were lying on the floor.

Nobody had ever escaped before.

Boyle tightened his grip on the rosary beads. Once again, he had underestimated Rachel, forgot what a resourceful cunt she could be—which was, ironically, one of the things he absolutely loved about her. Rachel reminded him so much of his mother.

A little over two weeks ago, Rachel had faked being sick, refusing to eat for days, and when he went into her cell to check on her, she attacked him and broke his nose. He fell to the floor and she kicked him in the head until he passed out.

The keys she took from his pocket didn't unlock the padlock for the basement door. Those keys were in his office. And that was where he found her, tearing the place up, looking for his other set of keys, maybe even his cell phone. Maybe Rachel had found the spare set of handcuff keys. He hadn't noticed they were missing. He was still cleaning up the mess she made.

He should have left Rachel inside her cell. He should have come to Belham alone, as originally planned, grabbed Carol and then, after he returned home—*then* he should have made a separate trip to bury Rachel.

Instead, he had been lured by the idea of burying Rachel next to his mother in the Belham woods around Salmon Brook Pond. He hadn't been to his old burial ground in years—so long, in fact, he had forgotten where he had buried her.

Boyle had made maps of all his burial spots. He couldn't find the recent map he had made showing where his mother's remains were buried. Boyle, never good with directions, had to rely on memory. It had taken nearly four hours to find the spot, followed by another hour of digging. When he left the woods, the idea of burying Rachel next to his mother had consumed him for days. He couldn't let it go. Now, because he had put desire before discipline, Rachel was lying in a hospital bed in Mass General.

The ICU doors opened and out stepped a *stunning* woman with shoulder-length black hair and dark brown eyes. She was young, with a perfect face and flawless skin. She was dressed in snug but stylish jeans, hip black high-heel shoes and a midriff shirt that showed a teasing hint of her soft, flat belly. Boyle guessed she was somewhere in her early to mid-twenties. The young woman stepped into the waiting room and picked up a box of tissues. The box was empty. She threw it in the trash. All the grieving men in the waiting room were watching her.

The woman was aware she was being admired. Instead of sitting down, she buttoned up her coat, turned around and gave them her back. Boyle's mother used to do that when she caught men she didn't like gawking at her. If they were handsome, she'd give them her full attention. If they were rich, she'd give them her body.

The young woman crossed her arms over her chest and stared at the ICU doors. She was waiting for someone. Not her husband. She had no rings on her fingers. Maybe she was waiting for her boyfriend. No. The boyfriend would have come out with her.

She was clearly upset, but she was not going to cry, not here, not in front of *these* people.

Boyle could get her to cry. Beg, too. He could make her shed that fake, WASPy exterior faster than a snake shed its skin.

He picked up the box of tissues next to him, stood and walked toward her. He could smell her perfume. Some women couldn't carry it well. She did.

Boyle held out the box. The woman turned around, looking angry at being disturbed. Her expression softened a bit when she saw his suit and tie, his nice shoes. He wore a wedding ring and a Rolex watch. He looked professional and put together. He looked trustworthy.

"I didn't mean to bother you," Boyle said. "I just thought you could use this. I've already gone through a box myself."

After a moment's consideration, she took a tissue and carefully dabbed at the corners of her eyes, not wanting to ruin her makeup. She didn't thank him.

"You have someone in there?" She nodded to the ICU doors.

"My mother," Boyle said.

"What does she have?"

"Cancer."

"What kind?"

"Pancreatic."

"My father has lung cancer."

"I'm sorry," Boyle said. "Was he a smoker?"

"Two packs a day. I'm going to quit. Swear to God." She made a sign of the cross to emphasize her commitment. "I'm sorry if I seemed rude. It's just—it's this goddamn waiting. I'm tired of waiting for my father to, you know, let go. That probably sounds cold, but he's in so much pain. And then there's the waiting for the doctors. They *love* to keep you waiting. I'm waiting for his highness right now."

"I know what you mean. I wish I had family to lean on, but I'm the only child, and my father died years ago."

"I'm in the same boat. My father is my family. After he goes"—she took in a deep breath to steady herself—"it's just me."

"What about your husband?"

"No husband, no boyfriend, no mother, no kids. Just me."

Boyle thought about the empty cell in his basement and wondered if this woman would be missed if she disappeared. He hadn't captured one so beautiful before. She had just the right amount of weight on her. The heavier ones lasted longer in the basement. The skinny ones never lasted, unless they were very young, like Carol.

"Do you live around here?" Boyle said. "I only ask because I think I've seen you around the neighborhood. I live across the street, in Beacon Hill."

"I'm from Weston, but I come to Boston a lot. I have friends who live on the Hill. What's your name?"

"John Smith. And yours?"

"Jennifer Montgomery."

"Your father wouldn't be Ted Montgomery, the real estate developer? He owns a bunch of buildings in my neighborhood."

"No, he owns a perfume business."

Boyle could easily find out his name and where he lived.

The ICU doors opened. A doctor stepped out, spotted Jennifer Montgomery and headed toward her.

"Good luck," Boyle said, and slipped inside the ICU doors before they shut.

Boyle quickly took in his surroundings—the security cameras pointed at the desk, the medical equipment in the corner that monitored each of the ICU patients. Down at the far end of the corridor he saw the patrolman sitting in a chair set up in front of Rachel's room. He wasn't worried about the security cameras. He would change his appearance the next time he visited.

The nurse behind the counter was looking at him. "Can I help you?"

"Could I have a box of Kleenex? My cousin's rather upset."

"Of course."

When the nurse reached behind her to grab a box of tissues, Boyle memorized the names on the clipboard holding the visitor sign-in sheet. He'd have to figure out a way to sign in without leaving fingerprints.

Boyle took the box of tissues, thanked her. "Which room is Mr. Montgomery? I'd like to drop off some videos for him tomorrow."

"He's in room twenty-two. Just make sure you bring VHS tapes. We don't have DVD players in here."

Boyle checked Montgomery's room. It was three down from Rachel's. Perfect.

Boyle walked out of the ICU and headed down the corridors. He dumped the box of tissues in a wastebasket.

As he waited for the elevator, he thought about Jennifer Montgomery. She was young. That was important. The younger ones could go the distance. The women in their late forties to early fifties didn't last as long. He didn't like bringing them home, but he had to take women of all ages, colors and sizes so the police wouldn't make a connection. It was important to randomly select his victims. Boyle had studied police work. There were many books on such things, and there was the internet. Information was everywhere.

Boyle thought about the crime scene investigator, the redhead. He had never abducted someone from law enforcement before. That one was definitely a fighter. Like Rachel.

The elevator doors opened. Boyle slipped his hands inside his pant pockets, his fingers feeling around the lips of the plastic sandwich baggies holding the chloroform-soaked rags. He always carried them in case he decided to abduct someone while he was on the road; and he always carried a bag in each pocket since that night years ago when he grabbed a young girl at the home of the friend who had seen him in the woods—

He stopped walking. That red hair, those striking green eyes . . . No, it couldn't be the same person.

Boyle pushed the thought aside. It would have to wait until he returned home. He went back to imagining all the wonderful things he could do with Jennifer Montgomery in his basement.

CHAPTER 17

Darby pulled behind the patrol car parked across the street from the Cranmore house. The street was eerily quiet. She had been expecting a media circus.

"Where is everyone?" Darby asked the patrolman dozing behind the wheel.

"Downtown, at the press conference. Mother's there, too."

"I'm going to take a look around."

"Shout if you need anything."

Last night and early this morning, much of her time had been devoted to processing the house and the space underneath the porch. She had examined the outside area around the house with a flashlight and had failed to find anything.

Still, as she examined the ground and bushes, a part of her secretly hoped to find some overlooked piece of evidence that would break open the case. After two full sweeps, the only thing she had to show for her efforts was mud on her boots and pant cuffs.

Standing back in the driveway, next to the boyfriend's car, she breathed away her frustration. The fading sunlight reflected a deep, dark red against the windows and puddles.

Okay, we know you pulled into the driveway and then entered the house, most likely using a key because there's no evidence to suggest you tampered with the locks. You shot the boyfriend and then grabbed Carol and struggled briefly inside the kitchen door. Even though it was late, raining hard and thundering, you couldn't risk dragging her kicking and screaming outside because it might wake someone up and call them to the window, so you knocked her unconscious before taking her out. You tossed Carol over your shoulder—it would be easier to move that way, and it would keep your hands free. Then you ran down the stairs to your van. You use a van because it can transport one or more bodies in privacy. You opened the back doors and put Carol inside, next to Jane Doe—only she wasn't there.

Darby imagined Carol's abductor running down the driveway, panicking, his head whipping around the sheets of driving rain as he searched for Jane Doe.

How far had he searched? And for how long? Did he drive around the streets looking for her? What made him decide to give up and go home?

Another thought hit her, causing Darby to reach for the notebook and pen tucked in her shirt pocket: What if he had stayed close by and saw Jane Doe being escorted out of the porch? What if he followed the ambulance? She made a note to tell Banville to increase security around Jane Doe.

Darby wondered about the intruder's reaction when he learned Jane Doe had only been a few feet away, hiding behind the garbage barrels underneath the porch.

Why was Jane Doe in the van?

Possible answer: He was planning on getting rid of her because she was sick.

But where was he going to dump the body?

No, he wouldn't dump the body. He'd bury it someplace where no one would find it. Was the plan to abduct Carol first and then bury Jane Doe somewhere in Belham?

Too risky. What if Carol woke up? If he had Carol, he'd want to bring her home.

Maybe he had changed his mind about burying Jane Doe and decided to abduct Carol instead.

Darby moved to the porch. The small white door was sealed with evidence tape. She pressed her forehead against the cool, damp wood.

I fooled him real good this time, Terry. I knew what he was going to do when he put me in the van, and I was ready.

A car door slammed. Darby turned and saw Dianne Cranmore marching up the driveway, a framed picture of her daughter clutched in one hand.

Dianne Cranmore was somewhere in her mid- to late thirties, with bleached hair and a round face heavy with makeup. She reminded Darby of the women she sometimes spotted in the nicer bars in Boston, women from Chelsea and Southie who fought hard to appear charming and sophisticated as they trolled for men who could transport them away from their crummy jobs and even crummier lives.

Carol's mother spotted the badge dangling around Darby's neck. "You're with the crime lab," she said.

"Yes."

"May I talk to you for a moment?" The woman's eyes were puffy and bloodshot from crying.

The patrolman Darby had talked to earlier was now standing in the driveway. "Miss Cranmore, why don't we—"

"I'm staying right here," Carol's mother said. "I want to ask her some questions. I have a right to know what's going on—and don't you tell me again I don't. I'm getting goddamn sick and tired of the way you people keep pushing me around."

"It's okay," Darby told the patrolman. "Why don't you give us a minute?"

The patrolman adjusted his cap and walked away.

"Thank you," Carol's mother said. "Now please tell me what's going on with my daughter's case."

"We're conducting a thorough investigation."

"Which is police talk for 'I'm not telling you jack shit.' My daughter is missing. *My* daughter. Doesn't that mean anything to you people?"

"Mrs. Cranmore, we're doing everything we can to find—"

"Please, please, *please* don't start in with that again. That's all I've heard over the past twenty-four hours. Everyone's working real hard, everyone's chasing down leads—yes, I know all about it. I've answered all your questions, and now it's my turn. You can start by telling me about the woman you found under my porch."

"I suggest you talk with Detective Banville—"

"What about when my daughter's dead? Will someone talk to me then?"

Dianne Cranmore's voice cracked. She clutched the picture of her daughter tightly against her chest.

"I understand how you're feeling," Darby said.

"You have kids?"

"No."

"Then how can you stand there and say that you can understand what I'm going through?"

"I guess you're right," Darby said. "I can't."

"When you have kids of your own, the love you'll feel for them . . . It's more love than your heart can ever hold. Like it's going to burst inside your chest. That's what it feels like. It feels a thousand times worse when you're wondering if they're hurt and calling out for you to come help them. Only you don't know that. All you people, this is just a job for you. When you find her dead, you all get to go home. What do I get? Tell me, what do *I* get?"

Darby didn't know what to say, felt she should say something.

"I'm sorry."

Carol's mother couldn't hear her. She had already turned and walked away.

CHAPTER 18

Sheila's nurse, Tina, was busy putting together a tray of food when Darby stepped into her mother's kitchen.

"How is she doing?"

"She had a good day. A lot of her friends called to say they saw you on TV. I saw it, too. Going underneath the porch was very brave."

Darby thought back to the day her mother delivered the news of the diagnosis, the way Sheila held her, arms steady and tough as steel, while Darby broke down.

The doctor had found the mole during a routine checkup. The Boston surgeon took out a good chunk of the skin cancer from her arm and many of her lymph nodes. He couldn't reach the melanoma that had already settled inside her lungs.

Sheila had refused chemotherapy because she knew it wouldn't help. Two experimental treatments had failed. Now it was just a matter of time.

Darby dropped her backpack on the kitchen chair. Stacked near the back door were two cardboard boxes full of carefully folded clothes. She spotted a pink cashmere sweater. Darby had bought the sweater for her mother this past Christmas.

Darby pulled out the sweater and was pierced by a memory of her mother standing in front of Big Red's closet. It was a month after the funeral. Sheila, holding back tears, had touched one of his flannel shirts and then pulled her hand back as though something had bitten it.

"Your mother cleaned out some of her closets today," the nurse said. "She asked me to drop them off at St. Pius on my way home. For their fund-raiser."

Darby nodded. Packing up the clothes, she knew, was her mother's way of trying to help ease her through her grief.

"I'll drop them off," Darby said.

"Are you sure? I don't mind."

"I drive by St. Pius on my way to work."

"Before you drop off the clothes, you may want to go through the pockets. I found this." The nurse handed Darby a picture of a pale, freckle-faced woman with blond hair and striking blue eyes taken at what appeared to be a picnic.

Darby had no idea who the woman was. She put the picture on her mother's tray. "Thanks, Tina."

Sheila was sitting up in bed, reading the new John Connolly mystery. Darby was glad for the soft lighting from the two lamps. It made her mother's face look less gaunt, less sick. The rest of her was covered up by blankets.

Darby placed the tray across her mother's lap, careful of the IV drip for the morphine.

"I hear you had a good day."

Sheila picked up the picture. "Where did you find this?"

"Tina found it the back pocket of a pair of jeans you're donating. Who is she?"

"Cindy Greenleaf's daughter, Regina," Sheila said. "You and Regina used to play together. They moved to Minnesota when you were around five, I think. Cindy sends me Christmas cards every year with Regina's picture."

Sheila tossed the picture inside the wastebasket and glanced briefly at the wall behind the TV.

After the diagnosis, Sheila had taken the pictures from downstairs and more from the photo albums, had everything framed and hung on every amount of available wall space so she could see them from her bed.

Seeing the pictures made Darby think of the wall outside Carol Cranmore's room. Then Darby thought of Carol's mother, her words about how having children was more love than your heart can hold. The love you felt for your child, Darby had been told, was all-consuming, and all-encompassing. It owned you until you were buried.

"The woman you found underneath the porch looks like a famine victim," Sheila said.

"It looks even worse up close. She had scars and cuts all over her body, and these sores."

"What happened to her?"

"I don't know. We don't know who she is or where she came from. She's being treated at Mass General. Right now, she's sedated."

"Do you know her condition?"

"She's got sepsis." Darby told her mother about her discussion with Jane Doe's doctor and what had happened at the hospital.

"Survival rates for sepsis depend on things like the patient's overall health, how effective the antibiotics work against the infection, the patient's immune system," Sheila said. "Given what you told me about Jane Doe's low blood pressure, some of her organs starting to fail, I'd say she's gone into septic shock. The doctor's in a tricky situation, trying to treat the sepsis while keeping her sedated."

"So prognosis doesn't look good."

"I don't think so."

"I hope to God she wakes up. She might know where Carol is—she's the missing teenager. Carol Cranmore."

"I saw it on the news. Any leads?"

"Not much, I'm afraid. Hopefully, we'll find something soon." Hopefully. Hope. Darby was spreading it around too thin. It left her nerves feeling frayed and vulnerable.

She sat down in her father's old recliner. It had been brought up from downstairs and set up next to her mother's bed so she could sleep here at night.

At first, Darby wanted to be here in case her mother woke up and needed something. Now Darby wanted to be here so she could hold her mother when the time came to say good-bye.

"I ran into Carol's mother about an hour ago," Darby said. "Talking to her, seeing what she was going through, it made me think of Melanie's mother. Do you remember the first Christmas after Mel disappeared, you and I were in the car, on the way to the mall or something, and we saw Mel's parents standing out in the cold, nailing a piece of plywood with Mel's picture to a telephone pole on East Dunstable Road?"

Sheila nodded, her pale face pinching tight at the memory.

"Everyone in town knew about Victor Grady, and Mel's parents were standing out there in the bitter cold either refusing to give up hope, or refusing to face the truth," Darby said. "I wanted you to stop the car and you drove past them."

"I didn't want you to suffer anymore. You had suffered enough."

Darby remembered looking in the car's side-view mirror, watching as Mrs. Cruz turned her back to a blast of wind, clutching the sheets with Mel's picture against her chest so they wouldn't blow away. Melanie's mother grew smaller until she finally disappeared, and right then, Darby wanted to throw the door open and run back there and help them.

Was Helena Cruz's love for her daughter just as intense now, after two decades? Or had she learned how to mute it, make it less sharp and easier to carry?

"There was nothing you could have done to help them," Sheila said.

"I know. I know they blamed me for what happened to Mel— they probably still do."

"What happened to Melanie wasn't your fault."

Darby nodded. "Seeing that look on Dianne Cranmore's face . . . I just wanted to do something to help her."

"You *are* helping her."

"It doesn't feel like we're doing enough."

"It never will," Sheila said.

CHAPTER 19

Daniel Boyle unlocked the basement door and moved around the desk, walking past the computer monitors and the mannequins dressed in the costumes he wore. What he was looking for was inside the next room. He took out his keys and unlocked the filing cabinet.

The hanging file folders were arranged chronologically with his most recent projects near the front for easy access. The older projects were in the bottom drawer. The folder marked BELHAM was in the far back.

Dust rose from the folder as he flipped past the yellowed newspaper clippings of Victor Grady. In the back he found the bundled stacks of Polaroids.

The colors had faded in the pictures, but Melanie Cruz's face was clear enough. She stood behind the locked bars of the wine cellar. The other five pictures showed what he had done to her. Boyle stared at the pictures and felt the beginnings of an erection.

He had taken other pictures—ones of Melanie Cruz lying dead in the ground out in the Belham woods. Those pictures, along with a map showing where she was buried, had been burned away in the fire. Boyle remembered how he had set the fire but couldn't remember where he had buried Melanie Cruz or the other women.

He picked up the stack of pictures belonging to a teenage girl with dark red hair and striking green eyes. He removed the elastic bands and flipped over the first picture.

The teenager's name was Darby McCormick. She bore a striking resemblance to the crime scene investigator he had seen at the hospital.

But was it the same person?

Boyle took out his cell phone and dialed information to get the number for the Boston Crime Lab. The operator connected him. Less than a minute later, he was listening to the lab's automated phone system instructing him on how to contact someone at the lab. Two choices: enter the person's extension or the first four letters of the person's last name.

He punched in the letters and flipped through pictures of a heavy-set blond woman named Samantha Kent. Boyle remembered how she had refused to eat. How she got weak and then sick. How he had brought her out to the Belham woods to strangle her and was interrupted by Darby McCormick and her two friends— Melanie Cruz and the blond girl he later stabbed inside the foyer. What a mess that was. He was trying to remember the blonde's name when the voice mail picked up.

"You've reached the office of Darby McCormick. I'm either away from my desk or on another line—"

Boyle hung up and leaned back against the wall.

CHAPTER 20

Boyle stared up at the wall crammed full of pictures of the women he had hunted over the years. Sometimes he sat here for hours, staring up at the faces and recalling what he had done to each of them. Pleasant thoughts to pass the time.

Tacked to the bottom corner was an old picture of Alicia Cross. She had lived two streets over, on the other side of the woods behind his house. She was riding her bike along a long stretch of empty road when he pulled up next to her. Alicia's mother, Boyle had told the twelve-year-old, had sent him to come get her and take her to the hospital. Alicia's father had been in a serious car accident. Alicia was so upset she left her bike on the road and got into his car.

She was too scared to fight, too small to fight. Boyle was sixteen and strong.

For an entire week—the second week of his mother's month-long vacation in Paris—police and volunteers combed through the woods and surrounding neighborhoods. Boyle watched them through his bedroom window. For three days, police and volunteers from the neighborhood searched the woods around his house. He recalled the long summer afternoons he sat by the window, listening to Alicia's mother call out her daughter's name over and over again while he stimulated himself.

At night, he would go downstairs into the wine cellar and remove Alicia's restraints. Sometimes he chased her through the dark basement. There were many places to hide.

While that was fun, nothing compared to the hot, blinding rush of excitement Boyle felt when he strangled her.

The night he killed her, he couldn't sleep. Strangling Alicia was magnificent, but it wasn't as fulfilling as watching the fear in her eyes, the way she stared at the rosary beads on the floor while she feebly clawed at the rope around her neck.

Boyle felt a tremendous sense of power—not the power to kill, no, that was too easy. What he held in his hands was the power to alter and shape destinies. He could change the shape of the world around him any way he wanted. Gripped in his hands was the power of God.

Early the next morning, while it was still dark, Boyle headed out into the woods with a shovel. When he came back for the body, he found his mother standing in the kitchen. She had come back from her Paris trip early. She didn't say why, didn't ask why his clothes were so dirty or why he was sweating. She made him take her luggage and shopping bags up to her bedroom and then spent the rest of the day sleeping.

Later that night, he dumped Alicia's body in the grave. Boyle stood over her body, gripped with a peculiar sadness. He shouldn't have killed her. He should have strangled her until she passed out. That way, when she woke up, he could do it all over again, as many times as he wanted.

Boyle heard a branch snap behind him. He turned around and saw his mother, her face clear in the moonlight. She didn't look angry, or sad, or disappointed. She looked blank.

"Hurry up and bury it," was all she said.

She didn't talk to him during the long walk back to the house.

He spent the time wondering what would happen. Two years ago, when she caught him strangling a cat, she sent him to his room. She waited until he fell asleep and then came in and hit him with the buckle end of a belt. He had the scars to prove it.

His mother locked the front door. "Did you keep her in the house?"

He nodded.

"Show me."

He did. Alicia's rosary beads were on the floor. They must have fallen from his pocket.

"Pick it up," his mother said.

He did. By the time he stood, his mother had locked the door to the wine cellar.

During his two-week confinement, he used the same slop bucket Alicia had used for her bathroom needs. He slept on the cold concrete floor. His mother didn't visit him. She didn't bring him food.

Trapped alone in the cool dark that never went away, Boyle never cried or called out for his mother. He used the time constructively, thinking about what he would do next.

He had some wonderful ideas for his mother.

One day he woke to voices. There was a vent in the adjoining room and he could hear his mother talking to someone upstairs—the police. His mother had called the police. Panic gripped up and then floated away when he heard his grandmother's voice.

"You can't leave him down there forever," Ophelia Boyle was saying.

"Fine," his mother said. "You can take Daniel home with you. I've been thinking he should be spending time with his father, anyway. Should I bring Daniel by the club or the office?"

Boyle had been told his father had died in a car accident before he was born.

"This isn't the first time Daniel's done something like this," his mother said. "I told you about the animals who disappeared around here last summer—and let's not forget the time Marsha Erickson caught him peeking inside her daughter's window in the middle of the night."

Boyle thought about his cousin, Richard Fowler. Richard was Marsha's friend. He had been inside her house several times, had stolen her money and lacy underwear—Richard was the one who had put the sleeping pills in Marsha's beer. When she passed out, Richard called Boyle and said to come over. The two of them spent a wonderful night playing with Marsha inside her bedroom. Her parents were away for the weekend.

After that weekend, Boyle would often wake up in the middle of the night, remembering what he had done to Marsha. Several times he would venture outside and stand by her bedroom window to watch her sleep, imagining all the new and wonderful things he could do to her—only this time she would be conscious. It was more fulfilling when they fought back. He thought about the prostitute Richard had choked to death in the backseat of his car. She didn't pray to God or beg for her life; she fought back with everything she had and might have hurt Richard severely if Boyle hadn't come back with the rock.

His grandmother's voice snapped Boyle out of his daydream: "Daniel is your problem, Cassandra. You're going to have to figure out—"

"I want him gone."

"You had your opportunity," his grandmother said. "I told you about the doctor in Switzerland who would have gotten rid of the bastard with a simple operation, but you absolutely refused because *you* wanted to blackmail—"

"What I wanted, Mother, was for you to protect me. Daddy climbed into my bed, he put his hands between my—"

"You've punished me sufficiently, Cassandra, and you've certainly used the situation to your advantage. I met all of your demands. I built you this brand-new house, filled it with everything you wanted. I bought you expensive cars—I've given you everything you wanted on top of the princely sum of money you demanded. Now you've run through the money. I'm not giving you any more."

"And you keep forgetting that Daddy was the one who got me pregnant," his mother said. "That . . . *thing* downstairs is your son, not mine."

"Cassandra—"

"Get rid of him," his mother said. "Or I will."

Days later, his grandmother opened the door. She told him to shower and get dressed in his best suit. He did. She told him to get in the car. He did. Four hours later, when she pulled up in front of a military school that specialized in treating what she called "troubled boys," she told him not to call home for any reason. His grandmother would handle all financial matters. She gave him a private number to call.

Boyle never called her. The only person he ever talked to was the only person who wanted to talk to him: his cousin Richard.

During his two years at Vermont's Mount Silver Academy, Boyle had learned discipline. When he graduated, he enlisted in the army. There he learned how to put planning and organization above the secret need that burned like a supernova in the center of his mind. He had to apply that same discipline now, to this situation.

Daniel Boyle, forty-eight, went into the other room and stared at the green glow coming from the six monitors set up on the shelf. Rachel Swanson's cell was dark. The other five cells were occupied. They were sleeping. Carol Cranmore seemed to be coming awake.

CHAPTER 21

Boyle's cell phone rang. It was Richard. Boyle heard traffic in the background. Richard was calling from a pay phone. He always called from a pay phone. He was always so careful.

"I've been thinking about Rachel," Richard said. "Do you still have Slavick's Colt Commander?"

"I have it."

"Good. Now listen to me. I want you to take Carol back to Belham."

"No."

"Danny, we need to get rid of her."

"I don't want to."

"You're going to drive Carol back to Belham."

"No."

"You're going to bring her out into the woods and shoot her in the back of the head—and make sure you leave the body out in the open. I want her to be found quickly."

"I want to keep her," Boyle said.

"After you shoot her, I want you to plant Slavick's blood on her clothes and underneath her fingernails. The police will think she fought him off before he shot her. The police will come in and investigate, and they'll find the blood belongs to Slavick. It will match the blood you left at Carol's house."

"Let's play with Carol for awhile. You know what the girls are like when they see the basement for the first time."

"We can't risk it. There's too much trace evidence in the basement. We don't want the police to find anything on her to connect her to Rachel."

"What are we going to do about her?"

"I'm still thinking about it."

"She's at Mass General. I know her room number."

"We'll talk about it when I get there. I'll see you in a couple of hours."

"Wait, there's something I need to tell you," Boyle said. "It's about Victor Grady."

"Grady? What does Grady have to do with this?"

"Do you remember the names of the three girls who saw me strangling Samantha Kent?"

"I know two of them are dead."

"I'm talking about the redhead, Darby McCormick."

Richard didn't answer.

"She's the teenager who left her backpack in the woods," Boyle said. "You went into her house and she fractured your arm with the hammer—"

"I know who she is."

"Do you know she's a crime scene investigator for the Boston Crime Lab?"

Richard didn't answer.

"She's working on Carol Cranmore's case," Boyle said.

"The Grady case is closed."

"I don't like the idea of her snooping around."

"Forget Grady. He's a dead end. Get Carol ready."

"Let's keep her just for tonight. Just give me one night—"

"Do it," Richard said, and hung up.

Boyle only needed a moment to get organized.

He tucked the Colt Commander in the shoulder holster under his vest. He slipped the silencer and stun gun in his right vest pocket so it was handy. The plastic bags holding rags soaked with chloroform were already in each pocket. He made a mental note to cut Carol and collect some of her blood. He wanted to plant it inside Slavick's house. It would be easy to do. Boyle had a set of keys to Slavick's house and shed.

Boyle was about to lock up the filing cabinet when he pulled the drawer back out and removed the old mask made of stitched-together strips of Ace bandages. He hadn't worn it in years. Smiling, Boyle slid the mask over his head and picked up the rope from the wall.

CHAPTER 22

Carol Cranmore sat on a cot, underneath a wool blanket that felt stiff and scratchy against the bare parts of her skin. She didn't know how long she had been awake. She knew she wasn't wearing Tony's shirt anymore. The clothes she was wearing—sweatpants a little too tight and a baggy sweatshirt—smelled of fabric softener.

She had no memory of being undressed. The only memory she had was the one she kept replaying over and over in her mind—the stranger pushing a foul-smelling cloth over her mouth.

Carol buried her hands in her hair. *This isn't supposed to be happening to me. I'm supposed to be at school today. I'm supposed to have lunch with Tony and then I'm supposed to go to the mall with Kari because Abercrombie & Fitch is having a huge sale and I've saved up money from babysitting because I'm a good person I shouldn't be here oh God why is this happening to me?*

The panic felt like a monstrous tide rising above her. Carol drew in a sharp breath and all the fear and terror were rushing through her, rushing up her throat, and she was screaming it into the dark room, screaming until her throat was raw, screaming until she had nothing left.

The darkness didn't go away. Carol closed her eyes and prayed to God—prayed hard. She opened her eyes. The darkness was still here. And she needed to pee. Was there a toilet hidden somewhere in this pitch-black room?

Carol swung her legs off the cot and felt something with a hard edge bump up against her foot. She reached down, hands moving across the shape. It was a cardboard tray holding a wrapped sandwich and a soda can. Whoever had brought her here had not only dressed her before putting her to bed, he had taken the time to wrap a blanket around her to make sure she was warm and had brought her food.

Carol wiped the tears from her face. She removed the Saran Wrap and took a bite of the sandwich. Peanut butter and jelly. She washed it away with the soda. It was Mountain Dew, her favorite.

As Carol ate, she wondered, for a brief moment, if her abductor may have been her father. She had never met him before—she didn't even know his name. Her mother referred to the man as "the donor" and that was it.

If her father had abducted her—stories like that were all over the news, it did happen—he wouldn't lock her up in a room with no lights. No, her father hadn't brought her here. Someone else had.

Carol finished the rest of the Mountain Dew, wondering if there was a light switch on the wall.

The wall behind her had the same rough, sandpaper-like texture as the floor. Concrete, probably. She rubbed her hands up and down along the wall above her cot and failed to find a light switch. But that didn't mean there wasn't one in here.

Carol got her bearings. Okay, here was the end of the cot. Two choices: left or right. She decided to go left and started moving her hands across the wall, counting her steps as she searched for a light switch. She counted all the way to eighteen when the wall ended. No place to move but left.

Nine steps and her shin bumped into something hard. She reached down and felt something cool and smooth. She kept running her hands over the curves and then she felt water and it came to her: a toilet. Good. She wanted to pee but that could wait. Keep moving.

Ten steps and here was a sink.

Eight more steps and her hands were feeling around the controls for a shower. She turned the knob slightly, heard water run through the pipe and then felt it splash her head and face. She was locked in a small, cold room with a cot, a toilet, a sink and a shower. A light switch *had* to be close by. Her captor wouldn't let her live in the dark, would he? *Please God, please let me find a light switch.*

Six more steps and the wall ended. Ten more steps. The wall turned left and Carol followed it with her hands, counting one, two, three, four—wait, here was something rough and hard and cold. It was metal. She kept moving her hands along the metal, up and down and across.

It was a door but not like any door she knew about. This door was very wide and made of steel. No doorknob or lever. If Tony were here, he would know what it was. When his father wasn't busy being a drunk, he was a contractor, and a pretty good one—

Tony. Had he been brought here, too?

"Tony? Tony, where are you?"

Carol stood in the cool dark, listening hard over the blood pounding in her ears.

A voice called out from far away, sounding garbled, as though it were traveling underneath water.

Carol yelled Tony's name again, as loud as she could, and

pressed her ear against the cold steel. Someone was trying to talk back to her. Someone was out there, but the voice was too far away.

An idea floated up from out of the depths of Carol's mind, surprising her: Morse code. She had read about it in history class. She didn't know Morse code, but she knew enough to work with it.

Carol knocked twice on the door. Listen.

Nothing.

Try again.

Two more knocks. Listen.

Two knocks came back, faint but clear.

A panel inside the door swung open to a burst of dim light. Staring at her from the other side was a face covered with dirty bandages, the eyes hidden behind pieces of black cloth.

Carol stumbled backward into the darkness, screaming as the steel door slid open.

CHAPTER 23

B oyle took out the gun, about to enter Carol's room when his mother spoke to him for the first time in years:

You don't have to kill her, Daniel. I can help you.

Boyle's breath was hot and stale underneath the mask. Carol was bunkered underneath the cot, begging him not to hurt her. He didn't want to lose Carol—he didn't want to lose any of them, not now, not after all his hard work and planning.

You can keep her, Daniel. You can keep all of them.

How?

Why should I tell you? After what you and Richard did to me when you came back home? I kept your secret for all those years, and you repaid me by burying me alive out in the woods. I told you then you'd never get rid of me, and I was right. You kill all these women who remind you of me and I'm still with you—I'll always be with you, Daniel. Maybe I'll just let the police come and take you away.

They won't find me. Everything leads to Earl Slavick. I've already planted the pictures on his computer. I've printed out the maps from his computer so the FBI can trace him. With one phone call I'll lead them to Slavick's doorstep.

But that doesn't solve your problem with Rachel, does it?

She doesn't know *anything*. She doesn't—

She made her way into your office, remember? She went through your file cabinet. Who knows what she found in there?

She's never seen my face. And I have Slavick's blood. I slipped inside his house with the copy of the keys I made and I put the chloroform rag over his face while he was sleeping and I took his blood, the tan carpet fibers from his bedroom—

You're very smart, Daniel, but you made a mistake with Rachel. She outsmarted you, and when she wakes up—and you know she will—she'll tell the police everything she knows, and they'll come and take you away. You'll spend the rest of your life locked inside a small, dark room.

I won't let that happen—I'll kill myself, if I have to.

You don't have to kill Carol, but you have to kill Rachel. You need to kill her before she wakes up. I know how to solve your problem with Rachel. Would you like me to tell you?

Yes.

Yes what?

Yes, please. Please help me.

Will you do what you're told?

Yes.

Shut the door.

Boyle did.

Go back to your office.

Boyle did.

Take a seat. That's a good boy. Now here's what you need to do . . .

Boyle listened to his mother explain what needed to be done. He didn't ask any questions because he knew she was right. She was always right.

When she finished, Boyle stood and paced the room, pausing several times to stare at the phone. He wanted to call Richard, but Richard had strict orders never to call him on his cell phone. Boyle knew he should wait until Richard arrived to tell him about the plan but he couldn't wait. Boyle was too excited. He needed to talk to Richard now.

Boyle picked up the phone and dialed Richard's cell. Richard didn't pick up. Boyle hung and dialed again. Richard picked up on the fourth ring. He was angry.

"I told you to *never* call this number—"

"I need to talk to you," Boyle said. "It's important."

"I'll call you back."

The wait was excruciating. Boyle rocked back and forth in his chair, staring at the phone, waiting for Richard to call back. Twenty minutes later, he did.

"We can connect Rachel to Slavick," Boyle said.

"How?"

"Slavick's a member of the Aryan Brotherhood. When he was living in Arkansas, at the compound for the Hand of the Lord, he tried to abduct an eighteen-year-old woman and failed—he would have gone to jail if the woman had been able to pick him out of a lineup. He also trained at their weapons facility, worked in their gun shop. And he firebombed black churches and synagogues."

"You're not telling me anything I don't already know."

"Slavick's planning his own underground movement here in New Hampshire," Boyle said. "I've been inside his compound. He has fertilizer bombs in the shed, and in his basement there's a batch of homemade explosives—plastic explosives. We can use them to create a diversion to get to Rachel."

"You want to bomb the hospital?"

"When a bomb goes off, it creates instant chaos. People will think it's a terrorist attack—they'll be reliving nine-eleven all over again. While everyone's running around, nobody will be paying attention to us. One of us can slip inside and kill Rachel, pump some air through her IV line and she'll go into cardiac arrest. It will look like she died of natural causes."

Richard didn't answer. Good. He was thinking about it.

"If we bomb the hospital, not only will we kill Rachel, we can bring the FBI into this sooner," Boyle said. "Once Slavick's DNA profile finds its match on CODIS, the FBI will be here at lightning speed to take over the case."

"You're right about that. If Slavick's identity makes it into the press, the feds will have a PR nightmare on their hands. Where's Slavick now? At home?"

"He's in Vermont for the weekend, interviewing potential members for his movement," Boyle said. "The GPS unit is still attached to his Porsche. I can tell you where he is right now, if you want."

"If we go ahead with this, you'll have to move—quickly."

"It's time I move again anyway. I've been thinking about heading back to California."

"You can't go back to Los Angeles. They're still looking for you there."

"I was thinking of La Jolla, someplace upscale. We should use this opportunity to get rid of Darby McCormick. Make it look like an accident. I have some ideas."

"We'll talk some more when I get there."

"What about Carol? Can I keep her?"

"For the moment. Don't let her out of the cell yet."

"I'll wait for you," Boyle said. "We can play with her together."

CHAPTER 24

Darby had set up a temporary work space in her old bedroom. The bed was gone, replaced by her father's desk. It faced the two windows overlooking the front yard.

Before leaving work, she made copies of the evidence report and the pictures. She tacked the pictures on the corkboard above the desk and then settled into the chair with the evidence file.

For awhile, she was aware of every sound—the tick of the grandfather clock from downstairs, her mother's soft snoring from down the hallway. Then she was lost in the file.

Two hours later, her head felt crowded, thoughts tripping over one another. It was closing in on eleven. She decided to take a break and went downstairs to make some tea.

The box of clothing was still by the door. She saw the pink sweater and had a new memory—alone in the house at fifteen, the weekend after her father's funeral, his down vest with its smell of cigars pressed against her face.

Darby pulled the sweater from underneath the pair of ripped jeans and sat on the floor. The hum of the refrigerator filled the kitchen. She rubbed the cashmere between her fingers. Soon this would be all that was left of her mother—her clothes with their fading whispers of perfume, memories frozen in pictures.

Darby stared at the spot where Melanie had stood begging for her life. She stared at the wall with its coat of paint that hid Stacey's blood. Victor Grady was sealed between these walls, now and forever, along with memories of her father, and Darby couldn't understand how Sheila could move through these rooms day after day competing with these two totally separate but equally powerful ghosts.

A car raced by, blaring rap music.

Darby found she was standing. Her hands trembled as she bent to pick up the sweater. She didn't know why she was sweating.

It was closing in on midnight. Best to get some sleep. Tomorrow morning she and Coop were going to head out early to the Cranmore house. With a few hours of sleep and a fresh eye, she was hoping to find something she might have overlooked or missed.

Upstairs, Darby laid in the recliner, cold beneath the comforter. When sleep finally came, Darby dreamed of a house with mazes of dark hallways and shifting rooms, doors that opened to black holes.

Carol Cranmore was also dreaming.

Her mother stood in the doorway of her bedroom, saying it was time to wake up and get ready for school. Carol could still see the smile on her mother's face when her eyes fluttered open to pitch-black darkness. She felt the itchy blanket wrapped around her and then remembered where she was and what had happened to her.

Panic flared and then, oddly, disappeared. And as strange as it sounded, she still felt sleepy. The last time she had felt this exhausted was last summer, at Stan Petrie's all-weekend party down in Falmouth where they drank all night and played touch football all day at the beach.

Carol wondered about the food again. Was it drugged? The sandwich had left a slight chalky taste in her mouth—it had tasted funny even when she was eating it—and some time later, after the man with the mask shut the door, she had grown real tried, which surprised her. She shouldn't be tired. She should be wide awake with fear, but she could barely keep her eyes open. And she needed to pee again. Badly.

She crawled out from underneath the cot, stood and immediately swung her right hand out, feeling for the wall. There it was. How many steps until the wall ended? Eight? Ten? She staggered forward, blinking, eyes wide open in the darkness that wouldn't go away. This must be what a blind person felt like.

She found the toilet and sat down. For no reason at all, she saw the desk in her room with its window view of the ugly street and the trees with their beautiful leaves having turned gold, red and yellow. She wondered what time it was, whether it was day or night. Was it still raining?

By the time she flushed, Carol felt better. Awake. Now she had to deal with the fear.

Carol knew she had to come up with a plan. The man who had brought her here would be coming for her again. She couldn't fight him off with her hands. Maybe there was something in here she could use—the bed. The bed was made with these steel rods. Maybe she could try and dismantle it, grab one of the rods and use it as a bat and knock him unconscious.

Carol felt her way through the darkness, thinking about the person who was trapped down here with her. She hoped to God it was Tony. Maybe Tony was awake, wandering around his room right now, looking for something to use to defend—

Carol bumped headfirst into something solid, a scream escaping her lips as she stumbled backward, almost tripping.

Not a wall, it definitely wasn't a wall, didn't have its hard, rough flatness. What was it then? Not the sink either. This was something new and different. What was it? Whatever this thing was, it was blocking her path.

A tiny green light glowed in the darkness, directly in front of her.

The man with the mask was standing behind a camera.

The flash went off, the bright white light piercing her eyes. Blinded, Carol stumbled back. She bumped into the sink, tripped and fell to the floor.

Another flash.

Carol crawled away, bright spots of lights dancing and fading in front of her eyes. Another flash and she bumped her head against the corner of the wall. She was trapped.

CHAPTER 25

Darby drove out early the next morning, while it was still dark.

Half a dozen patrolmen were busy redirecting the traffic on Coolidge Road in order to accommodate the swelling numbers of state police cruisers, unmarked detective cars and news vans that were clogging up the streets near Carol Cranmore's house. Small armies of volunteers were gathered, getting ready to canvass the neighborhood with fliers bearing Carol's picture.

Darby's attention turned to the state troopers holding the leashes of search and rescue dogs. She was surprised to see them. Because of statewide budget cuts, search and rescue dogs weren't ordinarily called out to the scene of missing or abducted people.

"I wonder who's picking up the tab for the dogs," Coop said.

"The Sarah Sullivan fund, I bet." Sarah Sullivan was the name of a Belham girl who was abducted from the Hill several years ago. Her father, Mike Sullivan, a local contractor, had set up a fund to cover any additional expenses related to a missing person's investigation.

Darby had to wait for the cops to move the blockades out of the way. When she turned the corner, the crowds of reporters and TV crews saw the crime scene vehicle and descended on them, shouting questions.

By the time they finally reached the house, her ears were ringing. Darby shut the front door and placed her kit in the downstairs foyer. The copper smell of blood grew stronger as she climbed the stairs.

Dianne's bedroom was in the same neat, tidy condition as it had been the other night. One of the dresser drawers was half open, as was the closet door. On the floor was a safe, one of those portable fireproof models people used to store important documents.

Carol's mother had probably come here to pack up some clothes while the house was being processed as a crime scene. Darby remembered standing in her own bedroom, packing up clothes for her stay at the hotel while a detective watched from the doorway.

Darby stepped into Carol's room. A gold, predawn light was visible through the windows. She looked at the surfaces covered with fingerprint powder, trying to tune out the sounds of dogs barking and reporters shouting questions over the constant blaring of car horns from Coolidge Road.

"What are we looking for, exactly?" Coop asked.

"I don't know."

"Good. That should help us narrow down our search."

The teenager's clothes hung on wire hangers inside the closet. A few shirts and pants were marked with the kind of stickers and price tags often used at thrift stores and yard sales. The shoes and sneakers were arranged in two neat rows by the season: the summer sneakers and sandals in the back, and in the front row, the fall and winter boots and shoes.

The window set up by the desk overlooked a chain-link fence and the neighbor's yard with its clothesline stretched from the back porch to a tree. Below, in the overgrown weeds, was a wooden ladder half-buried in the dirt. Crushed beer cans and cigarette butts littered the ground. Darby wondered what Carol thought of this view, how she managed to push it aside so it wouldn't get to her.

The top of the desk was clean and neat. An assortment of colored pencils was organized in glass jars. The middle drawer contained a decent charcoal sketch of her boyfriend reading a book in the brown chair from downstairs. Carol had left out the duct tape in the drawing.

The folder underneath the drawing held magazine and newspaper clippings of biographical profiles of successful women. Carol had underlined several quotes in red ink and made notes in the margins like "important" and "remember this." Written on the inside of the folder, in black marker, was a quote: "Behind every successful woman is herself."

A three-ring binder contained articles on beauty secrets. The section marked "Exercise" was devoted to dieting tips. For inspiration, Carol had pasted a picture of an extremely thin quasi-celebrity wearing big, round sunglasses.

"As fun as this is, I'm not much use to you up here. I'm going to take a look at the kitchen again. Holler down if you find anything."

Carol's bedding had been stripped and bagged. Darby sat on the sagging mattress and looked out the window at the television cameras. She wondered if Carol's abductor was watching.

What was she looking for, exactly?

What common trait did Carol Cranmore share with the other missing women?

Both Carol and Terry Mastrangelo were average-looking at best. In her picture, Terry had a frumpy, exhausted look Darby had seen in lots of single mothers. Carol was five years younger, a senior in high school. She was the better looking of the two, razor thin, with sharp blue eyes set against pale, freckled skin.

No, it wasn't a physical attraction; Darby felt sure of that. The trait these two young women shared was something beyond the surface, something she couldn't see.

The problem was that Darby didn't know Carol beyond the framed pictures on the hallway and the pieces of evidence collected in bags—she didn't know Terry Mastrangelo at all. At the moment, both women were snapshots frozen in pictures.

Terry Mastrangelo was a single mother.

Dianne Cranmore was a single mother.

Was Carol's mother the intended target?

Granted, Dianne Cranmore was a full decade older than Terry, but age didn't seem to be a factor in the abductor's selection process. The idea was still turning over in Darby's mind when she stood and headed back to the mother's bedroom.

Dianne had spent good money on the comforter and sheets. She had some decent jewelry, but nothing worth stealing. Well-worn clothes hung inside the closet. It looked like she splurged a little on nice shoes.

Across from the bed was a cheap bookcase holding framed pictures of Carol as a baby. Two shelves were crammed with paperback romance novels plucked from library book sales. The books and trinkets on the bottom shelf were coated with dust—except for the three black leather-bound albums. Those had been moved.

Had Dianne pulled them out last night? If she did, why had she returned them? Maybe she wanted another picture of Carol—the one that was printed on the flyers.

Darby snapped on a pair of latex gloves and settled on the carpeted floor to examine the bottom shelf.

Mounted underneath the shelf, tucked in the far corner so it was safely out of view, was a small black plastic box half the size of a sugar packet. Sticking out of one side, a quarter inch in length, was an antenna.

A listening device.

Grabbing the penlight from her shirt pocket, Darby lay on her back and examined the black box. It was secured to the wood by a Velcro mounting strip. No wires, so it was most likely battery operated.

There were devices on the market that could be turned on and off remotely to save battery power; some were voice activated. They all had different transmitting ranges. What she needed to know were the specifications of this device.

Darby leaned in closer, hoping to find the manufacturer's name and model number. She didn't see it. The manufacturer's stamp was most likely located on one of the sides flush against the wood, or on the back of the unit. In order to find it, she'd have to tear the device away from the Velcro strip. There was no way to do that quietly.

And if he's listening right now, he'll hear it and know we've found the listening device.

Darby stood up, legs fluttering, and hustled back to search Carol's room again.

CHAPTER 26

Darby found a second listening device underneath Carol's bed, mounted against the frame. Like the first device, this unit had been placed in such a way that she couldn't find the manufacturer's name or model number.

Two listening devices. She wondered how many more were inside the house.

Here was something else to think about: If Carol's abductor had taken the time to install listening devices inside the house, was he was also monitoring police radio and cell phones? They sold police scanners at Radio Shack, and cell phone frequencies were just as easy to pick up, if you had the right equipment.

Coop was in the kitchen. She caught his attention, pressed a finger to her lips, then wrote what she had found on his clipboard.

He nodded and started to search the kitchen. Darby went outside.

Bloodhounds and their handlers were searching the woods, their barks echoing through the pleasantly warm air. Standing on the front porch, she dialed Banville's number and watched a man limp his way over to a telephone pole and use a staple gun to tack up a leaflet holding Carol's picture. She wondered if Carol's abductor was sitting in his car right now, listening.

Darby remembered the monitoring equipment the feds had used in a case she and Coop had worked on last year. The equipment was big and bulky. If Carol's abductor was using similar equipment, it would need to be placed in something like the back of the van.

Banville picked up.

"Where are you?" Darby asked.

"On my way back from Lynn," Banville said. "I got a call early this morning about our boy LBC. He's been crashing at his girl-friend's house for the past two months. He's got a size nine foot, doesn't own any boots, and we have two witnesses who will swear LBC was with them the night the Cranmore girl was taken. I think we can safely scratch him off our list. We've rounded up all the local pedophiles. They're at the station right now."

"How soon before you're back in Belham?"

"I'm already here. What's going on?"

"Tell me where you are."

"I just stopped off for coffee at Max's on Edgell Road."

Darby knew the place. "Stay put. I'll be there in ten minutes."

Before she left, she checked in with Coop. Darby headed back out, deciding to walk to the diner. It would be quicker than driving through all the traffic, and she could use the time to organize her thoughts.

Daniel Boyle stood across the street, watching Darby McCormick walking fast down Coolidge, head down and hands stuffed in her windbreaker pockets. He wondered where she was going.

For the past hour, while he had been papering the nearby houses with fliers, tucking the sheets underneath windshield wipers and inside mailboxes, he had been listening to Darby and her partner's movements inside the house over his headphones. The iPod tucked in his pocket was actually a six-channel receiver that allowed him to switch between the six listening devices he had planted inside the house.

He had listened to the chatty conversation between Darby and her partner inside Carol's room. After her partner left, Darby had rustled about the bedroom for a bit, opening drawers, before heading back to the mother's bedroom. Lots of movement in there, especially near the bottom shelf of the bookcase where he had placed one of the listening devices.

Then Darby headed back to Carol's bedroom again, and after half an hour or so of searching, she went back downstairs to the kitchen. There was no conversation between Darby and her partner. A few minutes later, she was standing on the front porch, making a call on her cell phone.

Why did she have to come outside to make the call? If she had found something interesting, some new piece of evidence, why not make the call from inside the house? Why did she have to step outside?

Boyle had placed the listening devices in strategic locations where no one should be looking. Had she found them?

Clearly, she had discovered *something*. When she was on the phone, she had seemed either nervous or excited—and she kept looking around the street as if she knew he was here, mixed in with all the volunteers. She had watched him limp his way over to the telephone pole and put up a flier. He had adopted the limp because he wanted to stay close to the house. The cop handing out the fliers had no problem with it.

Boyle watched Darby take a right onto Drummond Avenue. He wanted to follow her and see where she was going.

No. Too risky. She had seen him. He should leave, just to be safe.

Boyle switched the receiver to the listening devices inside the kitchen and limped his way back to his car. All he heard was the echo of footsteps.

The reception on the iPod grew dimmer. The receiver inside his car had a much broader range. The police were no doubt looking for a van, so he had opted for his recent purchase, an old Aston Martin Lagonda, the same car his grandfather/father had owned. The car's engine and transmission were brand-new, but the outer shell was in desperate need of a new paint job. The paint had started to fleck and peel in several places, especially around the pockets of rust.

Boyle picked up his new BlackBerry phone. Richard had given it to him last night. It was equipped with encryption technology so it couldn't be overheard by the police or anyone trying to listen in on a scanner. The stolen phone had been reprogrammed so the calls couldn't be traced by the phone company.

"What's Darby doing?"

"She's still walking," Richard said. "I wonder if she found the bugs you left in the house."

"I'm wondering the same thing. What do you want to do?"

"I think we should assume she found them. Where did you buy them?"

"I didn't. They're homemade."

"Good. She can't trace them. Do you have any extra ones?"

"I do."

"We should plant some of them inside Slavick's house."

"Do you still want to go ahead with the plan?"

"Absolutely," Richard said. "We need to throw them off the scent. I'll call you later."

Boyle started his car and drove away from the commotion to find a quiet street.

Twenty minutes later, he was driving through a more upscale neighborhood. No cars sitting on blocks here, no welfare mothers sitting on their porches. This neighborhood had lots of nice lawns and neatly painted houses.

As Boyle examined the homes, he recalled how he wasn't that far away from where Darby used to live. He wondered if her mother was still living there. That was easy enough to find out.

There, the white house. The door behind the screen door was open. Someone was home.

Boyle drove to the end of the street. He put on a pair of gloves and reached under the seat for the padded mailer. He rolled the window down, turned the car around and tossed the mailer onto the porch steps of the white house.

By the time Boyle reached the highway, he felt relaxed and in control. The plan was in motion. Now all he needed to do was to get himself a FedEx or UPS truck and a body.

CHAPTER 27

Darby found Banville sitting in a red vinyl booth in the back corner, nursing a cup of coffee. No one else was around him. Taped to the window facing the small parking lot was a poster board holding Carol Cranmore's picture.

"I found listening devices inside Carol's house," Darby said after she sat down. "I don't think they've been there that long, since none of them are coated in dust."

"You said listening *devices*. How many did you find?"

"At the moment, four—one in the mother's bedroom, one in Carol's room, the other two mounted on top of the kitchen cabinets. I don't know the make or the model number of the bugs. That information is most likely stamped on the back, and I can't examine them because each one is mounted by Velcro. There's no way to rip the bug off without making any noise."

"And if we try to do that and he happens to be listening in, he'll know we found the bug."

"That's the problem. If I try to remove the bugs, he'll hear us. If I dust it for prints, the fingerprint brush will make noise against the mike and he'll hear us. And if I did happen to find a print, I'd have to use a tape lift to transfer it.

"The other problem is the power source," Darby said. "They

run on batteries. He can't leave them on all day, so there's a good chance they're remotely operated. He can turn them on and off to conserve battery power. If I had the device's make and model, I could do a simple Google search and find the product specs. It would give us an idea of how long the batteries last, if it's remote-operated, and the transmitting range. Some have a radius as much as half a mile, and almost every one of them can transmit through walls and windows with crystal-clear clarity."

"How do you know so much about bugs?"

"One of the first big cases I worked on was a mob case. Thanks to the feds, I got a crash course in listening devices. Judging by what I saw at the house, I doubt these devices are that sophisticated. They may even be homemade."

"Funny you should mention the feds. I got a message this morning from the Boston office. The site profiler here in town wants to talk to me."

"What did he want?"

"I haven't talked with him yet."

"I think our guy took Carol out of the house and put her in the back of a van—only when he opened the doors, he found that Jane Doe wasn't there. He searched for her, couldn't find her, and at some point decided he had to leave. But before he did, he went back inside and planted the bugs in strategic locations so he could listen to us as we moved through the rooms. I think it's safe to say he was listening to us last night. How many people do you have guarding Jane Doe's room?"

"At the moment, just one."

"Increase it. And make sure they check the ID of every person who comes inside the ICU."

"I'm already doing that. The press found out she's at Mass

General. They did a live news feed outside the hospital. It was all over the news."

"And Jane Doe?"

"As of nine this morning, she was still sedated."

"I think it would be a good idea if you have someone put together a list of names of every volunteer helping search for Carol Cranmore. Check licenses, too, see if you have anyone from out of town. Any luck locating Terry Mastrangelo's family?"

"We're working on it." Banville returned the coffee cup to its saucer. "About these devices you found," he said. "Do you have any idea about the kind of monitoring equipment our guy would be using?"

"Depending on the bug's frequency strength, it could be something as simple as an FM receiver. I've heard of receivers disguised as a Walkman, but again, the range would be rather short. If he was using something like that, he'd have to be close to the house. To listen from a longer range, you'd need more sophisticated equipment—bulky stuff that's not so easy to conceal."

"So right now our guy could be sitting in his van parked somewhere near the Cranmore house."

"Please don't tell me you're thinking of having patrol cars do a sweep of the area," Darby said. If Carol's abductor spotted patrolmen stopping people in their cars, he wouldn't hesitate to leave the area. He might even panic and kill Carol.

"It's tempting, sure, but it's too risky," Banville said. "No, what I was thinking was how we could use this to our advantage."

"You set up a trap."

"You sound like you've already got something in mind."

"First, we need to figure out the frequency range of the listening devices. Then we set up roadblocks—we lock down every possible way he can escape. You put me in one of the rooms with Coop, and as we're talking about made-up evidence, you track down the frequency."

"That's not a bad plan. Tracking down the frequency, though, we're not set up for that."

"The feds are. They come in, they'll find out what frequency those devices are transmitting on, and they can narrow it down. We need to move on this soon. I'm pretty sure those listening devices operate on batteries. We might have a day or two before they die."

Banville stared out the window, at the people heading into the diner. She couldn't read anything in his face. Every emotion, from surprise to sadness, was carefully sealed behind the same blank mask he always wore.

"This morning a reporter from the *Herald* cornered me and asked if I'd like to comment on the connection between Carol Cranmore and a missing woman by the name of Terry Mastrangelo."

"Jesus Christ."

"Tell me about it. So now, in addition to everything else, I've got to deal with a leak." He was looking at her now. "Who else knows about Mastrangelo?"

"Everyone at the lab," Darby said. "What about you?"

"I've tried to keep that information locked down to a few key people. The problem is, in a missing person investigation, especially one of this size, it creates a real competitive environment. Reporters want to be the first to get the inside scoop, and they're willing to pay for it. You'd be surprised at the kind of money they offer."

"Someone approached you?"

"Not me. They know better. But there are plenty of guys in the department who need extra cash for child support payments or maybe they got their eyes on a new set of wheels. Who else at the lab knows about the bugs?"

"At the moment, just me and Coop."

"Keep it that way."

"My boss wants me to update him," Darby said. "You're putting me in an awkward position."

"As far as he's concerned, I was the one who found the listening devices. You don't know anything about it."

"What about using the reporter? Have him plant a story about how the crime lab is planning on going through the house, say, tomorrow night because we're looking for certain key evidence. That way we can guarantee he'll be listening."

"I was thinking the same thing. Let me make some calls, and I'll get back to you. You want a ride back to the house?"

"I'm going to grab some coffee and then I'll walk back. The fresh air helps me think."

Darby's phone rang as she was standing in line. It was Leland.

"AFIS came back with a hit on Jane Doe's prints at one a.m. this morning. Her name is Rachel Swanson, from Durham, New Hampshire. She was twenty-three when she disappeared."

"How long has she been missing?"

"Almost five years. I don't have the details yet, just some preliminary stuff. Any luck at the house?"

"I struck out." Darby didn't like lying to Leland, but this was Banville's investigation, and he had decided how he wanted to play it out.

"I found Neil Joseph in the squad room and asked him to pull up the case file, see what's listed on NCIC," Leland said. "I've already talked with someone at the state lab in New Hampshire. They're going to fax over what they have for evidence."

"I'm on my way."

CHAPTER 28

By noon, Darby had learned most of the facts on Rachel Swanson's disappearance.

In the early morning hours of New Year's Day, 2001, twenty-three-year-old Rachel Swanson said good-bye to her close friends in Nashua, New Hampshire, and made the hour's drive back to the Durham, to the house she had recently moved into with her boyfriend, Chad Bernstein, who had skipped the party because he was ill. Lisa Dingle, a neighbor returning home from her own New Year's Eve celebration, saw Rachel's Honda Accord pull into the driveway sometime around two a.m. Rachel waved to her neighbor and entered through the side door of her house.

An hour later, Dingle, an insomniac, was still up reading in bed when she heard a car start. She glanced up from her book and saw Chad Bernstein's black BMW backing out of the driveway.

Five days later, when Lisa Dingle learned that both Bernstein and his girlfriend were missing, she called the police.

Police focused their attention on Bernstein. The thirty-six-year-old software engineer had been previously married, and the ex-wife was all too willing to tell police the stories about her former husband's physical abuse. She knew her ex was capable of hurting a woman, and the police knew it, too. The former wife had called 911 three times. During their last argument, Chad had pulled a knife and threatened to kill her.

Bernstein traveled extensively around the country for business. Three times a year he visited his office's London branch. A thorough investigation of Bernstein's house failed to produce his passport. The BMW was never found.

At quarter to one, the New Hampshire state lab faxed over the evidence report from the case. There was no sign of a forced entry, but boot prints were discovered in a flower bed outside one of the back windows—a man's boot print, size eleven. A mold of the footwear impression was taken, and the forensics technician Darby spoke to promised to send out a comparison sample via FedEx later today.

"So instead of shooting Chad Bernstein, our guy abducts the boyfriend," Coop told Darby. They were jogging through the Public Garden, having decided to take advantage of the unusually warm fall weather and clear their heads. "The question before us is why."

"It makes the pattern less noticeable," Darby said. "Plus this guy is smart enough to abduct women from different states, so when a detective gets on NCIC or VICAP, he can't find a common denominator except missing women—and women disappear all the time, right?"

"And he mixes up the pattern at the crime scenes. Terry Mastrangelo was abducted outside of her house. Rachel Swanson was grabbed when she came home, and then he took her and her boyfriend somewhere. Then our guy goes inside Carol Cranmore's house, shoots the boyfriend and leaves with her."

"If Rachel Swanson hadn't escaped, we'd be looking in all the wrong places."

"You know what I keep wondering? How long has he been doing this?"

"We know he's been doing it for at least five years," Darby said. "Now we've got to figure out what he's using these women for. I'm hoping the blood from the house finds a match on CODIS."

"I keep playing around with those letters you found on Rachel Swanson's wrist. I can't see the pattern. Any new thoughts?"

"Nothing beyond what I told you before about it being directions for something."

They jogged up a set of stairs and then ran over the bridge overlooking the swan boats, heading toward the Common. Darby had to run fast to keep up.

Twenty minutes later, Darby spotted a hot dog cart and stopped running. "I need to eat something before I pass out," she said. "You want anything?"

"I'll take a bottle of water."

While she ordered a chili dog loaded with onions and a Coke, Coop made small talk with a female jogger dressed in very tight spandex. Darby noticed two professionally dressed women eating their lunch on a bench; they were staring at Coop. Darby wondered if Carol's abductor had done that, had sat on a bench somewhere like the Public Garden, waiting for someone to catch his eye.

Was it as simple as that? Darby hoped the selection process wasn't some random intersection. She very much wanted to believe all three women shared one single common denominator.

Darby handed Coop his water. A moment later, he joined her on a bench set up across from rows of colorful mums arranged around a water fountain.

"You know what's missing from this hot dog?" Darby said.

"Real meat?"

"No, Fritos."

"The stuff you eat, it's amazing you don't have an ass the size of an elephant."

"You're right, Coop. Maybe I should just eat heads of lettuce like your last girlfriend. It was great when she passed out at the Christmas party."

"I told her she should splurge and have some ranch dressing with her celery sticks."

"Seriously, do you ever feel guilty for being so shallow?"

"Yes. I cry myself to sleep every night." Coop shut his eyes and leaned back against the bench to soak up the last of the afternoon sun.

Darby shook her head. She gathered up her trash and brought it over to the garbage can.

"Excuse me." It was the good-looking blonde Coop had been speaking to a few minutes ago. "I hope you don't think this is too forward of me, but that guy you're sitting with, is he your boyfriend?"

Darby finished chewing. "He was until he came out of the closet," she said.

"Why are all the good-looking guys gay?"

"It was for the best anyway. The man is hung like a cocktail weiner. His name is Jackson Cooper, lives in Charlestown. Warn all your friends."

Coop was eyeing Darby when she came back. "What were you two talking about?"

"She was asking for directions to Cheers."

"Darb, you grew up in Belham."

"Unfortunately, yes."

"You remember the Summer of Fear?"

She nodded. "Victor Grady made six women disappear that summer."

"One of his victims was from Charlestown, this girl named Pamela Driscol," Coop said. "She was friends with my sister Kim.

They were at some party one night, and Pam walked home and vanished. Pam was . . . She was just this really nice person. Very shy. She used to cover her mouth when she laughed because she had an overbite. Every time she came over she brought me a Hershey's Kiss. I can still remember her sitting in my sister's bedroom, listening to Duran Duran records and giggling about how cute Simon LeBon was."

"I thought the bass player was better looking."

"He didn't do it for me." Coop's face turned serious. "When Pam disappeared, everyone in town thought we had a boogeyman prowling around at night. My mother was so paranoid, she made my sisters move up to the second floor. She wanted an alarm system, but we couldn't afford one, so she convinced my old man to change all the locks on the house and install some extra deadbolts. Sometimes at night I'd wake up and hear a noise, and it would be my mother running around downstairs making sure the doors and windows were locked. My sisters wouldn't walk anywhere alone. Not that they could. Charlestown had instituted a curfew because of what happened to Pam."

Coop wiped the sweat from his face. "Wasn't one of Grady's victims from Belham?"

"There were two," Darby said. "Melanie Cruz and Stacey Stephens."

"Did you know them?"

"We went to school together. I was friends with Melanie— good friends."

"So you know what I'm talking about," Coop said. "That's what this case reminds me of, that same kind of fear."

They jogged back to the station and hit the showers. Darby was drying her hair when her cell phone rang. The caller was Dr.

Hathcock from Mass General. It was difficult to hear her over the screaming.

"What did you say?" Darby asked.

"I said Jane Doe just woke up. She's yelling for someone named Terry."

CHAPTER 29

Darby was relieved to see two additional patrolmen stationed outside the ICU doors.

"Doc's waiting for you inside," the chubby one said with a wry grin. "Enjoy."

Darby was wondering what he meant when she saw the tall, balding man huddled against the wall around the corner from Rachel Swanson's room, having a private conversation with Dr. Hathcock. The man's name was Dr. Thomas Lomborg. He was the hospital's director of psychiatry and author of several best-selling books on deviant criminal behavior.

"Damn," Coop said, patting down his pockets.

"What's wrong?"

"I forgot to pack my pompous asshole repellent."

"Play nice."

Darby flinched at the painful cry coming from down the corridor: *"TERRY!"*

Quick introductions all around. Lomborg spoke first.

"I gave Jane Doe a mild sedative to calm her down. As you can hear, it hasn't had much of an effect. Dr. Hathcock and I both agree her physical condition is still too risky to handle an antipsychotic drug, and I'm a bit leery of prescribing one until I can diagnose her mental condition. Dr. Hathcock told me Jane Doe believes you're this person named Terry?"

"She did the other night, when I found her under the porch," Darby said. "Her name is Rachel Swanson."

"Is Terry a real person?"

"Yes, she is. I can't get into specifics, but Terry and Rachel knew each other for an extended period of time."

"Can you at least tell me the circumstances of their relationship? It might help me with a diagnosis and possible treatment."

"They endured the same trauma," Darby said.

"Which is?"

"I don't know."

"And Rachel Swanson? Can you tell me anything about her?"

"Nothing that would be helpful," Darby said. "Has she spoken at all? Said anything beyond calling out for Terry?"

"Not to my knowledge." Lomborg looked to Dr. Hathcock, who was shaking her head.

"TERRY, WHERE ARE YOU?"

"I want to go in her room and see if I can talk to her again," Darby said.

"I'll be in there when you question her," Lomborg said.

"Rachel won't talk if you're in there—if anyone is in there. She wouldn't talk until I was alone with her."

"Then I'll listen outside the door."

"I'm sorry, but I can't allow that," Darby said. "For whatever reason, this woman trusts me, and I don't want to do anything to jeopardize that trust."

Lomborg stiffened. The dark circles under his eyes were covered with a light concealer so he'd look good for the camera crews camped out in front of the hospital.

"Are you going to record your conversation?" Lomborg asked.

"I am."

"I want a copy before you leave."

"You'll get one after it's been reviewed."

"This is not only highly irregular, it's against hospital procedure."

"TEEERRRRRRRRY!"

"Dr. Lomborg, I don't want to argue, I want to get in there and calm Rachel down," Darby said. "What would you suggest I do?"

"That's difficult to say, since I don't have much information about the case, or the circumstances causing her trauma. She's in a highly agitated state because she wants out of her restraints. Under no circumstances are you to do that. Despite your success the previous evening, Rachel may not be as receptive this time. She attacked a nurse."

"Yes, I know. Dr. Hathcock told me what happened yesterday."

"I was referring to this morning's incident," Lomborg said. "A nurse, thinking Rachel Swanson was still sedated, reached across her face to change a bandage, and Rachel bit her arm. Speaking of which, what's this business about the numbers and letters she wrote on her wrist?"

"We don't know." *Come on, you stuffy bastard, let me in there.*

"You need to try and convince her that we're here to help. She seems to think she's being kept somewhere. That's all I can tell you."

Rachel Swanson screamed for help, her bed thumping against the floor.

"Those two gentlemen standing outside her door, the ones dressed in hospital whites, they're psychiatric orderlies," Lomborg said. "They know how to restrain patients, if it comes to that."

"That's fine, but I don't want them or anyone else looking through the window. It might scare her." Darby took out her microcassette recorder. It was a small model, easily concealed inside a shirt pocket, and held a brand-new ninety-minute tape.

"I know you're anxious to get in there," Lomborg said, "but please understand this: If anything happens to you, the hospital will not be held liable. Are we clear on that point?"

Darby nodded. She pressed the RECORD button and tucked the recorder in her shirt pocket.

It seemed to take a long time to reach the door.

Gripping the cold steel handle, Darby fished for some scrap of memory, some thought or image she could use to keep her anchored against the rising tide of fear. The summer when she came back home for the first time, Sheila told her there was nothing in the house that could hurt her and held her hand as they walked through the house together. Her mother wasn't here, and nobody was going to hold her hand. Nobody was holding Carol Cranmore's hand.

Darby took in a deep breath and held it as she opened the door.

CHAPTER 30

Rachel Swanson's body was drenched in sweat. Her eyes were clamped shut and she was whispering to herself, as if saying a prayer.

Darby walked toward the bed, taking slow, quiet steps. Rachel Swanson didn't stir, didn't move. When Darby reached the side of the bed, she leaned in close to make out the words caught between Rachel's pinched, wheezing voice:

"One R L three R L."

Rachel was chanting the words she had written on her arm.

"Two L R two R L R R S L—no R, the last one is *R.*"

Darby placed the tape recorder on the pillow. She waited a moment, listening as Rachel Swanson counted all the way to six and then started over.

"Rachel, it's me. Terry."

Rachel Swanson's eyes flew open, focused. "Terry, oh thank God you found me." She tugged at her restraints. "He's got me. He's got me good this time."

"He's not here."

"Yes, he is. I saw him."

"There's no one in here but you and me. You're safe."

"He came to me last night and put on these handcuffs."

"You're in a hospital," Darby said. "You . . . accidentally attacked a nurse."

"He injected me again and before I fell asleep. I saw him look around my cell."

"You're in a hospital. There are people here who want to help you—I want to help you."

Rachel moved her head up off the pillow. Her bloody and nearly toothless smile made Darby want to scream.

"I know what he's looking for," Rachel said, her arms and legs straining against the restraints. "I took it from his office. He can't find it because I buried it."

"What did you bury?"

"I'll show you, but you've got to find a way to help me out of these handcuffs. I can't find my handcuff key. I must have dropped it."

"Rachel, do you trust me?"

"*Please,* I can't . . ." Rachel started crying. "I can't fight him anymore. I don't have anything left."

"You don't have to fight anymore. You're safe. You're inside a hospital now. There are people here who are going to help you get better."

Rachel Swanson wasn't listening. She eased her head back against the pillow and shut her eyes.

You're not getting anywhere. Try something else.

Darby slipped her hand inside Rachel's, the woman's bony fingers lifeless and rough against her skin.

"I'll protect you, Rachel. Tell me where he is, and I'll find him."

"I told you, he's *here.*"

"What's his name?"

"I don't know his name."

"What does he look like?"

"He doesn't have a face. He keeps changing his face."

"What do you mean?"

Rachel started shaking.

"It's okay," Darby said. "I'm here. I won't let anyone hurt you."

"You were there. You saw what he did to Paula and Marci."

"I know, but I'm having trouble remembering. Remind me what happened."

Rachel's bottom lip quivered. She didn't answer.

"I saw the letters and numbers you wrote on your wrist," Darby said. "The letters are directions, aren't they? L equals left, R equals right."

Rachel opened her eyes. "It doesn't matter if you go right or left or straight, they all lead to dead ends, remember?"

"But you found a way out."

"There's no way out of here, there are only places to hide."

"What do the numbers mean?"

"You've got to find the key before he comes back. Look under my bed, I might have dropped it there."

"Rachel, I need—"

"FIND THE KEY!"

As Darby pretended to look around the floor, she wondered if Rachel would reveal more information if she wasn't in her restraints. Lomborg would never allow it—not without him being in the room, not without the orderlies present.

"Did you find it, Terry?"

"I'm still looking."

Think. Don't let this opportunity slip away. Think.

"Hurry, the door's going to open any minute," Rachel said.

No one was standing outside the door; no one was even near the door. As much as she hated the idea, Darby wanted to go consult that stuffy prick Lomborg and see if he had any ideas.

"I can't find it," Darby said.

"It's here, I just dropped it."

"I'm going to get help."

Rachel Swanson bucked against her restraints. *"DON'T LEAVE ME ALONE WITH HIM, DON'T YOU DARE LEAVE ME ALONE AGAIN."*

Darby grabbed her hand. "It's okay. I won't let him hurt you, I promise."

"Don't leave me, Terry, please don't leave me."

"I won't leave you. I'm not going anywhere." Using her foot, Darby pulled a chair over and sat down. Think.

Okay. Rachel thinks we're still trapped, so let's go along with the delusion.

"Who else is in here with us?"

"There's no one left," Rachel said. "Paul and Marci are dead, and Chad . . ." Rachel started crying again.

"What happened to Chad?"

Rachel wouldn't answer.

"Paula and Marci," Darby said. "What are their last names? I can't remember."

No answer.

"There's someone else down here with us," Darby said. "Her name is Carol. Carol Cranmore."

"There's no one named Carol in here."

"She's sixteen. She needs our help."

"I haven't seen her. Is she new?"

"Where is she?"

Think, don't blow it.

"I heard her cry out for help," Darby said, "but I can't see her."

"She must be on the other side. How long has she been down here?"

"A little over a day."

"She's probably still sleeping. He always makes them sleep when they first get here, puts drugs in the food. The doors won't open for awhile, then. There's still time."

"What's he going to do to her?"

"Is she tough? Is she a fighter?"

"She's scared," Darby said. "We need to help her."

"We need to get to her before the doors open. You've got to get me out of these handcuffs."

"What happens when the doors open?"

"Get me out of these handcuffs, Terry."

"I will, just tell me—"

"I've helped you, Terry. All those times I showed you where to hide, all those times I protected you—now it's your turn to help me. *Get me out of these goddamn handcuffs right now.*"

"I will. Let's call out to Carol and tell her what to do."

Rachel Swanson stared at the ceiling.

"Carol needs our help, Rachel. Tell her what to do."

The tape ended with a loud click. Rachel didn't move, didn't look; she just kept staring at the ceiling.

Darby flipped the tape over and started recording.

It didn't matter. Rachel Swanson refused to speak.

CHAPTER 31

Darby was exhilarated and scared, running on fumes of hope. She pushed the door open, wanting to find a pen and paper, afraid that if she didn't write everything down she'd lose it. She reminded herself she didn't have to rush. The whole conversation was caught on tape.

The crowd outside Rachel Swanson's room had doubled. Darby scanned the faces, looking for Coop—there he was, at the far end of the hallway, talking on the phone behind the reception area. He hung up just as she reached him.

"That was the lab," Coop said. "Leland just got a call from Banville. A package with Dianne Cranmore's name was found on the stairs of a house in Belham, about twenty minutes away from where Carol lives. The return address has Carol's name on it. As far as I know, nobody saw who dropped it."

"What's in the package?"

"Don't know yet. It's on the way to the lab."

"I want you to head back to the lab and wait for the package. Ask Mary Beth to do a search for two more names—Paula and Marci. I don't know their last names. Tell her to limit the search to New England."

"And what are you going to do?"

"I need to talk to Lomborg."

"Be nice," Coop said.

Lomborg's mood had not improved. He crossed his arms as he listened to her idea about temporarily removing Rachel Swanson's restraints.

"There is absolutely no way in hell I'll allow that," Lomborg said.

"What if we move her to a psychiatric facility? We'd be better equipped there, and you could watch her over a monitor." Some rooms, Darby knew, were equipped with cameras to watch patients.

Lomborg looked like he was about to take the bait, but Dr. Hathcock was shaking her head.

"We can't move her until the sepsis is under control," Hathcock said. "She seems to be responding to antibiotics, but that could change. The next forty-eight hours are critical."

"Carol Cranmore might not have that kind of time," Darby said.

"I hear you—and God knows I'd do anything in my power to help you find that missing girl," Hathcock said. "But my first and primary responsibility is my patient. I can't allow her to be moved until the sepsis is under control—and I can't allow her to be taken out of the restraints. She's hooked up to IV lines. In the mental condition she's in, she'd probably rip them out."

"Could we take them out for a short period of time? Say, an hour?" Darby was desperate, willing to clutch at any possibility.

"It's too risky," Hathcock said. "We need to get the sepsis under control. I'm sorry."

Alone inside the woman's bathroom, Darby splashed cold water on her face until her skin was numb.

Darby ran her wet hands against the cool porcelain edges of

the sink. During the first year of Mel's disappearance, Darby often touched things, their textures a way of reassuring herself that she was alive. As she dried off her hands, she prayed for Carol to be clever, to find a way to survive.

Coming out of the bathroom, Darby rounded the corner, heading for the elevators. Mathew Banville was in the waiting room. Standing next to him, dressed in a sharp suit, was Special Agent Evan Manning.

CHAPTER 32

Time had been kind to Evan Manning. His short brown hair was a bit grayer, but he was still lean and fit, his face still seriously handsome.

What Darby remembered clearly, even after all this time, was the quiet intensity he carried in his face. Evan Manning, she saw, was looking at her that way right now.

Banville did the introductions. "Darby, this is Special Agent Manning from the Investigative Support Unit."

"Darby," Evan said. "Darby McCormick?"

"It's nice to see you again, Special Agent Manning." Darby shook his hand.

"I don't believe this," Evan said. "You still look the same."

"How do you two know each other?" Banville asked.

"I met Special Agent Manning when he worked the Victor Grady case," Darby said.

"The auto mechanic who abducted those women back in eighty-four?"

"That's him."

"Eighty-four," Banville said. "That would make you, what, about fourteen?"

"Fifteen. I knew two of Grady's victims."

"He killed one of them, didn't he? Shot a young girl in a botched abduction, if I remember correctly."

"He stabbed her." In a flash Darby saw her foyer walls splashed with Stacey Stephens's blood. "As for the other women, we're pretty sure Grady strangled them."

"How did you know they were strangled? The police never found the bodies."

"Grady recorded some of his . . . sessions with his victims. On a couple of the tapes, the women made sounds that were consistent with someone being strangled—at least that's what I read in the reports." Darby turned to Evan for confirmation.

"Grady kept the audiotapes in a lockbox hidden in his basement," Evan said. "The heat from the fire damaged most of the recordings."

Banville nodded, satisfied by the explanation. "Special Agent Manning is the new division head of the ISU's Boston office. AFIS alerted him early this morning when Rachel Swanson's fingerprint was identified. He's offered us access to his labs, anything we need."

"I understand you were in there talking to Rachel Swanson," Evan said. "Did she tell you anything useful?"

"She mentioned the names of two more missing women. We're looking into that right now. The whole conversation's right here." Darby held up the tape recorder. "What about this package that's on the way to the lab?"

"It's a padded mailer," Banville said. "I have no idea what's in it."

"I'm going to head over. Rachel's done speaking to me at the moment." She turned to Evan. "Why was the FBI alerted about Rachel Swanson's fingerprints?"

"I'll explain everything when we get to the lab. My car's in the garage. Can I offer you a ride?"

Darby looked to Banville for direction.

"I've already filled in Agent Manning on what we've found," Banville said. "I'll meet you at the lab as soon as I finish up here."

CHAPTER 33

"How long have you been working as a criminalist?" Evan asked after the elevator doors shut.

"About eight years," Darby said. "I did an internship in New York for about a year, and when the Boston lab had an opening I applied for the job and here I am. How long have you been working in Boston?"

"About six months. I needed a change of scenery."

"Getting burned out?"

"I was getting dangerously close. The last case I worked on nearly did me in."

"Which one?"

"Miles Hamilton."

"The All-American Psycho," Darby said. The former teenage psychopath, now confined to a mental asylum, was believed to have murdered more than twenty young women. "I hear he's gearing up for a retrial because of possible tainted evidence by one of your profilers."

"I don't know anything about that."

"Will Hamilton get a retrial?"

"Not if I have anything to say about it."

The elevator doors chimed open. Evan suggested they leave through the back entrance—no reporters there.

The sun was bright and strong as they jogged across the street to the parking garage. Evan didn't speak again until they were pulling onto Cambridge Street.

"Banville told me about the listening devices you found."

"I'm surprised you persuaded him so easily," Darby said. "I was expecting more of a fight."

"Banville is under the spotlight. He needs to be able to say he exhausted every resource when the Cranmore girl turns up dead."

"I don't think she's dead."

"Why's that?"

"Rachel Swanson was kept alive for almost five years—Terry Mastrangelo for two. That may buy us some time."

"Right now one of his victims is lying in a hospital room. If he's smart, he'll kill the Cranmore girl, bury her body someplace where we'll never find her and then blow town."

"Then why would he bother with the listening devices?"

"I think he's hoping to discover just how much we know about him so he can change his tactics before he moves on," Evan said. "What are your thoughts?"

"He seems very organized, very careful and methodical. I think he watches these women for a long time, gets to know their habits and routines—I think he had a key to Carol's house. He brings his victims to a private place where nobody can see or hear them."

"And what does he use them for?"

"I don't know."

"You think it's something sexual?"

"There's no evidence of that, although there's always some sexual component to these sorts of cases. Did Banville tell you about the evidence we found at the house?"

Evan nodded. "Our lab is still trying to identify the paint chip."

"You didn't seem surprised Carol's abductor left a package."

"He's trying to establish control. It's what most psychopaths do when cornered."

"Is that what you think we're dealing with here? A psychopath?"

"Hard to say. I'm not a big fan of labels."

"I thought you profiling types lived for labels—and acronyms. There's your fingerprint system. AFIS. You have CODIS—"

"You can't slap a label on every type of behavior," Evan said. "Have you considered the possibility that the man you're looking for abducts these women simply because he likes it?"

"There's a motivating reason behind every type of human behavior."

"What made you interested in this field?"

"Are you profiling me, Special Agent Manning?"

"You're avoiding the question."

"I took a criminal psychology course in college. After that, I was hooked."

"Banville told me you went on to get a doctorate in criminal psychology."

"I'm not a doctor yet," Darby said. "I still have to do my dissertation."

"Which is?"

"I have to pick a case and analyze it."

"And you picked the Grady case."

"I've been toying around with the idea."

"What's stopping you?"

"There are some missing pieces in the case file," Darby said. "Riggers, the detective who handled the Belham case, didn't leave much detailed information in his notes."

"I'm not surprised. In addition to being an idiot, the man was lazy. Tell me what you know and I'll see if I can fill in the blanks."

"I was able to look over the evidence files—the chloroform-soaked rag Grady dropped in the woods behind my house and the dark blue fibers he left behind in the bedroom door. I also read a copy of the fed's lab report. I know they identified the manufacturer of the rag. They narrowed down their search to automobile shops in Massachusetts, New Hampshire, and Rhode Island. The blue fibers matched the same brand of coveralls used at the North Andover automobile shop where Grady worked."

"We found all that out later, after Grady died."

"I read that," Darby said. "I also read about Grady's criminal record. He had two counts of attempted rape."

"Correct."

"According to the case file, Riggers was investigating about a dozen or so possible suspects. What made him move Grady to the top of the list?"

"A tip came through on the hotline about Grady. The caller, a regular customer at the garage where Grady worked, called in and said he saw a pearl necklace on the floor of Grady's car. The necklace appeared to have blood on it."

"But why didn't the caller report it to the police? Why did he call the hotline?"

"Because one of the missing women, Tara Hardy, was last seen wearing a pink cardigan sweater and a pearl necklace," Evan said. "That picture ran in the papers for weeks. It was all over the TV. The caller thought it might have belonged to her. The hotline was being flooded with calls. Everyone was trying to cash in on the reward money."

"And then what happened?"

"Riggers, wanting to be the hero, took it upon himself to search Grady's house. Riggers found clothing belonging to several of the missing women and left to get the search warrant. The problem was one of Grady's neighbors saw Riggers invite himself into the house."

"Making the evidence he found inadmissible."

"If he had played by the book, we probably would have nailed Grady before he killed himself."

"Did his suicide surprise you?"

"It did at first. Later, we discovered his family had history of mental illness. His mother was bipolar. If I remember correctly, his grandfather committed suicide."

"I saw that in the notes."

"My guess is Grady got spooked after Riggers went through the house. The day he killed himself, we went to the garage where he worked with a search warrant. I think he felt the walls starting to close in on him and took the easy way out."

"The case file mentioned that Riggers was bothered by the fire," Darby said. "He thought someone might have killed Grady and started the fire to burn away evidence."

"The fire bothered me too. What bothered me more was what Grady used to kill himself—a twenty-two."

"I'm not following."

"Cops generally use a twenty-two as a throw-down piece. You ever hear a twenty-two go off? Makes a small pop, you can barely hear it. If someone slipped inside Grady's house and shot him, you wouldn't hear it, especially if something like the TV or the radio was turned on. There were rumors someone clipped Grady. I'm sure you heard them."

"No."

"I was at Grady's house the night of the fire," Evan said. "I was watching his house. I would have seen someone."

Darby had seen Grady's house once, at night. She had driven

there on her own, about a month or so after coming home. She had hoped seeing the blackened shell of the house would somehow keep the nightmares away. It didn't.

"There's one question you can answer for me," Darby said.

"You want to know if Melanie Cruz was on one of those tapes."

"The audiotapes were given to the federal lab for analysis. No copies were ever forwarded to Boston police."

"The heat from the fire either damaged or destroyed most of the recordings. It took months to have them enhanced. We had the victims' families provide us with voice samples for comparison purposes. Melanie's parents gave us a home movie. Because of the condition of the audiotape, we couldn't get an *exact* match, but our voice expert agreed that, in all probability, the voice on the tape belonged to Melanie Cruz. The parents didn't feel the same way."

"They heard the tape?"

"They insisted on it. I played the part where Melanie . . . She was calling out for help. The mother shut the tape off and said, 'That's not my daughter.' She said her daughter was still alive and we had to find her."

Darby saw a snapshot of Helena Cruz turning her back to a cold blast of wind, clutching the sheets with Mel's picture against her chest so they wouldn't blow away.

"Did Mel say anything on the tape?"

"Not much that I recall," Evan said. "Mostly I remember her screaming."

"Was she in pain?"

"No, she was scared."

Darby could tell there was more. "What did Mel say?"

Evan paused.

"Tell me," Darby said.

"She kept saying 'Put away the knife, please don't cut me anymore.' "

Images flashed through Darby's mind—Mel's terrified face, the black tears from her mascara running down her cheeks. Stacey Stephens lying on the kitchen floor, blood spurting between the fingers clutched against her throat. Mel screaming as the man from the woods cut her.

Folding her arms around her chest, Darby stared out the window at the fast-moving traffic and thought back to that cold winter evening in the Serology Lab. The box of evidence from the Grady case sat on the counter. She remembered holding the rag that had been used on Melanie—the rag that would have most likely been used on her if she had gone downstairs.

"If you decide to go ahead and examine Grady's case for your dissertation, let me know," Evan said. "I'll make you copies of everything we have, including the audiotapes."

"I may take you up on that offer."

"Tell me about your conversation with Rachel Swanson."

For the next twenty minutes, Darby took him through her first encounter under the porch, finishing with what had happened in the hospital room.

Evan didn't speak. He seemed preoccupied with his thoughts. Darby could feel the man's fierce intelligence at work. To be so freakishly smart might be a gift, but Darby was sure it was a lonely one.

"Banville is mulling over the idea of using a reporter to set up a trap," Evan said.

"You don't sound convinced."

"If we blow the trap and he slips away—if he suspects we're on to him—he won't wait to kill Carol Cranmore."

CHAPTER 34

Since 9/11, every package and letter coming inside Boston Police headquarters was taken downstairs to the basement levels and X-rayed.

Darby paced the well-lit marble lobby full of patrolmen and detectives. The pacing helped keep her mind clear and focused.

Twenty minutes later, she was running the package, a medium-sized brown padded mailer, up the set of stairs. She didn't want to waste time waiting for the elevator.

Two white adhesive labels were on the front. The one in the center contained Dianne Cranmore's name and mailing address. The label in the upper left-hand corner contained only two words: "Carol Cranmore."

Both labels were the same size. Both had been fed into a typewriter—most likely one of those old-fashioned manual models that used an ink ribbon. Darby saw the spots where the ink had smudged on some of the words.

Coop had everything set up inside Serology. Waiting with him were Evan and Leland Pratt. Coop, clipboard in hand, stepped aside to give her some room.

Darby set the mailer on a sheet of butcher paper. After measuring the mailer, she took several pictures, first with the lab camera, then with the digital. The digital pictures would be emailed to the federal lab where Evan had people waiting.

Darby flipped the mailer over and looked for a manufacturer name or any unusual markings. All it said was "No. 7."

"Sometimes the manufacturer stamps its name inside one of the glued seams," Evan said. "Check when you take it apart."

Darby pinched the pull tab between her gloved fingers and opened the mailer. Small gray particles—the shredded filler used for the padding—swam in the air. She turned the mailer over and gently shook out its contents.

A folded white shirt fell onto the butcher paper.

Darby pried open the mailer's lip. There was nothing else in there.

She unfolded the shirt. A cold balloon of fear filled her stomach when she found the pictures, three in all.

Darby transferred the pictures to a separate sheet of butcher paper resting under the soft afternoon sunlight coming in through the windows.

Here was a picture of Carol Cranmore dressed in gray sweats, scared as she walked with her hands outstretched in a room of concrete walls and floors. There was a drain by her bare foot.

Here was Carol on the floor, stunned and frightened, staring up at the person behind the camera.

The last photograph was Carol stuck in a corner, a scream frozen on her face.

Evan stared down at the pictures with his cold and penetrating gaze. "Is Carol Cranmore blind?"

"No, she isn't," Darby said. "Why?"

"The way she's walking, bumping into the wall, I thought she might be blind. He must have surprised her in the dark, then."

Darby held the first picture in her hand, staring at it as though it were a window into Carol's dark prison cell. Seeing the terror captured on Carol's face made Darby feel closer to the teenager.

She flipped the pictures over. Taped to the back of the third picture were several strawberry blond hairs. Carol's hair.

Darby took in a deep breath. *Okay. Let's do this.*

"Coop, I have some writing on the back of the photo, bottom right-hand corner." Darby swung over the desk magnifier to read lettering. "H as in Henry, P as in Peter, one-seven-nine. There's no processing stamp."

Coop was standing next to her. "Could be a photo printer," he said. "The letters and numbers you found are probably the paper's stock number."

Darby checked the back of the second picture. Same writing in the same bottom corner.

"Let's get the hairs over to DNA," Darby said. "Coop, finish up with the mailer. I'll work on the shirt."

Evan left to listen to the tape alone in the conference room.

The white shirt, a man's size large, hung on a hanger, suspended above a table covered with a sheet of butcher paper. Darby worked a spatula over the shirt, scraping for trace evidence that might have been stuck. It was tedious, painstaking work. The entire time she had to fight the urge to rush.

"Got something," Pappy said.

Lying on the white paper, mixed in with the dirt and flecks of rust, was a single tan fiber. Darby grabbed it with a pair of tweezers and tucked it inside a glassine envelope.

Next, she moved the light magnifier over the trace evidence.

"I have a black speck here, could be a paint chip," Darby said. "There are several of them."

It was coming up on five. Evan had people standing by the federal lab for another hour. She gathered the glassine envelopes and distributed them through the lab before heading to check on the fingerprints.

Coop had used ninhydrin on the mailer. The paper was a dark purple. The mailer had been carefully cut open along the seams.

"The outer shell is a mess of fingerprints," Coop said. "I have comparison samples from the woman who picked up the mailer. The inside of the mailer is clean. No fingerprints, but he did use latex gloves. I found a tiny piece of it stuck on the mailer's self-adhesive lip but I didn't find any prints."

"What about the pictures?" Darby asked.

"They're absolutely clean. I may have some luck with the adhesive sides of the tape and the labels. I'm about to do that next."

"Okay, you have anything else?"

"Just the name of the mailer—Tempest," Coop said. "It was stamped under a fold. That's all I've got. Mary Beth just called. She's down in Missing Persons. She has something on the two names Rachel Swanson mentioned."

CHAPTER 35

Stomach grumbling from hunger, Darby pushed open the conference room door.

"—wasn't able to trace it," Banville was saying to Evan.

"Trace what?" Darby asked. She took the seat next to Leland and handed him a file folder.

"Dianne Cranmore received a call at her home an hour ago," Banville said. "The answering machine picked it up. It was a message from Carol saying she needed to talk to her mother and would call back in fifteen minutes. She did but didn't stay on long enough for a trace. Dianne Cranmore confirmed it was her daughter. One of my guys dropped off a copy of the tape. We were just about to listen to it."

Banville hit the PLAY button on the tiny microcassette recorder and leaned back in his seat. Evan finished typing on his laptop. Darby folded her hands on the table and stared at the recorder sitting a few inches away.

On the tape, the phone picked up. "Carol? Carol, it's me, are you okay?"

Darby heard stifled tears, the clearing of the throat.

"Carol, honey, is that you?"

"Mom, it's me. I'm . . . He hasn't hurt me."

Swallowing. Rapid breathing.

"Where are you?" Dianne Cranmore said. "Can you tell me?"

"I can't see anything, it's too dark."

"Where . . . What can I—Carol, listen to me—"

"He's here inside this room. He's got a knife."

"You need to protect yourself, like I showed you."

Click.

Banville shut off the recorder.

Evan looked to Leland. "With your permission, I'd like to send this tape to our lab. We can enhance the background noises, see if there's anything there. I'd also like to send the mailer and pictures. Questioned Documents can identify the type of typewriter used on the mailing labels and see if it matches another case."

Darby could tell Leland wanted to say no, but he was boxed in a corner where he couldn't. The FBI's Document Section was composed of seven different units that investigated anything to do with paper. The Boston lab simply couldn't compete.

"As long as we share everything," Leland said. "I take it the federal government has improved its communication."

"See for yourself." Evan reached across the table and dialed the number on the conference phone.

The sound of the phone ringing echoed over the speakerphone.

A voice picked up: "Peter Travis."

"Peter, Evan Manning. I'm calling from the Boston lab. I'm with lab director Leland Pratt and the forensic investigator on this case, Darby McCormick. Also joining us is the lead investigator, Detective Mathew Banville, from the Belham police. They may have a question or two for you, so I'm going to tell them to just jump right in."

"Absolutely," Travis said.

"Did you get all the digital pictures I sent you?"

"I've got them loaded up on my screen. The quality of the writing on the mailing labels isn't all that clear. I'll need the originals if you want me to identify the typewriter."

"You'll have them. Let's start with the pictures first."

"HP one-seven-nine is the brand of photo paper published by Hewlett-Packard. The paper is manufactured specifically for digital photo printers. You slip the memory card in, or you download the digital pictures from your computer or disc key, and it prints out a three-by-five picture."

"That's the same size we have here."

"I can take ink samples from the picture and try and narrow down the type of printer cartridge, but you're talking about a very big market," Travis said. "You're not going to find Traveler that way."

"Traveler?" Darby asked.

"We'll get to that in a moment," Evan said. "Go ahead, Peter."

"I can match the photo to the printer, if you have the printer."

"I don't have a printer, I don't have a suspect, and a seventeen-year-old girl is missing. What about analyzing the pictures using digital image processing techniques?"

"It's not a bad way to go. The problem is digital photography has evolved to such a point where you can doctor photographs without leaving any evidence."

"Meaning our guy could have, say, erased a window from the photograph."

"He could have erased a window, added a window—he could add and delete whatever he wanted if he knows how to operate the software. Given our past experiences, I doubt he'd leave anything in there that would lead us to his doorstep. I did find a new piece of evidence you can add to your list. Hold on a moment."

A brief sound of pages being snapped back. "Okay, here it is," Travis said. "The mailer he used most likely belongs to a small paper company named Merrill, based out of Hollis, New Hampshire. The company went under in ninety-five. They don't make them anymore."

"So our guy has a stockpile of them in his house."

"It's a strong possibility. I'd add it to your list. However, I'd like to reserve my final judgment until I've had a chance to examine the mailer."

"You'll have it on your desk tomorrow morning," Evan said.

"The footwear impression recovered from the Cranmore home belongs to Traveler. It's manufactured by Ryzer Gear, their Adventurer model."

"And the paint chip?"

"We struck out. The sample is not in our system. That's all I've got on my end. How did you make out with the shirt?"

Evan looked to Darby.

"We've recovered one tan fiber," Darby said. "The fiber matches the one we found in the foyer of the Cranmore house. The hair taped to the back of the picture is a similar match for Carol Cranmore. Fortunately, a root bulb was attached, so we can get a DNA sample. We struck out on the fingerprints on the mailer. It's a wipe."

"Any questions for Peter?" Evan asked the room.

There weren't any.

"Peter, I need you to contact Alex Gallagher, tell him to analyze an audiotape," Evan said. "It will be in the package I'm sending out today. You have my cell phone?"

"I do. I'll be in touch."

Evan hung up.

"I have some information on the two names Rachel Swanson

mentioned at the hospital," Darby said. "Missing Persons did a search and came up with two possible candidates from New England."

Leland handed her the folder. Darby removed the first sheet, a printed 8 x 10 color college graduation picture of a woman with plain features and curly blond hair. She placed it on the table.

"This is Marci Wade from Greenwich, Connecticut," Darby said. "She's twenty-six, lives at home with her parents. This past May, she drove to meet a former high school friend who was attending the University of New Hampshire. This friend lived about two miles from the campus. Marci drove home on a Sunday night and her car broke down on Route 95. She hasn't been seen since."

The second sheet Darby placed on the table was a printed picture of a good-sized woman, with round cheeks and a small portwine stain on her flabby chin.

"This is Paula Hibbert, a forty-six-year-old single mother and schoolteacher for a public high school in Barrington, Rhode Island. She asked her neighbor to watch her son so she could go and pick up a prescription for his asthma. She made it to the pharmacy but didn't make it home. They never found her or her car. She disappeared in January of last year.

"I don't know any details about the cases, or what they found for evidence," Darby said. "Both labs are closed for the day. We'll be on the phone first thing tomorrow morning. That's all I have. Now, Special Agent Manning, why don't you tell us about Traveler?"

CHAPTER 36

Evan swung his laptop around so it was facing the room.

On the screen was a picture of a Hispanic-looking woman with bleached blond hair.

"This is Kimberly Sanchez, from Denver, Colorado," Evan said. "She disappeared in the summer of ninety-two. Went out for a jog and never came back."

Evan clicked through the photos of eight more women. They were all Hispanic or African American, all in their mid-twenties to early thirties. They were all last seen last seen alone, driving away in their own cars, leaving a bar or their place of work late at night. The last trait they shared was that their bodies had never been recovered.

"The Colorado task force caught one lucky break," Evan said. "A witness leaving a nightclub saw the last victim getting inside a black Porsche Carrera with Colorado license plates. The same witness also recalled that the back bumper was dented.

"Police narrowed down the search of Porsche owners in the Colorado area. One of them, John Smith, was from Denver. When police went to question him, Smith wasn't home. Four days later, when Smith still hadn't returned home, police searched the house he was renting. Smith was already gone. He wiped the place clean before he left, but forensics managed to recover two key pieces of evidence—a small blood sample in a trash can and a boot print belonging to a Ryzer hiking boot, size eleven. It was an identical match to the boot print found in the dirt next to one of the victims' cars."

Evan clicked a key and on the screen was a picture of a white man with an overgrown beard and mustache. He had piercing green eyes and the kind of painfully thin face generally seen on heroin addicts.

"This is a picture of John Smith taken from his Colorado license," Evan said. "Neighbors said the back bumper of Smith's Porsche had been dented from a recent accident. They also filled us in on some other details. Smith went out a lot at night, was somewhat antisocial. Nobody knew what he did for a living, and nobody had been inside his house. Several neighbors recalled spotting the same crude tattoo on his forearm—a shamrock with the numbers six-six-six."

"The tattoos used by members of the Aryan Brotherhood," Darby said.

Evan nodded. "The ethnic backgrounds of the Denver women suggested a tie to the Aryan Brotherhood. Naturally, Brotherhood members claimed they didn't know Mr. Smith. The name isn't listed on any of our computers. We don't even know if John Smith is Traveler's real name."

"The blood sample you found," Darby said. "Did you find a match in CODIS?"

"We did. It belonged to one of the missing Denver women," Evan said. "After Denver, Smith set up shop in Las Vegas. This was toward the end of ninety-three. Here he changed his selection process. Over the next eight months, twelve women and three *men* vanished. The Vegas police didn't pay much attention to the cases, since people disappear from Vegas all the time. People go there down on their luck to indulge whatever vices they have; everyone comes and goes."

"What were the ethnic backgrounds of the victims?"

"The women were mostly white," Evan said. "The men were Jewish. One of the female victims, her car was left on the road. Someone messed with the ignition wires. Fortunately, a piece of evidence had been left behind—the Ryzer boot print.

"By the time I got involved, Mr. Smith had already moved on to Atlanta, his third stop. This was in ninety-four, and we had given his case a name: Traveler. The boot print was listed on VICAP and we were called in."

Evan shifted in his chair, springs squeaking. "Carrie Weathers, Traveler's fourth victim in Atlanta, was spotted getting inside a black Porsche Carrera. The witness said the car had a busted fender and Maryland license plates, but she didn't get a good look at the numbers. It was the first real break we had, so we asked local gas stations and garages to be on the lookout for a black Porsche with a dented fender coming in for fill-ups, repairs, whatever.

"We were in the process of running down registrations when a call came in at night from a gas station attendant working at a local Mobil station. A Porsche matching our description had just come in. A blond woman was in the passenger's seat. She was sleeping. She had too much to drink, the driver had said. I asked the attendant to secure the pump. I went to the station along with someone from the lab.

"The gas station attendant was very relaxed, very cooperative," Evan said. His voice sounded oddly detached, as though he were reading from a script. "He said he wrote the license plate down on his pad next to his phone. I followed him through the garage.

When I entered his office, he was standing behind me. He hit me on the back of the head. That was the last thing I remembered.

"When I woke up at the hospital, I was told he used the gas from the pumps to set the fire. At some point, I managed to crawl away, but I don't remember it because of the concussion. They identified the lab tech and the real owner of the gas station through dental records. They had both been shot with a Colt Commander."

"The same weapon used to kill Carol Cranmore's boyfriend," Darby said. She had the ballistics report in her folder. "You didn't recognize the gas station attendant?"

"This man was heavier, clean-cut with a shaved head," Evan said. "He looked nothing like John Smith. He was wearing a jacket, so I didn't see any tattoos. And he didn't fit the profile. He didn't ask many questions about the investigation, which psychopaths generally do. Obviously, I was wrong."

"Had he attacked a police officer before?" Darby asked.

"Not to my knowledge. But if John Smith is a member of the Aryan Brotherhood or some other white supremacist group, killing a police officer or any member of law enforcement means you move up through the ranks. It's a badge of honor."

"Still, it's odd that he would target you—and set up a trap," Darby said.

"It's what psychopaths do when they're cornered. Or maybe he was trying to send us a message—to let us know he was in control."

Evan's face took on a stillness that Darby found unsettling. "Traveler's a very smart, highly organized psychopath," he said. "He abducts women from different states and mixes up the methods of abduction so he won't attract any attention to himself. The victim selection is totally random so we can't find a pattern. He can hide underground for several months, which shows a remarkable amount of restraint. And as I've learned, his plans are well thought out.

"Everything Traveler does is about exerting control over his surroundings—that's why he sent the package to Carol's mother, why he placed the call to her. He wants us to know he has Carol and can kill her whenever he wants."

"Which is why we need to use the listening devices to bait him," Darby said.

"With what?"

"You," Darby said. "We use the *Herald* reporter, tell him you're here because Rachel Swanson woke up and told us some key piece of evidence and you want to take a look at the house. That way we can guarantee Traveler will be listening."

"If he reads my name in the paper, he might panic and decide to kill Carol and the other women and move on. He's done it before."

"Only this time he made a mistake at Carol's house," Darby said. "He left his blood behind—and one of his victims. Rachel Swanson could be the key to finding Traveler. He's going to want to stick around to see what we know about Rachel before he moves on."

Banville checked his watch. "I've got fifteen minutes left to call the reporter," he said. "I'm open to suggestions."

"We could wait until the sepsis is under control," Evan said, "and then move Rachel Swanson to a controlled setting at a psychiatric facility, take off her restraints and have Darby talk to her again."

"She may not want to talk again," Darby said. "You listened to the tape. She stopped talking to me. Have you found listening devices at any of the other victims' homes?"

"No, this is a first."

Darby looked at Banville. "I say we plant the story about the FBI wanting to go through the house to search for key evidence. Traveler will want to know what Agent Manning has found. If Traveler shows up, we'll corner him. We'll have all the streets blocked off so he can't escape."

"And if he doesn't show up?" Evan asked.

"He'll kill Carol—he may have already killed her," Darby said. "We need to use the listening devices. They're our best shot."

Evan was now looking at Banville. "This is your investigation. It's your call."

Banville rubbed a finger across his mouth. "Two missing women and a missing teenage girl . . . I agree with Darby. I say we go for it."

CHAPTER 37

All the florists in Beacon Hill were closed for the day. Darby was forced to pick through the anemic-looking flowers left inside the hospital gift shop. She took her time selecting the brightest colors she could find and made a nice arrangement.

ICU was quiet and calm now. Dr. Hathcock was gone for the day. Darby checked in with a nurse. There was no change in Rachel Swanson's condition.

It took some wrangling to convince the nurse to allow the flowers in the room. Darby placed the flowers on the sill underneath the TV. That way, when Rachel woke up, she would see the flowers. Maybe they would help convince her that she was no longer trapped in the dark room where Carol Cranmore now was.

Bleary-eyed and weary, Darby stumbled into her mother's room. Sheila was asleep.

A peculiar sadness gripped her. On the way over here, Darby had hoped her mother would be awake. Darby needed to talk. The selfishness of a child needing her mother. Darby wondered if she would ever outgrow it.

Sheila's eyes fluttered open. "Darby . . . I didn't hear you come in."

"I just got here. Can I get you anything?"

"Some ice water would be nice."

Downstairs, Darby filled a plastic tumbler with ice and water. She sat on the bed and held the cup while her mother sucked from a straw.

"Much better." Sheila's eyes were clear and focused, but she was having trouble breathing. "Did you eat? Tina made something resembling egg salad."

"I grabbed a sandwich at the hospital."

"What were you doing there?"

"Visiting Jane Doe," Darby said. "Her name is Rachel Swanson. She woke up today."

"Tell me about it."

"Why don't you rest? You look tired."

Sheila waved it off. "I'm going to have the rest of my life to sleep."

Darby wondered where her mother found the source of her bravery, what images she used to comfort herself for what was awaiting her.

She helped her mother sit up. When Sheila was comfortable, Darby told her about what had happened at the hospital.

"What about Carol Cranmore?" Sheila asked.

"We're still looking." Darby realized she was holding her mother's hand. "We have something, though. Something we might be able to use to help find the person who has her."

"That's good news."

"It is."

"So why don't you look happy?"

"If we don't do it the right way, he'll probably kill her."

"You can't control that."

"I know, but I pushed for this plan we're going to use tomorrow. Now I'm wondering if I made a mistake."

"What you want is for someone to assure you it's all going to work out."

"I smell a lecture."

"You were like that since the day you were born. You had to be in control of everything."

"Who says I'm not?"

Sheila grinned. "What you are is dedicated—and smart. Very smart. Don't ever forget that."

"The person we're after is smarter. He's been doing this for a long time. The other thing is, he might have other women besides Carol. They might still be alive. And if we don't catch him tomorrow, he might kill them."

Her mother's eyelids fluttered and then shut. "Promise me one thing."

"Yes, I'll save myself for marriage."

"Besides that," Sheila said. "Promise me you won't blame yourself if something goes wrong. You can't blame yourself for things you can't control."

"Sounds like good advice." Darby kissed her mother on the forehead and stood up. "I think I'll try some of that egg salad. You want anything?"

"I would love some gum. My mouth is so dry."

When Darby came back, she was asleep. Darby checked her mother's pulse. It was still there.

She went to the spare bedroom and tried reading the case file, but all Darby could see was Carol Cranmore in the pictures— Carol walking through her dark prison cell, hands outstretched; Carol bumping into wall, trapped, terrified.

Darby shut the file and brought her Walkman with her to the recliner. She listened to the conversation with Rachel Swanson and stared out the window, at the trees shaking in the breeze under the dark sky. Carol Cranmore was somewhere out there, swallowing darkness and fear in equal measures.

Hang on, Carol. Find a way to fight and hang on.

Darby thought about the listening devices and felt a flicker of hope spark inside her. It was small, but it would do. She shut off the Walkman, wrapped the blanket around her and waited for sleep.

CHAPTER 38

Carol Cranmore lay curled on her side on the hard floor underneath the cot, the wool blanket wrapped around her for warmth. She had stopped shaking, but her rapid heartbeat wouldn't slow down.

The man with the mask hadn't hurt her. He had pulled her up by her hair and told her to stop fighting and shut up or he wouldn't let her talk to her mother.

He stepped up behind her and pressed something sharp against her throat. It was a knife, he said. He told her what to say and then had her repeat it back to him. She did. Then he told her to repeat the words again, this time into a tape recorder.

Carol was still speaking when the tape clicked off. He removed the knife and told her to lie down on the floor, on her stomach. She did. He told her to close her eyes. She did. The door slid open and slammed shut, the loud sound vibrating through her chest. Locks clicked back and then she was alone again, trapped in the awful darkness.

At some point, she dozed off. Her head felt foggy, and her blanket was wet with drool.

She thought about the sandwich she had eaten earlier. The sandwich had left a funny taste in her mouth. Was it drugged? Why would the man with the mask want to drug her and make her sleep?

And why did he take those pictures? Was he planning on sending them to her mother along with the tape and ask for a reward? It didn't make sense. In the movies and on TV, they kidnapped rich people. One look at her neighborhood and you could tell nobody rich was living there. So why did he take those pictures?

Carol didn't know, but she was sure of one thing: the man with the mask was going to come for her again, and the next time he might hurt her. He might kill her. How was she going to defend herself?

Was there something in the room she could use?

Moving her fingers along the cot's edge, Carol felt the rough polyester fabric wrapped around the aluminum tubing. Was there a way to get a piece of that tubing out? She gave the cot a good shake, but it wouldn't budge. Why wouldn't it move?

Her fingers found the brackets and screws pinning the cot's legs to the floor. The cot was bolted to the floor.

Carol spent the next half hour struggling to break off a piece of metal tubing. No luck.

Her heart was pumping hard from the exertion and brought on new waves of fear, making her skin tingle. She pushed her fear aside. She had to keep her mind clear. She had to think. *Okay, what else is in here?*

Carol mentally pictured the room: shower, sink, toilet and cot. What she needed was something sharp, something she could use to stab him—

The toilet. She had helped one of her mother's boyfriends change some plastic thing inside the toilet tank, and she recalled the things inside there—the handle and the lever. They were both made of metal. Attached to the handle was a long piece of metal with a pointed end. She could use it to puncture skin. She could stab him with it, but it wouldn't do any serious damage.

She *could* use it on his eyes. Let him try to find her without his eyesight.

Carol navigated her way to the corner. Her shin bumped up against the edge of the toilet. She reached down and felt the toilet seat. She moved her fingers toward the tank. There was no toilet tank, just cold metal pipes dripping with moisture.

Panic set in. The voice inside her head, the one that sounded a lot like her mother's voice, urged her to push these thoughts aside, to calm down and think.

Carol didn't want to think. She stumbled through the dark until she found the steel door.

"Tony, can you hear me?" She banged her fists against the door. *"Tony! Where are you? ANSWER ME."*

A piercing sound, like the ringing of a school bell, made her jump.

The door was opening, *clank-clank-clank.*

Carol ran back to the cot and scrambled underneath it, grabbing the blanket and twisting it into a rope, hoping she could use it to defend herself if he came at her with something sharp.

The man with the mask didn't come inside.

Carol stared into the hallway of dim light. Lying on the floor, about ten or so feet away from her cell door, was a bottle of water and a sandwich wrapped in plastic.

Was he hiding around the corner?

Carol didn't see a shadow on the floor. Maybe he was standing far away from the door, waiting for her to come out. Was he waiting for her to come out there and grab the food? If she stepped out there, would the man with the mask attack her?

"Hello?"

Not Tony's voice—this was a woman's voice, faint but clear.

"Can anyone hear me?" the woman asked.

"I can hear you," Carol said. She wiped the tears from her eyes and watched the door, listening, getting ready to fight. "My name is Carol. Carol Cranmore. Where are you? Who are you?"

"My name is Marci Wade. I'm standing inside my room."

"Don't come out here," another woman yelled.

How many people were down here with her?

The ringing alarm sounded again. Her door was closing.

And then the screaming started.

CHAPTER 39

Darby's morning started at the Belham police station. It was six a.m. She stood with Coop in the back of the crowded conference room. Copies of today's *Herald* were visible everywhere she looked.

Carol Cranmore was the lead story: "Where Is She? Police on the Trail of a Possible Crazed Killer."

Darby had already read the article. There wasn't much meat in it, just speculation wedged in between lots of pictures. A photographer had captured a picture of Dianne Cranmore collapsed on the bottom of her porch stairs, hands in her hair as she wailed.

The last paragraph contained the bait:

A source close to the investigation revealed that police have discovered a key piece of evidence that could potentially break the case wide open. Crime scene technicians, assisted by federal lab consultants and Special Agent Evan Manning, from the FBI's Investigative Support Unit, will be going through the house today.

Now all Traveler had to do was to show up.

Banville took the podium. His hangdog face looked especially tired. Behind him, mounted on the wall, was a blown-up map of the streets surrounding Carol's house. Every possible escape route was marked off with red pushpins.

After the noise died down, he started to speak.

"FBI technicians on loan from the Boston office entered the Cranmore house last night and determined that the listening devices are active and transmitting on the same frequency. They're remote-operated, meaning they can be turned on and off in order to save battery power. The maximum range these devices can transmit is roughly a half-mile radius. At the moment, these devices are off.

"We'll have officers stationed in unmarked cars at key points within a half-mile radius of the house. Other detectives and patrolmen, pretending to be volunteers, will be covering the area with leaflets containing Carol Cranmore's picture and taking down license plate numbers.

"We can't assume he's sitting inside the back of a van," Banville said. "He's not using sophisticated surveillance equipment. It could easily be stored underneath a car seat. I was told that the receiver could be a device disguised in something as simple as a radio Walkman. It's even possible he can plug this device into his car stereo system and listen over the speakers. We all need to be on the lookout for a white male wearing headphones or sitting alone inside a car. If you see someone, call it in—and remember to use the frequency I've given you. Stay off your cell phones.

"We'll have three delivery trucks roaming the area. In each, FBI technicians will be monitoring the bug's signal once they turn on. Let them track it down. When they lock on to the signal, they'll call SWAT into action. Under no circumstances are you to approach the suspect alone. SWAT will take him down. Special Agent Manning, is there anything you'd like to add?"

Evan, standing in the far corner of the room, stared at the tops of his shoes for a moment before addressing the crowd.

"I know there's been some bad blood between police agencies and the Boston office. As far as I'm concerned, this is Detective Banville's investigation. We were asked to assist, and that's what we're here to do. We're all after the same goal—to find Carol Cranmore and bring her home. I don't care who gets credit for it.

"That being said, I can't stress enough how important it is for each of you to approach this cautiously. If you see someone or something suspicious, call it in immediately. We only have one shot at this, and we can't afford to spook him. Always assume he's watching, because he is."

Solemn nods and blank stares around the room.

Banville spent the next half hour explaining how the streets and roads would be blocked off. If Traveler was listening somewhere in that half-mile radius, there would be no way he could escape.

The meeting broke up. People got out of their seats.

Evan inched his way through the crowd to the back of the room.

"This could be a long waiting game," he told Darby and Coop. "Why don't you two head back to the lab, see if there's anything you can find about the tan fiber. I'll call you the second I find out something."

"Our boss wants us here," Coop said.

"There's no guarantee he'll be listening this morning," Evan said. "It could be sometime this afternoon. You'd be better off using your time at the lab."

"A case like this creates a lot of confusion—a lot of people are going to go straight for the collar, everyone wants to be a hero," Darby said. "If you find him, you're going to need people to secure the crime scene. We're going to need all the evidence we can get to nail him to the wall."

Evan nodded. "Let's keep our fingers crossed and hope he takes the bait."

Darby headed for the door. Carol's smiling face was everywhere she looked.

CHAPTER 40

A light rain fell over Boston, the highways clogged with traffic.

Daniel Boyle, sitting behind the wheel of the Federal Express van, clicked on the blinker and turned left, heading slowly down the ramp, the shocks groaning from the weight in the back.

Two policemen were guarding the delivery area. Boyle stopped in front of a long length of steel plating. He knew what it was. With a flip of a switch, the steel plating would turn over, revealing a set of road spikes that would puncture the tires of any fleeing vehicle.

An overweight cop with a jowly face lumbered his way through the rain. Boyle rolled down his window, face pleasant, smiling.

"Good morning, officer. This isn't my normal route—I'm just filling in for the day. I have a package for the lab. Could you tell me where to go?"

"You have to sign in first."

Boyle took the clipboard. His hands were covered in leather driving gloves. He wrote the name "John Smith" on the clipboard. The name matched the photo on the laminated FedEx badge clipped to his shirt pocket. Boyle had other supporting credentials ready, if needed.

He handed the clipboard back through the window. The fat cop's partner was busy looking around the van.

"Go down this ramp here, park in the back—you'll see the signs marked off pretty clearly," the fat cop said. "Deliveries are through that gray door back there. Follow the corridor to the front desk. Someone there will sign for it. You don't have to take the package up."

Boyle was about to ease off the brakes when the second cop said, "Back of your van is sagging quite a bit there, fella."

"Shocks are gone," Boyle said. "I've got three more stops and this baby's going in the shop. Rate I'm going, I'll be working until six tonight. Great way to start the day, huh?"

The fat cop, wanting to get out of the rain, waved him through.

A bump as Boyle drove the van over the steel plating. He headed down the ramp and into the garage. Security cameras were mounted high on the walls, sweeping the area. He pulled the FedEx cap low on his brow.

There were plenty of parking spaces for the delivery trucks. Boyle chose the one closest to the stairs.

Out of his seat and through the door behind him, Boyle grabbed the heavy package and headed inside.

The white surveillance van, complete with a periscope and microwave transmitters and receivers, was designed to look like a telephone repair vehicle. The driver was also dressed to look the part.

Darby sat next to Coop on a carpet-covered bench near the back doors. Across from her, seated on the opposite bench, were two members from Boston SWAT. Both men were sweating beneath their heavy combat gear. One was busy chewing gum and blowing bubbles, the other checking the impressive-looking Heckler & Koch MP7 machine gun strapped across his chest.

She had no idea what where they were. There weren't any windows. The tight space smelled of men's deodorant and coffee.

Banville was seated on a bolted-down swivel chair set up in front of a small but workable desk. He was having a private conversation with one of the FBI technicians. She wondered what was going on.

Another fed, a pair of headphones wrapped around his massive bald head, was listening to Evan's conversation in the house, sometimes pausing to talk to his partner, who was busy studying the screen of a laptop. It was hooked up to some futuristic-looking equipment being used to monitor the listening device's frequency. At the moment, the devices were turned off.

The call would come through. The FBI techs would lock on to the signal and Boston SWAT would get the call to move in. Boston SWAT was very good. They would move in hard and fast.

The wall phone started ringing. Darby tensed, digging her fingers into the edge of her seat.

Banville answered it. He listened for a full minute before he hung up. He shook his head.

"Bugs are still off," he said.

Darby rubbed her damp palms across her pants. *Come on, goddamnit. Turn on.*

The marble lobby of the Boston police station was very impressive. Boyle was sure hidden security cameras were watching him right now, recording his every move. Cops were everywhere. He kept his head bowed as he moved quickly toward the front desk.

The blue uniform sitting high behind the front desk was reading today's *Herald* by a banker's lamp. Boyle slid the big package across the wood.

"Want me to take this up?" Boyle asked. "It's pretty heavy."

"No, we'll take it from here. You need me to sign anything?"

"You're all set," Boyle said. "Have a great day."

Billy Lankin was still thinking about the FedEx truck. He didn't know much about cars, but he felt reasonably sure the problem with the delivery truck wasn't blown shocks.

Billy's partner, Dan Simmons, sipped his coffee as rain drummed softly against the roof above them.

"That's the eighth time you've looked in the garage, Billy."

"It's that FedEx truck. I don't like the looks of it."

"What do you mean?"

"The way the back of the truck is sagging," Billy said. "I don't think the shocks are blown."

"If it's bothering you that much, go take a look."

"I think I will."

CHAPTER 41

Boyle opened the door to the parking garage. The cop stationed out front, the one who had looked over the back of the truck, was checking the driver's side door.

Smile and play it cool.

"Something wrong, officer?"

"Since when do you guys lock up your truck? You don't trust us?" The cop grinned, but there was a warning behind it.

"Force of habit," Boyle said, returning the smile. "My normal route is in Dorchester. When I started out there, I was delivering a package and some kids vandalized my truck. Guess who was liable for all the damages?"

"You mind if I take a look in the back?"

"Sure." Boyle reached inside his jacket for the keys. He felt the Colt Commander tucked inside the shoulder holster.

Boyle unlocked the back door. The cop ran his tongue across his front teeth as he looked around at the boxes lined on the shelves. Boyle wondered if the cop was going to get inside the truck and start moving the boxes around. The fertilizer bombs were packaged in big boxes underneath the shelves. Boyle had left nothing to chance.

The cop moved his head out. "You better get those shocks looked at."

"I'm going to drop off the truck right now," Boyle said. "Have a good one."

Ten minutes later, Boyle was back on the road, heading toward Storrow Drive. He put on his headphones and tuned his iPod to the frequency of the small listening device he had planted inside the taped folds of the brown paper wrapped around the package.

A scrambling of noises, people talking, voices far and close.

A voice came over the headphones: "Christ, this thing's heavy."

Next, a loud thud, and then the same voice said, "Hey, Stan, do me a favor and pull the rest of the mail off the conveyor belt, will ya?"

"I thought you wanted me to go get us something to eat?"

"In a minute. This package just came in for the lab. I want to get it upstairs."

Boyle took out his BlackBerry and typed the message quickly with his thumbs: "Package delivered. About to go on X-ray machine. Test for explosives?"

Boyle hit send and waited. He wished he could talk to Richard. It would be certainly quicker and much easier than trying to type while driving.

Richard's message came through: "They'll see mannequin on X-ray and will rush to lab."

Boyle hoped Richard was right. He typed back: "Twenty minutes from hospital. Darby?"

Five minutes later, Richard's response came through. "She's in van, with SWAT. Will turn on listening devices in 30 minutes. Signal when ready."

Boyle hit the gas.

*   *   *

Stan Petarsky, one of three X-ray technicians hired by the Boston police, sat on a stool behind the controls, sipping coffee to clear his head. Last night, he had another humdinger of a fight with his wife about his drinking, and right now he didn't know what was worse—the pounding hangover or the sound of his wife's nagging voice ringing through his head.

A little nip from a bottle of Jim Beam would shut them both up. He'd have to wait until lunch, though, when the bar across the street opened.

The package was moving down the conveyor belt. When it reached the X-ray machine, he edged the controls until the package was in full view on the monitor, which was eye level with his face.

Stan stood up fast, knocking his stool over. "Jimmy, get over here."

"What?"

"Take a look at this." Stan stepped back so Jimmy could get a full view of the X-ray monitor.

Inside the brown-wrapped box were severed limbs and a head. Stan could make out the legs and arms. Next to the head was a hand wearing several rings and a watch.

Stan's stomach squeezed so hard he thought he was going to dry-heave.

Jimmy rubbed a shaking hand across his dry lips. "Back the package out of the X-ray for a minute. I want to see something."

Stan did. Jimmy put on his bifocals and examined the writing.

"Check out the name in the return address," Jimmy said. His face was pale.

"Carol Cranmore," Stan said. "So what?"

"So that's the name of the missing girl. Haven't you been following the news?"

"Christ Almighty. You think her body is in *there?*"

"You better call upstairs and tell them."

"You do it. I have to do the test for explosives first."

"You think there's a bomb stuffed up her ass?"

"Hey, I'm just following procedure."

"I need to make some calls. While I'm on the phone, you might want to do yourself a favor, chew on some mints or gum or something. I'm getting a buzz off your breath, hear what I'm saying?"

Darby shifted in her seat. On the laptop screen were two pairs of steady lines which reminded her of an EKG.

She was itching for something to happen, needed to get busy. She kept crossing her legs.

Coop leaned in close to her. "Is there something wrong with your ass?"

"Those devices should have turned on by now."

"Be patient."

Half an hour passed.

"I talked to my sister last night," Coop said. "Trish is going into the hospital tomorrow. They're going to induce labor."

"How long is she overdue?" Darby's attention was still on the laptop.

"Almost two weeks," Coop said. "They finally picked out a name for my nephew. Fabrice."

"She's naming the baby after an air freshener?"

"No, that's Febreze. I said Fa*brice.* It's French, like her husband."

"That kid better grow up with a thick skin."

"Tell me about it," Coop said. "Brandy thought the name sounded cool and hip."

"Brandy?"

"New girl I'm seeing. She's studying to be a cosmetologist. When she graduates, she wants to move to New York and name lipsticks."

"What does that mean? Name lipsticks?"

"Lipstick companies, they can't say colors like pink or blue. They've got to come up with cool marketing names like Pink Sugar and Loud and Lovely Lavender. Those are her names, by the way."

"Hands down, she's certainly the brightest woman you've dated."

The lines on the laptop's screen started vibrating.

"The listening devices are transmitting," the FBI tech said.

Darby grabbed the edge of her seat as the van sped up.

CHAPTER 42

The hospital bathroom reeked of Pine-Sol. Boyle was alone. He stood inside the last stall on the far left. He had already taken off his hat and FedEx jacket. The empty backpack, which had been strapped across his back, was now on the floor.

Boyle had worn green surgeon's scrubs underneath his clothes. He took off his boots and slipped on a pair of sneakers. After he tied a bandana around his head, he stuffed the boots and FedEx clothes into the backpack and opened the stall door.

He checked himself in the mirror. Good. A pair of stylish black-framed glasses was tucked inside his breast pocket. He put them on.

Boyle stuffed his backpack inside the garbage can. He took out his BlackBerry and typed: "Ready. In position."

Boyle opened the door and stepped out into the bright, busy corridor on the eighth floor. He walked down three corridors and stopped near the large bay windows overlooking the entrance for Mass General.

The only vehicles allowed near the main entrance were taxis and ambulances. He saw six ambulances parked out front. Two more ambulances were coming. Police were busy directing traffic. More police had been called in to handle the swelling crowd of reporters. They were huddled near the old brick building used for hospital deliveries.

Richard's message came through five minutes later: "Go."

Boyle reached inside his pocket. The detonator felt cold in his hand.

He walked away from the windows toward ICU. When he reached the waiting room, he hit the button.

A distant rumble, followed by glass shattering. Then the screaming started.

Stan Petarsky was trying hard not to think about the dead body inside the box next to his feet. He tried to think about something pleasant—like Jim Beam over ice—when the elevator door opened.

Erin Walsh, the pretty blonde he saw sometimes in the cafeteria, was standing in front of a door, talking on her cell phone and waving to him to come this way, to the stairwell. Stan picked up the box and carried it into Serology Lab.

Erin started taking pictures. Stan didn't want to stick around to see a severed body. He headed for the door, thinking about how to get his hands on some Jim Beam, when the package exploded.

CHAPTER 43

Darby had a new view: a monitor showing what was happening outside the surveillance van.

They were driving at a good clip down Pickney Street, three blocks away from the Cranmore house. The houses were a little better over here, but not by much. Darby spotted more than one car parked up on cinder blocks.

Karl Hartwig, one of the SWAT members, was kneeling in the center of the van, his face covered by the periscope. Everyone else was watching the laptop.

On the monitor and coming up close was a battered black van parked on the left-hand side of the road, near a grouping of trees making up a small patch of hilly woods.

Spikes danced on the laptop screen and leveled off.

"He's in the black van," the FBI tech said.

Hartwig talked into his chest mike: "Alpha-One, this is Alpha-Two, we have confirmation on a black Ford van with tinted windows and no license plates parked on Pickney Street, over."

"Roger, Alpha-Two. We're moving into position."

A moment later, the surveillance pulled over and came to a stop. The engine was still running, the floor vibrating beneath her feet. Hartwig moved the periscope.

On the monitor now, down the far end of the street from which they had just come, was a UPS truck. It traveled a few feet and pulled over. Darby caught a brief flash of black coming from the back of the truck and then it was gone.

The UPS truck didn't move. Darby knew it would stay there and block the street.

Static over Hartwig's mike, then "Alpha-Two, this is Alpha-One."

"Go ahead Alpha-One," Hartwig said.

"Alpha teams Three and Four are moving in position. Stand by."

"Roger, Alpha-One. Standing by."

The UPS truck swept past the woods. The third surveillance vehicle, a flower delivery van, made its way down Coolidge Road.

Traveler was blocked in.

The black van still hadn't moved.

Banville hung up the wall phone. "All the areas are blocked off," he said. "Everyone's in position."

"Alpha-One, all teams report ready to go," Hartwig said. "We're in position and standing by, over."

"Acknowledged, Alpha-Two. Prepare to engage."

"Copy, Alpha-One."

Darby felt the surveillance van pull away from the curb, stop and turn around. Hartwig locked up the periscope and crouched next to his partner near the van's back doors. Clipped to their belts were stun grenades—also known as flashbangs because of their blinding flash and deafening blast. An explosive entry had been authorized.

Darby watched the black van on the monitor. It still hadn't moved.

Hartwig turned to her and said, "The two of you are to stay in here until the area is secured, understood?"

The van slowed down.

Hartwig gave the signal to his partner. The van's back doors swung open.

The two SWAT officers jumped out into the light rain, leaving the back doors open. Darby moved out of her seat to get a better view.

SWAT officers were already positioned at the back of the Ford van, their gloved hands on the door—here came another SWAT officer running out from the woods, bringing up his pistol, targeting the driver's side window.

Hartwig gave the hand signal. A SWAT officer yanked on the door handle and the van's back doors open.

Hartwig tossed the flashbang grenade inside, and before Darby shut her eyes, she saw a man in a dark jacket sitting in front of a table holding some type of equipment full of small, blinking lights.

The grenade exploded in blinding light, the blast deafening. Hartwig came around and brought up his weapon, his laser scope targeted on the person's back. He was still sitting in front of the table. He hadn't moved, and his hands were hidden inside his jacket pockets.

"HANDS ON TOP OF YOUR HEAD, DO IT NOW, PUT THEM UP AND DON'T MOVE."

Traveler didn't move.

Darby felt the van come to a sharp and sudden stop. Banville was out of his seat, moving past her. Hartwig rushed into the back of Traveler's van.

"GET YOUR HANDS UP IN THE AIR RIGHT NOW. DO IT."

Hartwig threw Traveler to the floor.

Darby stepped outside, legs shaking from the time spent sitting. She wanted to be in there with the SWAT officer, wanted to see Traveler's face and look into his eyes when he said Carol's name.

Hartwig stepped out of the van, shaking his head. He said something to Banville.

Coop was standing next to her now. Traveler was lying on the floor. He wasn't moving.

Banville was heading back.

"What's going on?" Darby said.

"It's a dead body bound to a chair," Banville said. "That's what's going on."

"What? The grenade couldn't have killed him."

"He's been dead for several hours," Banville said. "Someone strangled him."

"Then what's with all that equipment?"

Banville didn't answer. He had stepped back inside the van, the wall phone already pressed against his ear.

"It's got to be him," the FBI tech said behind her. "The listening devices are being picked up in *that* van. Look, there's an L32 receiver in there."

"Maybe he's using the equipment to transmit the signal somewhere else," his partner said.

The commotion and noise, and the sight of eight SWAT team members hovering around the van had drawn the neighbors out of their homes. They stood on the front steps, many of them standing in the rain, wanting to know what was going on.

"Let's secure the scene," Darby told Coop.

Standing across the street was a girl no older than eight. She was dressed in a yellow rain slicker and held her mother's hand. The girl looked scared, on the verge of tears. Darby was watching her when the van exploded and blew the girl and her mother off the ground.

CHAPTER 44

An evacuation siren blared over the hospital speakers. Daniel Boyle pushed his way through the crowds of civilians, doctors and nurses running in all directions, people bumping into each other, some falling, everyone scrambling to find an exit, to get away from the dust and smoke filling the hallways.

The ICU waiting room was empty. The ICU doors were opened. Nobody was guarding Rachel's room. The two cops responsible for watching her had either been called away or had decided to leave.

Boyle ran down the hallway. The ICU nurses had left their post. He was alone. He looked through the window to Rachel Swanson's room. She was sleeping.

Boyle pushed open the door with his arm, careful about not leaving any fingerprints.

Hand already inside his breast pocket, he came back with the hypodermic. He clamped the plastic cap between his teeth, exposing the needle, his thumb drawing the plunger higher as he moved to the bed.

Boyle wished he could wake her up, wished he could watch Rachel scream one final time before she started convulsing.

The needle pierced the IV tube. Boyle pushed the air through the line.

A quick wipe of the line using his jacket cuff and he was moving back to the door. Hurry.

Cap back on the needle, the hypodermic tucked back inside his pocket. Hurry.

Out the door and walking swiftly down the hallway, nobody watching—

One of the hospital's security staff was standing next to the nurse's station. The man was dressed in a dark raincoat and wore an earpiece and a lapel mike. He was looking around the space, searching for the wounded when he spotted Boyle.

Boyle ran to him. "Everyone's gone," he said. "It's all clear."

An alarm sounded from behind the front desk.

The security man turned to look at the monitors. "What's going on?"

Boyle pretended to study the numbers on the monitor. "One of the patients has gone into cardiac arrest," Boyle said. "I'll take care of it. Make sure everyone gets to the stairwells."

"You sure I can't help you?"

"No, get going. I can take it from here."

The security man didn't move.

Very calmly, as if reaching for a pen, Boyle slipped his hand inside his white coat and undid the snap for the shoulder holster. He'd drop the rent-a-cop if he had to. Drop him first and then run for the stairwell.

No need. The security man had left. Boyle watched him leave, then turned the corner and headed for the bathroom. He grabbed his backpack from the trash and made his way toward a cop directing people into the stairwell. Boyle blended into the crowd of civilians and hospital staff.

The morning was filled with rain and sirens. He jogged down Cambridge Street and took the stairs for the T station.

Yesterday, on his way home from Belham, he purchased an electronic T pass at South Station. He swiped the pass through the magnetic card reader, leaving no fingerprints, and stood with the rest of the people watching the chaos below them. Smoke drifted from the crumbled ruins of the delivery garage. Fire trucks, ambulances, and police cars were coming from all directions. Shards of glass and pieces of brick and concrete covered Cambridge Street. Some of the store windows, Boyle saw, had been blown apart by the blast.

When the train pulled up, Boyle grabbed a window seat, took out his BlackBerry and typed a message to Richard: "Done."

To pass the time, Boyle thought about what he would do to Carol Cranmore once she stepped outside her room. Sooner or later, she would come out for her food. They all did.

But he couldn't wait forever, not now. The preparations for leaving were already made. He would have to kill them all soon—tonight, maybe.

CHAPTER 45

The right side of Darby's face throbbed as she helped Coop lift another wounded SWAT officer onto the stretcher. The officer was unconscious but breathing.

They carefully made their way over the wet debris, heading as fast as they could through the rain and smoke, toward the far end of the street where the wounded lay scattered on the ground. Dozens of them were being treated by the EMTs and doctors rushed in from Belham Hospital. The dead ones lay still under blue tarps weighed down by rocks.

Darby eased the officer onto a gurney. She was about to head back out when she spotted Evan Manning kneeling on the ground, lifting up a blue sheet to examine the face of one of the dead. She pushed her way through the crowds of medical staff shouting orders over the wail of the approaching sirens, the screaming and the crying.

She grabbed Evan by the arm. "Did you find Traveler?"

"Not yet." He seemed genuinely surprised to see her. "What happened to your face?"

"I was knocked down by the blast."

"What?"

"It's too loud here. Come this way."

Darby led him across the street and into the woods. The leaves protected them from the rain. It was quieter in here but not by much.

"I tried calling you on your cell," Evan said, wiping the water away from his face.

"I'm pretty sure I broke it when I fell. What's going on with Traveler?"

"All the roads are blocked off, but so far, we haven't found him."

"In order to have set off the bomb, he'd have to be close by, wouldn't he? We need to make sure the cops at the roadblocks are checking everyone they see. He could still be somewhere around here—he could be walking away right now."

"We're checking everyone. Listen, I've got to leave. I'm going to be tied up in Boston. It doesn't look good."

"What's going on in Boston?"

"There was an explosion inside your building. I don't know all the details yet."

Suddenly Darby had to sit down. There was no place to sit. She leaned back against a tree and filled her lungs deep, the ground shaky beneath her feet.

"Two of our mobile forensic units will be here early tomorrow morning—one here, one at the blast site in Boston," Evan said. "We can run the investigation from there. I need to get going. I'll call you later. Where can I reach you?"

She wrote down her mother's home number on the back of a business card and handed it to him.

"Your face is swelling up," Evan said. "You should put some ice on it."

Darby stepped out of the woods and stared at the wounded and the dead. Four bodies—no, five—were under the blue tarps.

An EMT was pulling another tarp over the body of another SWAT officer.

She turned away and looked in the direction of where the van had been. Now it was a smoldering black crater. The body of the man she had seen inside the van hadn't been found. Pieces of him were scattered among the debris. They'd be lucky if they ever identified him.

A firefighter dropped his hose. He yelled something she couldn't hear and then all four firefighters were running to the bloodied hand fighting its way out of the rubble.

That could have been me, Darby thought. *If I had been standing any closer to the van, I might be trapped or dead.*

Coop was heading back with another stretcher—this one holding a young woman. Her limp arms hung over the sides of the stretcher and bumped against the rubble as her lifeless eyes stared up at the dark gray sky, the rain washing away soot and blood from her face.

CHAPTER 46

By quarter to three, all the survivors had been found and moved. Firemen were still crawling around the blast site; two were standing by with hoses. ATF agents and members of the Boston Bomb Squad, dressed in coveralls and boots, sifted through the debris.

The man in charge of the blast site was Kyle Romano, a former Marine explosives expert and a fifteen-year veteran of the Boston Bomb Squad. He was a big, burly man with a dark red buzz cut and a face scarred by acne.

Romano had to shout over the steady rotor-thump of the news chopper hovering in the sky directly above them.

"It's definitely dynamite," Romano said. "You can tell by the way the metal's pitted. We also found pieces of a timer and what appears to be a metal footlocker. Given what you and everyone else told me, once those van doors opened, I'd say it sent a signal to the timer. You know the rest. Now I got a question for you."

Romano scratched his nose. His face was covered in soot and ashes. "I was talking to Banville, and he told me this guy you're after kidnaps young women."

"That's right."

"This has the markings of a terrorist attack. You pull something like he did today, it's guaranteed to draw attention. This guy you're after, everything about him suggests he doesn't want to be found."

"I think he's feeling desperate," Darby said.

"That's the same thing the profiler told me—Manning was his name. Evan Manning."

"What else did he tell you?"

"Not much. He was talking about the teenage girl that's missing." Romano shook his head, sighing. "Poor girl's as good as dead."

"He said that?"

"Not in so many words." Romano took a long pull from his water bottle. "That's all I know right now."

"Can I help with something?"

"Yes, you could point me to the piece of metal with the vehicle's VIN number on it. It's buried somewhere in this goddamn mess."

"I can help with the sifting," Darby said.

"We've got ATF here to help. Bomb cases are different from the ones you work on—no offense. I've got to clamp down on the scene. Too many people walking around here. Thanks again for your help."

The vehicle, its windows shattered from the blast, was part of the crime scene. Bomb techs were searching it for scraps of evidence. Darby couldn't drive it.

Darby couldn't find Coop. She'd have to walk home.

The press was everywhere. She walked past them, numb, and headed down a street only to realize it was closed off to allow investigators to sift through the debris.

When she stopped walking, she was standing near East Dunstable Road. There was Porter Avenue. Down the road was St. Pius. Half a mile up the road was the Hill. Sitting high above it was Buzzy's.

The pay phone she had used over two decades ago to make the call was still in the same spot, replaced by a new Verizon model with a bright yellow receiver. Darby wanted to call Leland to see what had happened at the lab. She checked her pockets. All she had was dollar bills. She went inside Buzzy's to get change.

The store was empty except for the teenage girl standing behind the counter. She was watching a news report about the bombing at Mass General on a small color TV set up on top of a mini-refrigerator.

"Could you turn that up?" Darby asked.

"Sure."

The reporter, who was live at the scene, didn't have much information but he had plenty of visual footage of the bomb that had exploded inside the delivery garage at Mass General. As he talked about eyewitnesses who had described hearing a large, thunderous booming sound, the camera kept playing various footage of the destruction. Darby saw the streets lined with debris and overturned taxis and ambulances. The front half of Mass General, which was made entirely of glass, had been blown apart. When she saw the smoking crater, her first thought was a fertilizer bomb. A fertilizer bomb, if packaged correctly, could have caused the amount of destruction she was seeing on the TV.

Dozens of wounded people were being moved to Beth Israel Hospital. Mass General patients were in the process of being evacuated to other area hospitals. There was no information on how many people had been killed.

"Were you there?"

Darby glanced away from the TV. The teenage girl was talking to her. She wore too much eyeliner and her face looked as though it had fallen inside a tackle box. Her nose was pierced, as were her bottom lip and tongue. Almost every available space on her ears was covered with pierced earrings.

"Were you at the bomb site?" the teenager asked. "Your clothes are, like, all dirty and ripped and stuff. And you've got blood on you."

"I was here in Belham."

"Oh my God, that must have been sooo freaky. Did you see any dead bodies?"

"I need some change for the pay phone."

Darby plunked her quarters down into the slot and dialed Leland's cell phone. When his voice mail picked up, she tried his home number. His wife answered.

"Sandy, this is Darby. Is Leland there?"

"Just a moment."

Darby swallowed. When Leland came on the line, she explained what had happened in Belham. Leland listened without interrupting.

"Erin called me while I was stuck in traffic," Leland said after she finished talking. "She said a FedEx package came into the lab early this morning. They brought it downstairs to X-ray and found what looked like a body stuffed inside the box, so they rushed it upstairs. The return address was Carol Cranmore's."

"Didn't they test it for explosives?"

"I don't know. If I had to guess, I'd say they saw the body and decided to rush it upstairs. I'm in the process of pulling the security tapes from the garage and the lobby.

"I was talking to Erin when the package blew up," Leland said. "I don't think she made it. Pappy was out in a junkyard in Saugus collecting paint samples when the bomb went off. The blast took out the lab, the evidence lockers . . . it's all gone."

Darby wanted to ask about any other survivors but couldn't get the words out.

"I'm afraid I have more bad news," Leland said. "The hospital called looking for you a few minutes ago. Rachel Swanson went into cardiac arrest. They couldn't revive her. They're going to do her autopsy this afternoon."

"He killed her."

"Rachel Swanson was sick, Darby. The sepsis—"

"Traveler needed to get to her. She was the key to finding him, and the only way he could do it was to create a diversion. What better diversion than bombing the hospital. The explosion creates a sense of panic—people start thinking it's a terrorist attack and run for cover. Nobody's paying any attention. Traveler moved in and killed her. Get someone over there and seal off the room—and pull the ICU security tapes."

"I already tried. ATF won't allow access," Leland said. "I just got off the phone with Wendy Swanson, Rachel's mother. Some- one at the New Hampshire lab must have called her. She called us, wanting to know what hospital her daughter was in. I had to tell the woman her daughter was dead."

"Do you have her number? I want to talk to her about Rachel."

"That's Banville's job."

"Banville's going to be tied up at the bomb site here in Bel- ham. I want to talk to the mother to see if I can find out anything about Rachel, maybe figure out why she was selected. She might know something that can help us find Carol."

Leland gave her the number. Darby wrote it down on her fore- arm.

A phone rang in the background. "I've got to take this call," Leland said. "Call me back if you find out anything."

Darby called her mother. The phone kept ringing. She hung up, wondering if she was too late. A cold nausea gripped her as she ran home.

CHAPTER 47

The nurse shut the door to Sheila's bedroom. Her mother was inside, fast asleep. Her lungs made a sick wheezing sound as she struggled to breathe.

"I had to increase her morphine level," Tina said, ushering Darby away from the door. "She's in a lot of pain."

"Did she see the news?"

The nurse nodded. "She tried calling you and couldn't get through."

"My cell phone is broken. I called from a pay phone. Nobody picked up."

"The explosion knocked down some of the phone and power lines—at least that's what they're saying on the news. She knows you're okay. A friend of yours stopped by and told her. I forget his name. Are you going back out? I can stay a while longer. It's not a problem."

"I'm in for the night."

Darby folded her arms and leaned back against the wall. She was afraid to move away from her mother's door. Walking away now, Darby felt she was saying good-bye.

"I don't think it will happen tonight," Tina said.

It took Darby a moment to gather the courage to ask the question. "When, do you think?"

Tina pursed her lips. "Any day now."

After the nurse left, Darby wrote a note to her mother saying she was home and taped it to the nightstand where she kept her glasses and pills. She kissed her mother on the forehead. Sheila didn't stir.

Darby headed into the shower. Standing under the hot water, she reviewed the things Rachel had said under the porch and at the hospital. Rachel had used the word *fighting* several times. *I can't fight him anymore,* Rachel had said. What had she said about Carol? *Is she a fighter? Is she tough?*

Fighter. Fighting. Was that the key? How would Traveler know they would fight back?

Did he pick them up from battered women's shelters? No. Those women predominantly *didn't* fight back. What then? Some place, they all had to connect at some place. *Please, God, let me find a common thread.*

When the water grew cold, Darby toweled off, threw on a pair of sweats and a sweatshirt and headed downstairs to the kitchen. She checked the phone. It was working. She put on her jacket and took the cordless and her pack of cigarettes out to the back deck. The rain was coming down harder now, drumming against the roof.

She went through two cigarettes before dialing the number for Rachel's mother. A man answered the phone.

"Mr. Swanson?"

"No, this is Gerry." His voice was terribly quiet. Darby was sure she heard someone crying in the background.

"Can I speak with Wendy Swanson? I'm calling from the Boston Crime Lab."

"Hold on."

A thin, trembling voice came on the line: "This is Wendy."

"My name is Darby McCormick. I wanted to call and tell you how sorry—"

"Are you the one who found my daughter underneath the porch?"

"I am."

"Did you talk to Rachel?"

"Yes, ma'am, I did. I'm sorry for your loss."

"What did Rachel say? Where was she all this time? Did she tell you?"

Darby didn't want to lie to the woman, but she didn't want to upset her even more. Darby needed Wendy Swanson to answer some questions.

"Rachel didn't say much. She was very sick."

"I saw the news story, the video footage, and I didn't once think it was Rachel. The woman you found looked nothing like my daughter. I didn't even recognize her. And I'm her mother." Wendy Swanson cleared her voice several times. "This person who took Rachel, what did he do to her?"

Darby didn't answer.

"Tell me," Rachel's mother. "Please. I have to know."

"I don't know what happened to her. Mrs. Swanson, I know this is a difficult time for you. And I wouldn't be calling you if this wasn't important. I need to ask you some questions about your daughter. The questions may sound odd, so please try and bear with me."

"Ask anything you want."

"Was Rachel ever in an abusive relationship?"

"No."

"Would she have told you if she was?"

"My daughter and I were very close. I knew all about Chad's background, but he never hit her—he never even raised his voice. Rachel wouldn't have put up with any of that. She had nothing but positive things to say about Chad. I think his ex-wife was a bit of a nut."

"Was Rachel ever assaulted by anyone?"

"No."

"Did she ever tell you about being stalked? Was someone following her?"

"No. If something like that ever happened, she would have told me. Rachel and Chad had a great relationship. They were going to get married. Rachel was . . . She was so smart, so hardworking. She paid her own way through college. She was taking out loans to go to law school. She never asked for anything, never got into any trouble. She was just a solid, well-grounded person."

Wendy Swanson broke down. She spoke through her tears. "The police told me that when someone goes missing, if they're not found in the first forty-eight hours that usually means they're dead. After the first year, I started to accept the fact that Rachel wasn't coming home, and that I may never find out what had happened to her. And then early this morning I get a phone call from a friend who works at the state lab and she says that Rachel was found in Massachusetts—was found alive. *Alive.* After five *years.* I got down on my knees and thanked God. And then I call to find out what hospital Rachel is in only to be told she's dead. Rachel was alive all this time and I find out and now she's dead and I didn't . . . I didn't get to talk to her. I didn't even get a chance to hold my baby's hand and tell much I love her and how sorry I am for giving up on her. I didn't even get to say good-bye."

"Mrs. Swanson, I'm—"

"I can't talk now, I have to go."

"I'm very sorry for your loss."

Wendy Swanson hung up. Darby squeezed the phone and, without realizing it, looked up at her mother's bedroom window.

CHAPTER 48

Darby stared out at puddles in what used to be her mother's garden, where Sheila spent her time before she got sick. As she smoked, she thought about Traveler's victims. Evan Manning said Traveler had selected them at random. If that was true, then it would be difficult to catch him. It was going to be difficult to catch him anyway, Traveler having thought through all the options, going to great lengths so he wouldn't be found. Maybe he had already killed Carol and the others. Maybe he was driving away right now. *No, don't think about that.*

A copy of every work email was automatically forwarded to her Hotmail account so she could access information from the road. Darby put out her cigarette and went inside, heading upstairs to check her computer. There was a message from Mary Beth regarding the crime scene photographs.

Mary Beth always took two sets of photographs—one using film, the other digital. Digital pictures were not admissible as evidence because they could be doctored. Mary Beth always took them so investigators had copies for their files.

Darby was in the process of reviewing them when she heard coughing. She poked her head out into the hallway and saw the thin crack of light at the bottom of her mother's bedroom door. Sheila was awake, watching TV.

When Darby eased open her mother's door, she could see pictures of the blast site reflected in her glasses.

"What happened to your face?"

"I slipped and fell. It looks worse than it is," Darby said. "How are you feeling?"

"Better, now that you're here." Sheila turned down the volume on the TV. "Thank you for leaving the note."

Darby sat down on the bed. "I tried calling, but the phone lines were down. I'm so sorry you had to go through that."

Sheila waved it off, but Darby could see where the worry still ate at her. Even in the soft light, her face looked haggard, leached of color. *Any day now.*

Darby laid down next to her mother and hugged her.

"You know what I kept thinking about today? The time you got caught in an undertow and almost drowned. You were eight."

Darby remembered the feeling of tumbling across the ocean floor, the water getting colder. When she finally resurfaced, she coughed up water for the next hour.

But it was the chill she felt while trapped underneath the water that refused to leave, even while she sat in the sun. The chill was still with her later when she was tucked in her bed underneath layers of warm blankets. The chill was a reminder that there were things in this world she couldn't always see, waiting to strike out when you least expected it.

"You didn't cry—your father was more shook up about it than you were," Sheila said. "He took you to get an ice cream, and you said—I'll never forget this—you said to him, 'Dad, you don't have to worry about me. I can take care of myself.'"

Darby closed her eyes and saw the three of them packed in the car, on their way home, the car smelling of the ocean and Copper-tone. The three of them together. Healthy and safe. A good memory there. She had lots of them.

"Coop stopped by," Sheila said. "He wanted me to know you were okay."

"That was nice of him."

"He's very nice—and funny."

"That's what he keeps trying to tell me."

"He looks like that basketball player, what's his name, Brady."

"Tom Brady. He plays football. He's a quarterback for the Patriots."

"Is he single?"

"He is."

"I think you two should go on a date. You're well suited for each other."

"I've tried, but sadly, Tom Brady won't return my phone calls."

"I was referring to Coop. He reminds me of your father, has that same quiet, confident way about him. Is he dating anyone?"

"Coop isn't the dating type."

"He said he's looking to settle down."

"Probably with one of his underwear models," Darby said.

"He thinks very highly of you. Told me how smart you are, how hardworking and dedicated you are to your job. He said you're the most trustworthy person he has ever met—"

Darby was asleep.

CHAPTER 49

Carol had spent the first few minutes after the door shut covering her ears to block out the god-awful screaming—and not just from one woman. Several women were somewhere outside her door and they were *screaming*.

What scared Carol even more were the banging sounds. *Bang,* scream, *bang-bang-bang*-scream, *BANG-BANG-BANG-BANG,* the frightening sounds growing louder and closer.

Carol had frantically searched her room again, trying to find something to use as a weapon, something she might have missed. Everything was bolted down, even the toilet seat. There wasn't anything she could use. The only thing in here was the blanket and pillow.

Hours had passed since that moment. Her door never opened, but that didn't mean the man with the mask wasn't coming back for her.

Standing alone in the dark room, Carol hadn't wasted her time feeding her fear. She had used that time to think of a plan.

Men, she knew, were vulnerable in one key area—their balls. One time Mario Densen put his meaty hand on her ass and gave it a tight squeeze. Mario was twice her height and almost triple her weight; but, wouldn't you know, the fat jerk crumbled like a deck of cards when her shin connected squarely with his crotch.

Carol had removed her sweats and, using the pillow, formed a ball underneath the blanket. This was her plan:

When the door opened, the man with the mask would think she was curled up underneath the blanket; she would be pressed up against the wall next to the door. After he stepped inside her room, she'd get behind him and kick him squarely in the crotch. Get in one good kick, and after he fell to the floor—they always did—she'd kick him in the face and in the head.

Carol, dressed in her underwear and bra, shivered inside the cool room. To stay awake and keep warm, she paced the small area near the door, knowing she had only six steps before she hit the wall. When she felt tired, when the fear started to trickle in, she pounded her hands against the wall to keep the anger close to her skin.

She thought about the tray of food and wondered if it was still in the hallway. The thought of food made her stomach rumble. She didn't need the food, she reminded herself. She could survive on water, and there was plenty of it from the sink. She had some water earlier, wanting to stay hydrated and to flush the drugs from her system—

Wait. The tray. The food was on a plastic tray. If she broke the tray, she could use the sharp pieces to defend herself. She could use it on his face. She could use it on his eyes.

Her door started to open, *clank-clank-clank*.

Carol pressed her back against the wall, tensing, eyes tuned to the square of dull light parting the darkness along the floor. Get ready, she had to think about getting ready, she only had one shot and she couldn't waste it.

The man with the mask didn't come into her room—he wasn't even standing outside her room. His shadow wasn't on the floor.

Music started playing—old-fashioned jazz stuff that reminded Carol of a time when men wore things like fedoras and went to places like speakeasies. No banging and no screaming.

Her door was still open. The last time, the door shut after a couple of minutes.

Was he waiting for her to come out there?

To get the tray, she'd have to risk turning the corner. She'd have to risk having him see her. If he saw her, then her plan of using the clothes and pillow underneath the blanket would be worthless.

She couldn't defend herself with her hands. The man with the mask was too strong. And he had a knife. She needed the tray. Carol edged closer to the opened door, listening for sounds, watching for movement, a shadow.

Now Carol stood at the corner. Carefully, she turned the corner and looked.

The plastic tray had been kicked down to the far end of the long hallway. Beneath the tray and looking black in the dim light was a pool of blood. It was coming from the woman lying face-down on the floor.

Don't scream, don't you dare scream or he'll hear you.

Carol bit her bottom lip and tried hard to clamp down on the scalding fear.

Get the tray.

Carol didn't move. She was thinking about the dead woman lying in all that blood. She wasn't moving.

You need to get the tray. If he comes back here with the knife—

Carol ran.

Her door started to clank shut.

Carol kept running. She focused on the tray, the prize. Keep running.

It seemed to take forever to reach the end of the corridor. She scooped up the tray, the blood warm and sticky underneath her feet. Carol turned around, about to run back to her room, when she felt the woman's hand clamp around her ankle.

Carol screamed.

"Help me," the woman said in a sleepy voice. "Please."

BANG, a door slammed shut.

Get back to the room.

I can't leave her—

She's dead, Carol, get back to the room now.

Carol ran back with the tray. She ran as fast as she could, legs pumping, dear God please help me, please let me make the door.

The door to her room was shut.

There was no handle. Carol clawed at the door, her bloody fingers sliding across the cold steel, trying to find a way to pry it open. There was no way to open it. The door was shut and she was locked out, trapped out here with the dead woman—

BANG, another door slammed shut, *BANG-BANG-BANG,* the man with the mask was coming for her.

CHAPTER 50

Darby woke to the still darkness of her mother's bedroom, her legs tangled around a blanket. Her mother must have put the blanket on. Darby had no memory of doing it.

Sheila's breath caught. Darby stood up, leaned in close to her mother and heard Sheila's soft, ragged breathing. Darby checked her mother's pulse. It was still strong.

But not for long. Soon, very soon, Sheila would be buried next to Big Red and then Darby would be alone—alone in this house with its lifetime of collected knickknacks and pictures, the dime-store jewelry her mother bargained down at flea markets and discount stores, all of it proudly stored in one of the few valuable items she owned—a beautiful handmade jewelry box handed down from two generations of McCormick women.

No more phone calls. No more words of encouragement. No more shared birthdays and holidays and Sunday night dinners in the city. No more conversations. No more new memories.

And how would she fight to keep the memories she had from fading? Darby thought of her father's goose-down vest, how she had worn it after he died, lost in its warmth and fading whispers of cigar smoke and Canoe aftershave, feeling close to him. What would she wear of her mother's to keep Sheila from fading? What had Helena Cruz held of Melanie's to keep her daughter's memory alive? Was Dianne Cranmore lying awake in this same darkness right now, sitting in her daughter's room leveraged between despair and hope, wondering where Carol was, wondering if she was all right, wondering if she was coming home or wondering if she was gone?

Darby lay back against her mother's bed, the pillow damp with sweat, and wrapped the blanket around her. For no reason at all she saw Rachel Swanson lying in her hospital bed, terrified. Now she was lying inside a morgue cooler with a Y-shaped incision stitched on her chest, the fear still sealed inside of her.

What about Carol? Was she awake now, breathing this same darkness?

Darby didn't know many things about herself, but she knew this much: she could not, would not, stop searching for Carol. Dead or alive, she would be found.

Darby went down the hallway to the spare bedroom. She clicked on the small desk lamp, turned on the computer and reviewed the photographs.

Here was Rachel Swanson with her strong, plain face and good hair.

Here was Terry Mastrangelo, average looking, black hair. Rachel's was brown.

Now Carol Cranmore, the youngest, her body having already produced the right amount of curves to get men to look her way. She'd be a knockout in the years to come. Darby had already ruled out physical attraction as a unifying connection. The women didn't even look the same. Was it something about their personalities?

Darby tried to imagine him sitting behind the wheel of a van, trolling through neighborhoods, searching for women who caught his eye. Had he just happened upon them and then decided to watch them for some period of time before devising an abduction plan?

Fact: he kidnapped these women and kept them somewhere they couldn't be found. They had no bodies, no evidence. Traveler was careful.

But he had made a mistake at Carol's house. He had left blood behind. Rachel Swanson had escaped. He planned on doing something to her—getting rid of her seemed the only rational explanation. Rachel was sick. She wasn't any use to him anymore.

And Rachel Swanson knew that. She had outsmarted him. She was a survivor. She had used her time to devise a plan and had escaped and Traveler had found her and killed her because he was afraid Rachel knew something that would help the police find him. What? What was she missing?

Frustrated, Darby grabbed her Walkman and listened to her taped conversation with Rachel.

"He's got me," Rachel said over the headphones. "He's got me real good this time."

"He's not here."

"Yes, he is. I saw him."

"There's no one in here but you and me. You're safe."

"He came to me last night and put on these handcuffs."

Darby hit STOP. Handcuff key. Rachel said she had a handcuff key. Darby hadn't found one underneath the porch.

She pressed the PLAY button and leaned forward, listening.

"I know what he's looking for," Rachel said. "I took it from his office. He can't find it because I buried it."

"What did you bury?"

"I'll show you, but you've got to find a way to help me out of these handcuffs. I can't find my handcuff key. I must have dropped it."

Darby stopped the tape again and hunted through the pictures.

Here was one of Rachel Swanson in the back of the ambulance. Her arms were covered in mud. The next three photos were close-ups of the wounds on Rachel's chest.

Here was a close-up photo of Rachel's hands. The fingernails were caked with dirt, the skin cut up and bleeding not from fighting but from *digging*.

Darby ran down to the kitchen and grabbed the cordless. Coop answered on the sixth ring.

"Coop, it's Darby."

"What's wrong? Is it your mother?"

"No, it's about Rachel Swanson. I think she hid something underneath the porch."

"We searched that area, including the trash, and didn't find anything."

"But we didn't search the ground," Darby said. "I think she buried something."

CHAPTER 51

The rectangular-shaped area underneath the porch was about half the size of a small bedroom. The ground was still muddy. Darby couldn't see any recent evidence of digging, so she started working in the far left-hand corner where she had first spotted Rachel.

Darby did the digging. She filled the bucket and handed it to Coop. He dumped the dirt on top of the sifter set up on a large garbage can lined with plastic.

They'd been at it for well over an hour, and the only thing they had to show for their efforts was a collection of rocks and glass shards.

Kneeling underneath the porch, her pants wet and soaked with mud, Darby handed Coop another bucketful for sifting. Carol's mother stood on the neighbor's back porch, watching them dig, her face twisted with worry and hope.

Coop ducked his head underneath the porch. "Just more rocks," he said, handing her the empty bucket. "What do you think?"

It was the third time Coop had asked the question.

"I still think she buried something in here," Darby said.

"I'm not saying you're wrong. I looked at the same pictures you did, and I agree she dug in here with her hands. But I'm beginning to think maybe she buried something only she could see."

"You heard the tape. She kept mentioning a handcuff key."

"Maybe she *believed* she had a handcuff key. The woman was delusional, Darb. She thought you were Terry Mastrangelo. She thought the hospital room was her prison cell."

"We know, for a fact, she escaped the van. I think she had a handcuff key. It's got to be around here somewhere."

"Okay, let's say you're right. What's a handcuff key going to buy us in terms of evidence?"

"What do you want to do, Coop? Sit around and wait for Carol Cranmore's body to turn up?"

"I didn't say that."

"Then what are you saying?"

"I know how badly you want to find something. But there's nothing here."

Darby grabbed the trowel and started digging at a feverish pace. She had to remind herself to slow down. She didn't want to damage any evidence with the trowel.

Rachel Swanson might have been delusional, but it was brought on by real trauma and not some imagined event. The woman had suffered unimaginable horrors over the course of five years. Mixed up in her fear were grains of truth. Something was buried here, Darby could feel it.

"I think the Dunkin' Donuts is open," Coop said. "I'm going to grab a coffee. You want one?"

"I'm all set."

Coop crossed the backyard, walking past the crime scene vehicle, which was still parked in its original spot from this morning.

Darby dug up two more pails and sifted the damp dirt on the screen. More rocks.

Forty minutes later, Darby had dug up about three-quarters of the area underneath the porch. The muscles in her legs and lower back ached. She thought about hanging it up when something caught her eye—a folded, corner section of what looked like paper sticking out from the dirt.

Darby moved the portable light into the hole. She used her gloved fingers to scoop away the dirt and then switched to the brush.

A handcuff key sat on top of the folded piece of paper.

"Looks like I owe you an apology," Coop said.

"Buy me dinner and we'll call it even."

"It's a date."

Once the photographs and documentation work were completed, Darby lifted the folded piece of paper out of the hole and set it up on top of the sifting screen.

Documents required special handling and care. Because paper was nothing more than pulverized wood and glue, when wet paper was allowed to dry, it turned to glue. Folded pages and papers stacked on top of one another would be stuck together and couldn't be pried apart.

"Any idea when these mobile forensic units are arriving?" Coop asked.

"I don't know, but if we wait too long, these pages will start to stick together and we'll be screwed."

As it turned out, Darby didn't have to wait long. By the time she finished bagging the handcuff key into evidence, a Ford 350 turned the corner at the far end of the street, towing a seventy-foot trailer with antennas and a small satellite dish.

CHAPTER 52

Darby borrowed Coop's cell phone and called Evan Manning. When he picked up, she got right to it.

"Sorry for the early call, but I've found some evidence at the Cranmore house—a folded wet piece of paper that was buried, along with a handcuff key, underneath the porch. One of your mobile units just arrived, and I need to open the paper before it dries. How soon can you get here?"

"Look across the street."

The trailer door opened. Evan Manning waved to her.

The mobile forensic unit contained all the latest equipment, all of it carefully designed to fit inside the long, narrow space. Everything looked and smelled new. Displayed on one of the computer monitors was the FBI's DNA identification system, CODIS.

"Where are your forensic people?" Darby asked as they walked.

"In the air," Evan said. "They're scheduled to touch down at Logan sometime in the next three hours. The other two mobile units have already started working the blast site in Boston. Does the paper have blood on it?"

"I don't know. I haven't unfolded it yet."

"We should suit up, just in case."

After they dressed, Evan handed out masks, safety goggles and neoprene gloves.

"The neoprene will leave indentation marks if we touch the paper," Coop said. "They'll show up during fingerprint processing. We should use cotton gloves over latex."

The examination room was cool and gleaming white. The work counter was small. Evan stood behind Darby to give her some space.

She transferred the paper to the clean work space. Using two pairs of tweezers, she went to work unfolding the paper.

Prying the pages apart was slow, painstaking work. In addition to being wet and flimsy, the paper was badly wrinkled and had started to tear in several places from having been folded and refolded so many times.

It was an 8 x 10 sheet of white paper. The side facing them was a printout of a computer-generated color map. Most of it was unreadable. The colors had faded and several spots had been rubbed away, most likely from the perspiration from Rachel Swanson's hands.

Two areas of the map were caked with mud. Other areas had absorbed the dirt's dark color. Some spots were covered in dried smears of blood and with some yellow liquid, either mucus or pus.

"Why did she fold the paper into such a tiny square?" Coop asked.

Darby answered the question. "That way she could conceal the paper inside a pocket, her mouth or, if needed, her rectum."

"I'm glad we suited up," Coop said.

Darby used cotton swabs to clear away the mud from the paper, careful not to rub off any more of the color toner. Carol's face kept flashing through Darby's mind as she worked.

Hidden beneath the mud were computer-printed directions in neat but faded lettering. At the bottom of the sheet was the URL of the website from which the map had been printed.

Darby had to use the magnifier to read the directions.

"It says '1.4 miles, go between two trees, go straight.' "

Evan moved behind her. "Any idea where the road is?"

"Hold on." Darby followed the trail of the printed road, stopping when she saw what appeared to be part of a number hidden underneath dirt. She used a cotton swab to clear it away.

"It's Route Twenty-two," Darby said. "There's a Route Twenty-two in Belham. It wraps around the woods on the other side of Salmon Brook Pond."

"Let's take a look at the writing," Evan said.

Darby turned the piece of paper over. On the back, written in a shaky hand with small lettering, were notes and what appeared to be names, all written in pencil faded from perspiration and the constant folding and refolding of the paper. Some of the writing was obscured behind crusted spots of dried blood.

Using the light magnifier, she examined the sheet for several minutes.

"Take a look at this." Darby stepped away from the counter to give Evan room.

"1 S R R 2R S," he said. "Does it match what Rachel Swanson wrote on her arm at the hospital?"

Darby had consulted her PDA, where she had transferred her notes. "Here's what she wrote on her arm: '1 L S 2R L R 3R S 2R 3L.' "

"Not only are they different, they're shorter."

"What's the next line say?"

Evan read the combination of letters and numbers.

"They're different—and longer," Darby said.

Evan moved the magnifier over the paper. "There are dozens of different combinations here."

Coop said, "How could directions change?"

"I don't know," Evan said. "I was thinking it might possibly be a combination to, say, a locked door until I saw this line. It says '3: STAY AWAY.' Terry Mastrangelo's name is written beside it with a question mark. And there are several other names here Rachel crossed out."

"She was keeping track of the names of the women kept with her all that time," Darby said, more to herself. "Any chance you have a Video Spectral Comparator in here?"

"The best I've got is the stereomicroscope." Evan grabbed the piece of equipment, set it up on the table and backed away from the counter.

Darby slid onto the stool and carefully transferred the paper to the stereomicroscope. She started her examination at the top, left-hand corner of the paper. Most of the names were illegible. Several names had been crossed out.

"There's a space here that looks like it's been erased," Darby said. "We can toy around with oblique lighting sources to see if we can pick up any indented writing."

"We're better off using infrared reflectography," Coop said. "It works well on revealing erased pencil marks and covered signatures. We can also use it on the areas that are crossed out."

"I'm concerned about fingerprints."

"The pencil won't wash away under any the solvents we use. My first choice would be to try an electrostatic detection apparatus to see if we can pick up any indented writing. It won't damage the document or any potential fingerprints."

"We might have a portable ESDA unit," Evan said. "I'll have to check the equipment list."

"I have a name—Joanne Novack." Darby spelled it as Coop wrote it down on the clipboard. "Next is K-A . . . I can't read the rest. Last name is Bellona or Bellora, I'm not sure. Below it is Jane

Gittle, maybe Gittles. There are additional letters but they're too faded."

"Let me see what I can find out about these names." Evan copied the names on a notepad and left the room.

Darby examined the rest of the document. Dozens and dozens of lines were written in Rachel Swanson's cryptic number and letter code.

Darby took extra pictures with the Polaroid for her own personal file while Coop set up the camera equipment for the close-up pictures. She stuffed the Polaroids in her back pocket and then jotted down the directions on a separate sheet of paper.

She tore the sheet off the pad. "I'm going to give these directions to Evan."

Stripped of her containment gear, Darby walked into the hallway. Evan wasn't in here. A laser printer was spitting out a sheet of paper. It was a picture of a woman with curly black hair and pale features—Joanne Novack, twenty-one, from Newport, Rhode Island. She was last seen leaving her shift at a local bar. She had been missing for almost three years.

Darby picked up the other two sheets.

Kate Bellora, nineteen, had the kind of sallow, haunted face Darby had often seen in battered women. Kate was a heroin addict and known prostitute. She was last seen working in the town she grew up in: New Bedford, Massachusetts. Nobody knew what had happened to her. She had been missing for almost one year.

The last picture held a photograph of a blue-eyed woman with feathered hair and freckles. Jane Gittlesen, twenty-two, from Ware, New Hampshire. Her abandoned car had been found on the side of a highway. Gittlesen had been missing for two years. She was married and had a two-year-old daughter.

Darby borrowed Coop's phone and dialed Banville's number.

He didn't answer. She explained what she had found, along with the directions, and stepped outside to find Evan.

He was standing near the crime scene van, talking to the Boston Bomb Squad commander, Kyle Romano. Dawn was breaking, the sun visible through the trees. The cool air still smelled of smoke.

Evan took a phone call. Romano walked away. Darby caught up with him and asked him if she could use the crime scene vehicle. She could. By the time she reached Evan, he had hung up.

"Any good news?" Darby asked.

Evan shook his head. "I need to head into Boston to take care of a few things."

"Romano gave me clearance to use the crime scene vehicle," Darby said. "I'm going to head out to the woods and see what's out there."

"I need you to stay here and work the evidence until the lab people arrive."

"There's nothing left to do until the paper dries. Coop and I will head out. I told Banville to meet us there."

Evan checked his watch. "I'll go with you," he said. "I want to see what Traveler left for us."

CHAPTER 53

Darby pulled off Route 22 and came to a stop in front of two trees. Between the trees was a dirt road. Someone could easily pull a car inside there and be hidden from the main road. She didn't spot any tire tracks on the ground.

"This looks like the place," Darby said.

Evan nodded. He had been unusually quiet during the drive, communicating with nods and short answers.

Darby killed the engine. She felt a building, jittery panic as she hefted her kit out of the backseat. Evan grabbed the shovels.

"It's going to be slow walking back there," Evan said. "You want me to carry that?"

"Thanks, but I can manage." Darby headed into the woods.

It *was* slow walking, steep and muddy from the rain. Twenty minutes later, the trail ended. In front of them now was an uneven terrain full of sloping ground packed with trees, rocks and downed tree limbs. They had to duck under tree branches as they walked.

Evan slung the shovels to his other shoulder. "You're awfully quiet."

"I could say the same about you. You've hardly said a word since we left."

"I've been thinking about Victor Grady."

"What brought him to mind?"

"The map you found," Evan said. "Riggers said he saw a map of these woods when he was in Grady's house."

"I don't remember reading anything about a map."

"It was destroyed in the fire. Riggers didn't remember much from the map, but he said it was for these woods. The thinking was Grady might have used this area as a possible burial spot, so we searched the woods. We never found anything."

"How much of the woods did you search?"

"About a quarter of it," Evan said. "I don't have to tell you how big these woods are. The Belham department ran out of money and the search was called off."

"So Grady's victims are probably still buried out here."

"I think so—at least that's what I believe deep in my gut. To find where they're buried, it would take a miracle."

Darby stopped walking. "This should be the place."

Below them was a sunny, wide-open patch of ground covered with leaves.

"I don't see any evidence of recent digging," Evan said. "In fact, I don't see evidence of anyone having been out here at all. Take a look at the slope. No boot prints."

"The rain we had might have washed them away. There's barely any tree coverage here."

"We should assemble a team to come out here and search."

"Look down there." Darby pointed to a boulder spray-painted with a small, white smiley face.

"Some kids could have done that," Evan said.

No. Evan was wrong. Kids wouldn't come all the way out here. This location was too remote and private. Digging out here late at night, Traveler wouldn't have to worry about being spotted or heard.

Darby headed down the muddy slope, wondering if Traveler made two separate trips out here—one time to dig the grave, the second to bury the body. Or did he do it all in one trip?

Darby placed her kit on top of the boulder. Next she set up the tarp. When examining burial spots, a team of people was used to help with the tedious task of turning over each leaf and setting it on a tarp while searching the ground for any potential evidence that might have been left behind.

"We should call in more people," Evan said. "It will make this go quicker."

"By the time we mobilize a group and get them out here, we'll probably be done." Darby grabbed a shovel. "Come on, let's get to work."

CHAPTER 54

Darby was hoping to find a cigarette butt, a candy wrapper or soda can—something with DNA that would place Traveler at this burial site. After sifting through the leaves for an hour, the only thing they found was an old penny. She bagged it into evidence, but she wasn't holding out any hope of finding a fingerprint.

"I say we start digging at the base of the boulder and work our way out," Darby said.

Evan agreed and handed her a shovel.

As Darby worked, the morning sun warm on her neck, her thoughts kept running back to what Evan had said about having searched through these woods for the remains of Grady's victims. Was Melanie still buried somewhere out here?

I'm sorry, Mel. I'm sorry you and Stacey never got the chance to live out your lives. I've tried hard to forget what happened. If you had lived, Mel, I know you would have done a much better job at remembering me. If there is such a place as heaven, I can only pray that if we ever meet you'll find it in your heart to forgive me.

The hole was rectangular in shape, about four feet deep. Darby tossed her shovel aside.

"I don't want to risk damaging anything with the shovel." She lay down on her stomach and reached inside the hole. "Do me a favor and grab the brush and hand trowel from my kit."

Darby used her gloved hands to scoop away the dirt. The wet dirt had seeped through her jeans. In the far distance she heard the sound of branches snapping back.

Evan stood over her, watching. He had retreated back into his stony silence. He had barely spoken while they dug.

Darby felt something hard beneath her fingers. She scooped away the dirt. At first, she thought it was a rock. But as she moved away the dirt, she had an idea what it was.

Staring up at her were the parietal and occipital bones that made up the human skull. Jane or John Doe was lying facedown in the grave. The skull was a dark, rusty color, and there wasn't any hair.

Evan handed her a brush from her kit. Darby scooped away more dirt, alternating between her fingers and the brush.

"I don't see any insect activity. No soft tissue . . . No muscle tissue, cartilage or ligaments. Fully skeletonized would be my guess."

Darby pointed to a dark web of lines on the ocular section of the skull. "These are dendritic impressions. You see these root etchings when a skull's been buried for a good amount of time. I should call Carter. He's the state's forensic anthropologist."

"How many people does he have working for him?"

"I'm not sure. Two, I think. Carter has experience in exhuming mass gravesites. He also works for a group that travels to third world countries—places where there are mass graves from genocide and wars."

The sound of branches snapping back grew louder. Someone was heading this way. *Probably Banville,* she thought.

"I wonder if there's a full set of remains buried in there," Darby said.

"This spot could be a dumping ground."

"The ground's too wet to use ground-penetrating radar," Darby said. The machines Carter sometimes used looked like futuristic lawn mowers. They required traction on hard, dry surfaces. "I'm going to call Carter. I don't want to dig any more and risk damaging whatever bones might be buried in here."

Evan glanced off at the trail. Darby looked over her shoulder.

Standing on the level ground above her were four men dressed in suits. The tallest of the bunch, a man with a crew cut, said, "Special Agent Manning, may I speak to you privately for a moment?"

"Who's that?" Darby asked.

Evan walked away without answering. Darby stood up and brushed the mud off her jeans.

Coop's cell phone vibrated in her back pocket.

Darby stripped off her gloves. The cell phone's signal was low, the reception scratchy. She barely heard Coop's voice. Darby told him to hold on a moment and paced the area until the static eased. She pressed a hand over her other ear.

"What did you say, Coop?"

"I said they kicked me out of the mobile lab."

"Who did?"

"Our good friends from Club Fed," Coop said. "The FBI has taken over the investigation."

CHAPTER 55

"It happened about twenty minutes ago," Coop said. "They're taking me downtown."

"Why?"

"They have some questions about the investigation. Has Manning said anything to you?"

"No." *But I have a feeling I'm about to find out,* Darby thought. "What reason did they give you for taking over the case?"

"They didn't. Two of their agents were killed by the bomb in the van, so I'm guessing they're using that as their way in. I can't talk long. I snuck away and borrowed Romano's phone."

"Is Banville there?"

"I haven't seen him. Look, I don't know what's going on, but I think it might have something to do with CODIS. After you left, the computer came back with a DNA hit. I saw it on the screen. Whatever it is, it's classified. I couldn't access it. Shit. Here they come."

"Call Leland," Darby said. "I'll see what I can find out."

Darby headed up the slope. Everyone stopped talking.

The tall man with the crew cut handed her a business card—Assistant Attorney General Alexander Zimmerman from the Department of Justice. *Oh boy.*

"Your business here is concluded, Miss McCormick," Zimmerman said. "Once you reach your crime scene vehicle, you're to turn over all materials and related evidence to Special Agent Vamosi. He'll escort you out. You're to follow Agent Vamosi to the Boston office."

A man with a pie-shaped face stepped up next to her.

"This is a missing persons investigation," Darby said. "You don't have any jurisdiction—"

"Two federal officers are dead," Zimmerman said. "That gives me jurisdictional control. If you have any questions, you can take them up with your attorney general."

"Why is there a classified DNA sample on CODIS?"

"Good-bye, Miss McCormick."

Darby turned to Evan. "Can I speak to you for a moment?"

"I'll talk to you later," Evan said. "You need to get going."

Darby's face reddened. She would never forgive him for the way he had dismissed her.

"You called them out here, didn't you?"

Evan didn't answer. He didn't have to. The look on his face said it all.

"You're trying my patience, Miss McCormick," Zimmerman said.

Darby didn't move, didn't take her eyes off Evan. "You know who Traveler is, don't you? Those listening devices were our best shot at finding Traveler, and you knew what he was capable of and let us walk right into that trap."

The skin on Evan's face tightened. He stared at her with the same cold, penetrating gaze she had witnessed at the lab.

"What about Carol?"

"We'll do everything we can to find her," Evan said evenly.

"I'm sure you will. I'll make sure I tell her mother what safe and capable hands her daughter is in."

Vamosi took her arm. It was either go or fight him.

"I need to get my kit," Darby said.

"I'm sorry, but it needs to stay here," Vamosi said. "We'll return it to you when we're done."

Two federal agents were going through the crime scene vehicle. An unmarked car blocked the trail. Darby had to wait while Agent Vamosi examined items of interest.

Her phone vibrated again. The caller was Pappy.

"I've been trying to reach you all morning. What are you doing with Coop's phone?"

"My phone's busted," Darby said, walking away from the Explorer. "What's going on?"

"I have some good news about the paint chip we recovered from Rachel Swanson's T-shirt. The German database came through with the ID. It's the car's original paint job. The color is called Moonlight White. It's a one-of-a-kind paint manufactured only in the U.K.—that's why we couldn't identify it. The paint was used exclusively for the Aston Martin Lagonda."

"The one from the James Bond movies?"

"The name was made famous in one of the James Bond movies, but the model I'm talking about, the Lagonda, is an early series two, manufactured in the U.K. in the late seventies— seventy-seven, I think. The vehicle was cleared for sale here in the U.S. in eighty-three. They made a conversion kit that had a color TV in the front as well as the back. Back in the day, they sold for 85,000 pounds, which works out to, by today's conversion standards, roughly 150,000 U.S."

Darby watched as Agent Vamosi went through her backpack. "That's quite the price tag," she said.

"I don't know how much they're worth now. They're probably more of an odd collector's item. Only about a dozen or so of these cars were sold in the U.S. We're talking about a very limited—and very select—pool of buyers. A car like that should be easy to track down."

"Where are you right now?"

"Sitting at home, still trying to absorb what happened. I was out yesterday collecting paint samples at a junkyard. It was a last-minute opportunity. If I didn't take it, I would have been inside the building when it . . . when it happened."

Agent Vamosi handed the backpack off to one of the agents and came for her.

"I didn't know your mother was sick," Darby said. "I'm sorry."

"What are you talking about?"

"I think you should see her. She'd love the company."

"Is someone there?"

"Yes. Listen, I need to get going. The FBI has some questions for me. I have to head down to the Boston office."

"The feds have taken over the investigation?"

"Correct," Darby said. "Who else have you told about your mother's illness?"

"No one but you."

"Keep it that way. I'll try you on your cell in a little bit." Darby hung up.

Vamosi stood in front of her. "Can I have the pictures in your back pocket, please?"

Darby handed them over.

"Are you in possession of any other materials related to this investigation?"

"You have everything," Darby said.

"For your sake, I hope so."

And then Darby was seated behind the wheel of the Explorer, the two agents motioning for her to leave. Vamosi had already pulled out. Darby followed. Her arms were shaking with anger, her eyes hot and wet.

She thought about Rachel Swanson. Rachel, with her confident smile and hard-won knowledge, had survived unbelievable pain and cruelty for years. Rachel, with her emaciated body full of scars and sores and broken bones, had kept a list of her fellow prisoners and planned for the moment of her escape. Now she was dead.

And what about Carol? Was she still alive? Or was she already buried in an unmarked grave? Buried like Mel where no one would ever find her?

On the other side of these woods was Route 86. Twenty-four years ago, she had seen a woman being strangled. She didn't know the woman's name or what had happened to her. But Victor Grady did. The man from the woods had come for her and Darby had survived. If she survived that, she could survive anything.

Darby knew what she had to do. When she saw the exit, she hit the gas and bounced up the ramp.

CHAPTER 56

Darby parked the crime scene vehicle in the delivery area behind a liquor store. Safe from prying eyes, she called Pappy back on his cell and quickly filled him in on what had happened. She asked him to repeat the information on the paint chip and wrote everything down in her pocket notebook.

"I meant to ask you this earlier: Who sent the paint sample to the Germans?"

"I did," Pappy said. "I sent them a sample in case the feds weren't able to identify it. Plus, the Germans said they would look at it right away."

"So as far as the feds are concerned, the paint chip wasn't identified."

"As far as I know. My contact at the federal lab sent me an email and said he struck out."

Evan Manning had told her the same thing.

"Darby, if the feds find me, I'll have to turn over what I have."

"Which is why you need to go someplace for the day."

"Well, I was thinking of heading over to the MIT library for awhile."

"Good. Stay there—and stay off your phone unless I call."

Next she called Banville on his cell.

"I take it you heard the good news," she said.

"Our federal friends are at the station right now, going through my office files and computer."

"What are they looking for?"

"Beats the hell out of me. They keep throwing out Title Eighteen as the reason for taking over the investigation."

"Title Eighteen," Darby said. "Doesn't that have something to do with the Patriot Act?"

"You've got it. It basically gives the FBI domestic investigative powers in cases involving terrorism. I don't know anything more than that. My guess is, by the way they're racing through here, we've stumbled across something potentially embarrassing and now they're here to sweep it under the rug. When it comes to burying secrets, nobody does it better than our government—especially this administration."

"I found an entire set of—"

"We shouldn't be talking over a cellular phone. Call me back in five minutes at this number."

Darby wrote it down and headed out to find a pay phone. There was one just outside the front doors of the liquor store. She went inside to get change and, armed with quarters, called Banville. She kept an eye on the parking lot, paranoid that Agent Vamosi was going to pull up at any moment.

Banville picked up right away. Behind him was the steady drone of traffic.

"Are they monitoring our phone calls?" Darby asked.

"When it comes to the feds, I don't take any chances. Tell me what you found."

"We found a skull. I had it partially dug up when the feds showed up and took over. Coop told me the feds got a hit on CODIS."

"I wonder if that's what triggered all of this."

"CODIS will give them a name and a last known address, but I have a way we can find Carol Cranmore." Darby filled him in on the paint chip.

"Aston Martin Lagonda," Banville said. "That's a very select market."

"The cars brought into the U.S. should be easy to track down since they had such a small production run. We'll concentrate our search on anyone living in or around New England. Traveler isn't flying into Boston, he's rooted somewhere close. What he does with these women requires privacy. We'll look for owners with isolated houses."

"Manning told us they couldn't identify the paint chip."

"So?"

"Maybe they were lying to us," Banville said. "Maybe they're already trying to track Traveler down through the paint chip."

"Or maybe Manning was telling the truth. Maybe their lab couldn't ID the paint chip and they're planning on tracking down Traveler through the map."

"I'm not following."

"The map was printed from a website," Darby said. "The website's URL was printed at the bottom of the page. They'll track Traveler down through an IP address."

"I have no idea what an IP address is. The computer stuff is way over my head."

"All the feds need to do is to identify the people who accessed this particular section of the map. They'll go to the company and have them print off a log of IP addresses—it's a unique string of numbers assigned to your computer every time you log on to the internet through your ISP—your internet service provider. Those IP addresses can be tracked down to an individual computer."

"So these IP addresses, they're like a digital fingerprint."

"Not only is it like a digital fingerprint, the IP address acts as an individual map which will lead the feds directly to Traveler's home. The feds will get a list of IP address and start targeting anyone living in and around New England. That's going to take some time. Tracking Traveler down through the make of the car will be quicker."

"Okay. Give me your notes again on the paint chip."

"Tell me where to meet you. It will be quicker."

"You need to go to the Boston office before you get into any more trouble."

"I want to help you. You're going to need people you can trust."

"It's not a matter of trust, Darby. The feds can't hurt me. I'm set to retire at the end of next year, but if they find out you're still investigating this case, they'll make your life difficult. I've seen it happen before. Too many times. Go downtown. I'll call and keep you up to date, I promise."

"If you want the notes, then I'm coming along for the ride."

"Getting involved in this could cost you your career. You may want to give that some thought."

"I want to find Carol Cranmore and bring her home. What do you want?"

Banville didn't answer. Darby spoke into the silence.

"We're wasting time. Carol may still be alive. We need to jump on this now."

"You said you're parked at a liquor store."

"Joseph's Discount Liquors on Palisades," Darby said. "I'm parked out back, in the delivery area."

"I still have one of the surveillance vans. We can run the investigation from there. Give me twenty minutes."

CHAPTER 57

At 1300 hours, the FBI's Hostage Rescue Team boarded a private business jet at the Quantico airstrip. They were coming from a debriefing on the Traveler case. This was what they knew:

In late 1992, nine Hispanic and African American women disappeared in and around Denver, Colorado. The lead suspect in the case, John Smith, had packed up and moved by the time police located his address.

Smith's home had been thoroughly cleaned, but forensics technicians for the Denver police recovered a partial boot print that matched a footwear impression found in the dirt next to the abandoned vehicle belonging to one of the missing women. An empty trash can sprayed with Luminol revealed a small area of blood. Analysis yielded two different DNA samples.

The first sample matched the genetic profile of one of the missing Denver women. The DNA profile was entered into CODIS, the FBI's Combined DNA Indexing System.

The second blood sample was also listed on CODIS, but the identity of the person was not made available to law enforcement agencies or forensic laboratories. The sample belonged to Earl Slavick, a member of the Hand of the Lord, a paramilitary white supremacist group whose ethnic cleansing agenda included the overthrow of the U.S. government. The group, it was believed, had played a role in the Oklahoma City bombing, although no firm link had ever been established.

Slavick was also a high-level FBI informant.

Slavick had been given early parole in the beating of a Hispanic woman in exchange for providing the FBI with detailed information of the group's activities at its secluded training headquarters in the Arkansas hills, not far from the Oklahoma border. As a member of the group, Slavick had been undergoing firearms training and bomb making when, in early 1990, he tried to abduct a Hispanic woman at gunpoint. Slavick dragged the woman, Eva Ortiz, into the woods. When Slavick tripped and fell, Ortiz ran away.

The woman had failed to pick Slavick out of a lineup. He was let go by local police.

When word of his botched abduction attempt finally reached the FBI, Slavick was already on his way to Colorado, under the alias John Smith, to start his own racial cleansing movement.

Given the highly sensitive nature of the case, all of Slavick's files were classified. His fingerprints and DNA profile were left on the computer databases. If a match was ever found, the FBI would be alerted to Slavick's whereabouts, while the reporting law enforcement agency or forensic laboratory would only see the code name the FBI had given to the case: Traveler.

Slavick's next stop after Denver was Las Vegas. Twelve women and three men vanished over a nine-month period. A footwear impression matched the one recovered in Denver.

When Slavick moved on to Atlanta in 1998, Special Agent Evan Manning was asked to help assist in the investigation of three missing women. Slavick, posing as a gas station attendant, had attacked Manning, who managed to crawl away before passing out. Like his many victims, Slavick vanished into thin air.

That changed this morning, at 0800, when CODIS matched the blood found at the home of an abducted Massachusetts teenager to the DNA profile of Earl Slavick.

As the jet lifted off, nobody talked. HRT knew they were flying to Pease Air Force Base in Portsmouth, New Hampshire. From there, a Black Hawk attack helicopter would take them to the command post set up in Lewiston.

Team commander Colin Cunney took off his headset. He took a few minutes to review his notes before standing up to address his crew.

"Okay, boys, listen up. The computer-printed map found early this morning was identified by our lab as having come from an online website specifically geared to hikers. Here's where we got lucky. Two weeks ago, the map was accessed by a man living in twelve Cedar Road in Lewiston, New Hampshire. Crisis Management is already on the ground. They did a visual sweep of the house. It's our boy Slavick."

"Hopefully he'll stay put this time," Sammy DiBattista said.

Nervous laughter echoed inside the cabin.

"A Black Hawk, courtesy of our friends at the Pease Air Force Base, made a run about an hour ago and got us a few aerial shots of the house," Cunney said. "The area's thickly settled with woods, so we can use that to our advantage. There are three buildings: the house, a good-sized garage where he keeps a number of vehicles—so far they've spotted two vans—and a bunker. The entire area is surrounded with fences covered with razor wire, security cameras, infrared trip alarms, you name it."

Cunney paused for a moment. He wanted his next point to sink in.

"Slavick spent a lot of time at the Hand of the Lord's training camp in Arkansas," he said. "Not only does he know how to shoot, he's considered somewhat of an explosives expert. You all know he destroyed a hospital with a fertilizer bomb and a homemade plastic explosive stuffed inside a FedEx box took down to the Boston Crime lab. Our man also killed two of our agents with dynamite packed inside a van. Going in, we've got to assume he's rigged some of the buildings.

"It will be nightfall by the time we arrive. Intel says there are other people on Slavick's property—probably some local weekend warrior assholes he's recruited for his movement. I want to hit him hard and fast. We're not going to have another goddamn firefight, not if I can help it."

The ghost of Waco passed through the faces.

Cunney looked to his two best snipers, Sammy DiBattista and Jim Hagman.

"Sam, Haggy, you're not to fire until you have the go-ahead from me, understood?"

Both men nodded. Cunney wasn't worried. He had seen these two men in actual combat and knew their capabilities.

"We don't know how many women Slavick's got trapped in there with him," Cunney said. "We're going in with the assumption they're alive. Rescuing those women is our primary objective. This is a tactical operation. There will be no negotiating.

"One last thing. This is strictly a home team affair. We don't have to worry about any interference from ATF or the locals. Crisis Management has assembled all the technical and tactical help we need. That's all I have right now. Questions?"

Sammy DiBattista asked the question on everyone's mind: "What do we do if Slavick decides to engage us?"

"Simple," Cunney said. "We take the son of a bitch down."

CHAPTER 58

The computers at the Massachusetts DMV were terribly slow. It took over two hours to assemble a twenty-page list of drivers who owned or had owned one of the twelve Aston Martin Lagondas imported into the United States.

Darby hunted through the sheets of tiny print for recent owners while Banville talked on one of the secured phones inside the surveillance van. More than four hours had passed since the feds had taken over the investigation. During that time, he had assembled a small group of detectives he could trust to handle the investigation discreetly.

Out of the twelve Lagondas, only eight were still active. The other four had been junked. Darby was in the process of compiling her notes when Banville hung up.

"Rachel Swanson died of an air embolism," he said. "Someone pumped air through her IV line. The feds confiscated it along with the security tapes for ICU."

"Wonderful," Darby said. The feds were certainly covering their tracks.

"We interviewed the ICU nurses, but nobody remembers anything but the news of the bomb. That's why Traveler bombed the hospital, didn't he? Create all that confusion and fear and the son of a bitch slipped right in."

"It was just like 9/11. Everyone is running around, trying to find an exit. Nobody is paying attention to anyone."

"Pretty slick." Banville rubbed his chin. "I'm still trying to figure out why he just didn't pack up and leave."

"Ego, maybe. None of his victims had ever escaped. Or maybe he was afraid Rachel knew too much and he didn't want to take the risk of her talking to us. Let me show you what I have on the car."

Darby picked up the sheets where eight names were highlighted. "The closest states with recent Lagonda owners are Connecticut, Pennsylvania and New York."

"Wasn't one of Traveler's victims from Connecticut?"

Darby nodded. "Take a look at this name."

"Thomas Preston, from New Canan, Connecticut," Banville said. "Owned the vehicle for two years, then sold it a little over two months ago. That Lagonda hasn't been registered yet."

"Traveler could be the guy who bought the car. Let's look into Preston first, see how long he's lived in Connecticut, and if he owns a van."

Banville reached across the console and grabbed the wall phone.

"Steve, it's Mat. Take a look at page fifteen. About halfway down the page, you'll see the name Thomas Preston from New Caanan, Connecticut. Find out everything you can about him. I need to know if he owns a van."

Twenty minutes later, the phone rang. Banville listened for a moment, then covered the receiver with his hand. "Preston doesn't have a record. He's fifty-nine, a lawyer, divorced and has lived in his house for the past twenty years. He's never owned a van."

Scratch Preston.

"We need to find out who Preston sold the car to," Darby said. "We need to find his name. Ask your man to get Preston's home number—get all of his numbers, business, cell phones, everything. And get the name of his insurance agency."

Banville relayed the information and hung up. "If the buyer is Traveler, and he gave Preston a phony name, there's no way we can track him."

"Let's keep our fingers crossed. We're overdue for some luck."

"Why did you want the name of his insurance agency?"

"The safest way to play it is to call and pretend to be someone from his insurance company. The guy's an attorney. You know how these guys act when you try to ask them questions about a criminal case. He'll bury us in legal bullshit and paperwork. It will be a week until he gives us an answer. But if we call and say we're from his insurance agency, he'll give us the info."

"I agree."

Banville's contact called back ten minutes later.

"Do you mind if I make the phone call?" Darby didn't want Banville's rough manner to turn away Preston.

Banville handed her the phone.

Darby tried the office number first. The secretary said Mr. Preston was on another line. Darby had to wait through several minutes of soft elevator music.

"Tom Preston."

"Mr. Preston, I'm calling from Sheer Insurance in regards to your Aston Martin Lagonda."

"I sold it about two months ago."

"Did you turn in the plates?"

"Of course I did."

"According to our records, the DMV says you didn't."

Preston went on the defensive. "I turned in the plates. If there's a problem, take it up with the DMV."

"Clearly some mistake has been made. Did you make a copy of the title?"

"I sure as hell did. I made copies of everything. Goddamn registry, if I ran my practice like they did, I'd be disbarred."

"I understand your frustration. Tell you what: Give me the name and address of the person you transferred the title to, and I'll see if I can save you a trip to the registry."

"I don't remember his name. The copy of the title's at home. I'll call you first thing tomorrow morning. What's your name again?"

"Mr. Preston, I really need to take care of this matter now. Is there someone you can call at home?"

"No, I live alone—wait, I mailed him the owner's manual."

"Excuse me?"

"When he came to pick up the car, I didn't have the original owner's manual," Preston said. "I couldn't find it. He wanted it and any other documentation I might have, so I told him I'd take a look. He gave me his address and I said I'd mail it to him. I wrote it down in my date book . . . Here it is. Fifteen Carson Lane in Glen, New Hampshire."

"What's the man's name?"

"Daniel Boyle."

CHAPTER 59

Banville's detective at the Massachusetts Registry had already coordinated efforts with New Hampshire's Department of Motor Vehicles. According to their computer records, Daniel Boyle had sold his van two days ago but hadn't turned in the plates. There was no information in his registry file about an Aston Martin Lagonda.

New Hampshire DMV was transmitting Boyle's license picture.

Coming up on the monitor was the driver's license for Daniel Boyle, a white male, forty-eight years old. Boyle had thick blond hair and a pleasant-looking face with dead green eyes.

Banville hung up and immediately started dialing another number. "Boyle had his home number disconnected three days ago."

"Looks like he's getting ready to move," Darby said.

"He may already be gone. We're trying to see if he has a cell phone. If he does, and if he's carrying it with him and it's turned on, we may be able to track down his location through his cellular signal. I don't have that kind of equipment here. We'll have to use someone from the phone company."

Banville was now on the line with the Glen County sheriff's office. Darby watched the GPS monitor. They were heading up 95 North at a fast clip. At their current speed, they would make it to Boyle's address in a little over an hour.

"The county sheriff, Dick Holloway, left for the day," Banville said after he hung up. "Dispatcher's paged him. The woman I talked to knows the area—six or so old homes surrounding a lake. It's pretty isolated, she said. She doesn't remember Daniel Boyle but knew his mother, Cassandra. She lived out there for years until she disappeared."

"The dispatcher remembered this?"

"Glen's a small area, with a tight community. The woman I talked to grew up there. She was surprised to hear Boyle living back home again. She thought the house hadn't been occupied in years.

"The dispatcher also told me another interesting tidbit," Banville said. "Back in the late seventies, Alicia Cross, a neighborhood girl, disappeared. They never found her body. She's going to have someone check the case to see if Boyle was ever a suspect."

Darby felt the pieces coming together. "How long will it take Glen County to mobilize their SWAT unit?"

"The SWAT members are from different counties," Banville said. "Once Holloway makes the call, we're talking an hour or two just to get them together."

"What about sending a patrol car out there to see if Boyle's home?"

"I don't want to run the risk of spooking him. This van is designed to look like a telephone repair truck. We're less than an hour away. I say we head over to Boyle's house and see if he's home. If the Lagonda's parked in his garage, we'll call Holloway and ask for backup."

"I don't think we should go with an explosive entry. If Boyle sees a cop on his doorstep, he may decide to go and kill Carol and the other women."

"I agree. Washington—he's the man driving us—I'll have him dress up as a phone technician. We have a couple of uniforms in here. His face hasn't been on TV, so Boyle won't recognize him. If Boyle sees a telephone repairman, he'll be more inclined to open the door to us. Once he does, we'll take him down."

CHAPTER 60

Daniel Boyle had lived most of his life out of suitcases. His army training had taught him to live only with the bare essentials. He didn't have much to pack.

The original plan was to leave Sunday, after he finished his business in the basement. That changed early this afternoon when Richard sent him a text message: "Remains found in woods. Leave now."

Boyle saw the breaking news report on NECN. Belham police had discovered a set of remains buried in the woods. The report didn't mention how the remains were found, or what had led police to the area. There was no video footage of the area, so he didn't know where, exactly, the remains had been found.

The women who had disappeared during the summer of eighty-four were buried out in those woods, but the police had never found the bodies. They couldn't find the bodies. The map he had left inside Grady's house had burned away in the fire.

The police had found a *single* set of remains. He wondered if they had found the remains of his mother/sister. If they had, if they managed to identify her, then the police would start asking questions, which would lead them here, to New Hampshire.

Rachel must have told the police something. But what could

she have possibly said? She didn't know anything about the Belham woods or how many women he had buried there. Rachel didn't know his name or where he lived—she certainly didn't know about where he had buried his mother/sister. What could Rachel have told them? Had she found something in his office? In the filing cabinet? The questions kept turning over and over in his mind as he packed the envelopes and laptop.

The first envelope contained two sets of false IDs—passports, driver's licenses, birth certificates and Social Security cards. The last two held ten grand in case, his seed money to help get him started in another city. After that, he could use his laptop to wire money from the private bank he used in the Caymans.

Boyle zipped up the suitcase. He didn't know regret or sadness. The emotional concepts were as foreign to him as the terrain on the moon. Still, he would miss this house, his childhood home, with its big rooms and privacy, the magnificent view of the lake from the master bedroom. What he would miss most was the basement.

Boyle clicked off the bedroom light. There was only one item left to pack.

He walked into the finished room over the three-car garage. He didn't turn on the lights; he could see fine by the moonlight coming in through the windows and skylight.

He walked past the walk-in closets still holding his mother's clothes and knelt on the floor next to the window overlooking the driveway. He peeled back the carpet, removed the loose floorboard and grabbed the well-oiled Mossberg shotgun and shells. He had used it only once, to kill his grandparents.

Boyle glanced out the window, about to stand when he saw someone below him, looking inside his garage.

It was Banville, the detective from Belham.

Boyle froze.

Banville was talking into his jacket. The detective was wearing an earpiece. A surveillance kit. Banville was talking into a vest mike.

They found you, Daniel.

His mother's voice.

They're coming to take you away, just like I said they would.

This was a mistake. He had carefully built a trail of evidence that led back to Earl Slavick. The blood, the padded mailers and the navy blue fibers, the pictures he had taken of Carol—everything led to Slavick. Banville shouldn't be here.

Why hadn't Richard called him? He was watching Banville.

Had something happened to Richard?

Boyle took out his BlackBerry. He didn't want send a text message and wait for an answer. He needed to know. Now. He called Richard's main number.

The phone kept ringing and ringing. Richard's voice mail picked up. Boyle left a message. "Banville's at my house. Where are you?"

A telephone van pulled into his driveway. The dim interior light clicked on. Sitting behind the wheel was a man dressed in a brown jacket, a Verizon patch stitched on his breast pocket. He was studying a clipboard.

So this was how they were going to do it. Have a telephone repairman ring the doorbell and when he opened the door they'd take him down. They wouldn't risk breaking in because they were worried he would kill Carol.

There's no escape for you, Daniel.

He wouldn't answer the door. They'd go away if he didn't answer the door. He would wait until they left and then he would drive away.

It's too late. They know you're home. The lights are on downstairs and in the garage—Banville's seen the boxes you left by the car. The police know you're getting ready to leave. If you don't come out, they'll come in.

He could sneak through the back door and head into the woods. He had the keys for the shed. The Gator was in there. Head out on one of the trails to the main road, then find a car and hotwire it—no, the Gator would be too noisy. He'd have to follow one of the trails on foot.

Banville brought other cops with him, Daniel. They have the house surrounded. You won't get far.

Boyle looked around the dark woods, wondering how many SWAT officers were hiding out there.

It's over, Danny. You can't escape.

"No."

They're going to lock you up on death row, in a place darker than the cellar.

"Shut up."

They'll probably extradite you to a place where they have the death penalty. They'll strap you down to a table and give you the needle and the last voice you'll ever hear before you suffocate to death will be mine, Danny. You're going to die alone, just like I did.

He wouldn't let them take him in. He wasn't going to die alone in some goddamn cage. He had to get to his car or the surveillance van. He knew a spot where he could dump it, run and then hide out for awhile until he could figure out a plan to disappear again.

The driver stepped out of the van. Banville had drawn his sidearm.

Boyle threaded four Super Magnum shells into the shotgun. He dumped the rest of the shells in his pocket and headed for the stairs.

CHAPTER 61

Darby watched the front of the house through the periscope.

On the way here, she had imagined finding a rundown house, some brooding structure with a sunken-in porch and broken windows. The house she was looking at resembled the ones she saw in upscale Weston, Massachusetts—a sprawling antique Colonial of massive rooms full of expensive furniture and the latest in electronic trinkets. Landscape lights lit up a nice brick walkway, the shrubs surrounding it neatly manicured.

An Aston Martin Lagonda, the front hood and sides marred with pockets of rust, was parked in the garage. Banville had radioed the news over her earpiece. Darby was rigged with the same surveillance kit used by the Secret Service—an earpiece and lapel mike attached to a small black box clipped to her belt.

Darby wanted to call for backup, but Banville didn't want to wait. Boxes were stacked next to the car; Boyle was about to move. Mobilizing the New Hampshire SWAT unit would take too long, and he had to consider the possibility that Carol and the other women might be somewhere in the house, alive. They needed to take Boyle down *now*.

Someone was home. A single light was on downstairs, coming

from the foyer, and Darby was sure she had spotted movement in the upstairs bedroom before the light turned off.

Glen Washington, the detective dressed in the brown coat and pants, rang the doorbell.

A phone was ringing. Not one of the wall phones. It was Coop's cell. She answered it.

"We've found Traveler," Evan Manning said. "He was living in New Hampshire. Hostage Rescue had to take him down. That's all I can tell you."

"You're sure it's him?"

"I'm positive. The man HRT took down is the man who attacked me at the garage. He's got the same tattoo on his forearm as John Smith. Do you remember what I told you about the mailer? The one with Carol Cranmore's clothes?"

Darby went back to watching the house. "You said they didn't make those mailers anymore. The company went bankrupt."

"I'm looking at a whole shelf-full of those mailers right now. They're a match. This person also has an old IBM electric type-writer, a computer, a photo printer and paper. I won't know for sure about the paper and the printer until I get them back to the lab. We also found several different types of listening devices."

"Where's Carol?"

Washington rang the doorbell again.

"We're searching for her right now," Evan said. "I'm sorry about what happened earlier. I didn't want it to go down that way, but it wasn't my decision."

The door to the front house opened.

Washington's voice came over her earpiece: "Good evening, sir. I'm with the telephone—"

A shotgun blast blew him off the front steps.

CHAPTER 62

Darby dropped the phone and watched as Banville brought up his handgun and fired two shots inside the doorway—*BOOM* and the shotgun blast splintered apart the door frame, chunks of wood raining down on Banville's back.

Darby scooped the cell phone from the floor. Evan was saying "Darby? What's going on? You there?" She hung up and dialed 911 to request medical assistance and backup.

Looking back through the periscope, she caught a fast glimpse of Banville heading inside the front door. Washington lay on his back, his hand scrabbling at his chest.

Darby opened the van's back doors and ran to the driver's side door, legs rubbery as she got behind the wheel, relieved to find the keys dangling in the ignition. She started the van and hit the gas hard, bouncing in her seat as she drove across the front lawn—*BOOM* over the earpiece. Banville fired back in a tight pattern, two shots each.

Darby stopped the van between Washington and the front door of the house and, using the van as a shield, got out and ran for the downed officer.

The fabric of his jacket was torn open from the shotgun blast.

No blood. Darby unzipped his jacket. Through the torn fabric she saw body armor with a trauma plate.

Washington's eyes, wild and glassy, looked up at her, his throat working, making wet, gurgling sounds.

Darby gripped him under the armpits. "Hold on, you're going to be fine," she said, repeating the words over and over as she dragged him across the lawn, the fierce wind blowing leaves everywhere.

Over the earpiece, new sounds between the gunfire: shouting and glass shattering.

Darby managed to hoist the upper half of the man's torso into the back of the van. Jumping back outside, she lifted the man's legs and pushed him back across the carpet.

Kneeling beside him, Darby removed the SIG Sauer pistol from his shoulder holster. She ripped open his shirt, buttons popping off, and undid the Velcro straps from the vest to relieve the pressure.

Glass breaking—not coming from the earpiece but from outside.

SIG gripped in her hand, she slammed the van doors shut.

Boyle was standing on the garage roof with a shotgun.

Darby dove to the ground—*BOOM,* the blast hit the back doors. Rolling to her side, she scrambled to her feet and ran to the driver's side door—*BOOM,* the blast ricocheting off the van's bulletproof plating.

Ears ringing, she brought the gun up over the front hood and aimed at the roof—

Boyle jumped onto the driveway.

He's going for the car, she thought and fired two shots.

Too wide. Both shots hit the side of the garage. Boyle stumbled and fired again—inside the garage. *Banville must be in there.*

Boyle turned and headed into the woods.

Darby followed, catching a glimpse of Banville inside the garage. She ran into the woods, chasing the sound of branches snapping ahead of her, running hard and fast like she did in her nightmares, branches and leaves whisking past her face and arms and hands.

A shotgun blast hit a tree close by. Her legs froze and she tripped and fell, tumbling hard against the ground full of rocks and downed branches. Darby got back up and heard Boyle running her way, coming closer, coming fast.

More footsteps crashing through the woods behind her— Banville. No sounds in front of her.

Where was Boyle?

Her eyes had adjusted to the darkness and she could see the ground in front of her, how it dipped and fell and leveled off. Darby headed up a hill, pushing her way through a thick brush of trees, the handgun big and awkward inside her clenched fist.

The ground leveled off. Left or right, make a decision, hurry.

She turned left and came face-to-face with Daniel Boyle.

Darby brought the handgun up. Boyle swung the butt of the shotgun hard against the side of her head. Bright sparks of pain danced in front of her eyes as she fell backward and hit the ground. Boyle stepped on her hand, crushing her fingers against the pistol, and pressed the hot muzzle of the shotgun against her throat.

BOOM and Boyle staggered backward against a tree. Banville came around and shot Boyle in the chest and still the shotgun came up and Banville shot him again and again, Boyle's face collapsing, deflating like a balloon as he slid down the tree in a wet, red trail.

CHAPTER 63

Darby's legs were shaky. She couldn't stand. Banville put his arm around her waist and escorted her away from the body. She kept turning around to make sure Boyle wasn't chasing her.

"He's dead, he can't hurt you," Banville said to her, more than once. "It's over."

By the time they exited the woods, the road wasn't dark anymore. Police cruisers were parked everywhere, their revolving blue and whites bouncing off the trees and windows of Boyle's home.

A red-faced cop stood in the driveway. Sheriff Dickey Holloway didn't mince words. He was good and pissed about having a shootout in his backyard.

Darby left them and headed into the house. Chunks of plaster had been blown out of the walls. The smell of cordite was strong. She stumbled through the rooms until she found the basement door.

The steps led to a nightmarish maze of corridors with very little light. Darby called out Carol's name as she wandered into dim and dusty rooms packed with old furniture and boxes. At the far end of the basement was a small wine cellar thick with cobwebs and reeking of mold.

Carol Cranmore wasn't here. Nobody was.

Banville was standing in the foyer when she came up the stairs.

"There's no prison cell downstairs," Darby said. "Boyle must have kept Carol and the other women somewhere else."

Holloway was in the bedroom, examining the suitcase on the floor. One of the windows had been blown apart.

"He barricaded himself in here and then escaped through the window," Banville said. "He shot at you from the roof."

The suitcase held a good amount of clothes and a laptop computer. The envelopes held lots of cash and several false IDs.

"Looks like he was getting ready to do some traveling," Holloway said. "You got here just in time."

"I'd like to take a look at the laptop," Darby said. "There might be something on there that can help us find Carol."

"Right now, you need to get that cut treated. All due respect, ma'am, you're bleeding all over my crime scene."

The EMT used a butterfly stitch on the split skin above her cheekbone and then gave her an ice pack to help keep the swelling down. She could barely see out of her left eye, but she refused to go to the hospital.

Darby sat alone on the back bumper of the surveillance van with the ice pack pressed against the growing lump on the side of her face and watched Holloway's men moving through the woods.

Seeing the flashlight beams crisscrossing through the woods brought back the piercing memory of watching the police search for Melanie. She had convinced herself Mel going to be okay. Mel never came home.

Please God, please let Carol be alive. I don't think I can live through this again.

Banville came out the front door. He sat down next to Darby.

"One of Holloway's men is a somewhat of a computer expert.

He turned on the laptop. Everything on there's password protected, he said. We're going to need someone who knows to bypass
the security or the files will be erased."

"I can call the Boston Computer Lab—they're in a different
building, so they weren't affected by the bomb," Darby said.
"They aren't on call. It will have to wait until morning. I'd rather
not wait that long."

"You have another idea?"

"You could call Manning. He might have someone—and he's
close by."

Darby shared the details of her phone conversation with Evan.
Banville didn't speak after she finished. He stared at the tops of his
shoes, jingling the change in his pockets.

Holloway emerged from the woods.

"We found a shed less than a quarter mile off the property. It's
locked up pretty tight. I'll show you the way. It's bumpy walking
back there, so watch your step."

The shed sat alone in a clearing, painted the same white color of
the house. The large bay door was locked down with twin
industrial-gauge padlocks to prevent anyone from gaining access—
or from escaping. There weren't any windows or a door.

They had to wait over half an hour for someone from the station to deliver a pair of bolt cutters.

Inside the garage area was a John Deere Gator holding dirt and
a shovel. Darby borrowed a flashlight and found dried spots of
what could be blood on the plastic seat.

Banville poked his head around a corridor. "Darby."

The narrow corridor was made of Peg-Board walls holding
lawn equipment. Banville stood at the far end. He took down a bag

of lime from a shelf and placed it on the floor. Cut inside the Peg-Board wall was a square with enough room to reach inside and turn a door handle.

First they had to take care of the padlock.

The secret room held two prison cells. Both were unlocked and empty.

Banville stood inside a room of gray concrete and stainless steel. No mirror or windows, just a small vent high in the ceiling. A surplus army cot was bolted to the floor. A floor drain was in the center of the room. Darby recalled the pictures of Carol she had seen at the lab.

"This must be where he kept her," Banville said.

Darby thought of the Gator with its shovel and bed full of dirt and felt the last dangling thread of hope slide away.

CHAPTER 64

Darby pulled Banville aside so they could talk privately.

"Hostage Rescue might have access to a chopper," Darby said. "If they do, and if it's equipped with infrared heat sensors, we can use it to search the woods, see if it can lock on to what's left of Carol's heat signature, depending on how deep she's buried and how long ago Boyle killed her."

"Holloway's already put out the call to the state police for assistance. By morning, the dogs will be here. We're going to cover every inch of these woods."

"A chopper can do a sweep of these woods in about a couple of hours."

Banville let out a long sigh.

"I don't like asking the feds for help any more than you do, believe me," Darby said. "But I'm thinking about Dianne Cranmore. You and I both know what happened here is going to be all over the news first thing tomorrow morning. I think we should tell the mother before she finds out on the news."

Banville handed over his cell phone. "You can make the call to Manning."

Darby stood alone on a dark trail, dialing Evan's number, Holloway's men busy behind her.

"It's Darby."

"I've been trying to reach you for over an hour," Evan said. "What's going on? The call was dropped. I kept calling and you didn't pick up."

"Did you find Carol?"

"No, not yet. What I did find, though, was more evidence—a pair of men's boots, size eleven, manufactured by Ryzer Gear. There's also a navy blue carpet in the bedroom. I think it will match the fibers you found."

"Did you find a prison cell? Like the one we saw in the pictures?"

"No."

"Carol's not there."

"What are you talking about?"

"First, I want to ask you a question about Hostage Rescue. Do they have access to a chopper?"

"A Black Hawk," Evan said. "Why?"

"Is it equipped with infrared heat sensors?"

"What's going on, Darby?"

"Find out and call me back on Banville's cell phone. Do you need the number?"

"I already have it. Now tell me what's—"

Darby hung up. Holloway's men were getting ready to search the woods for recently dug graves.

Half an hour later, Evan called back.

"The Black Hawk is equipped with infrared heat sensors."

"I'm going to need it to do a search of some woods," Darby said. "I'm looking for a buried body. Maybe several of them."

"Where are you?"

"First, you're going to tell me why your wonderful organization took over my case."

"I told you, it's classified—"

Darby hung up.

Evan immediately called back. "Booting you off the case wasn't my decision."

"I know. You looked real upset when it happened."

"You're putting me in an awkward position. I can't tell you what—"

"You're going to tell me what happened, right now, or I'm hanging up again."

Evan didn't answer.

"Good-bye, Special Agent Manning."

"What I'm about to say is completely off the record. If it ever gets back to me, I'll deny it."

"Don't worry, I'm well acquainted with how you federal guys operate."

"The man we took down was Earl Slavick, a former informant we had working inside a white supremacist group with suspected ties to the Oklahoma City bombing. While Slavick was feeding us information about his group, he had started his own racial cleansing agenda and abducted women from the area. I was called in to help out local authorities. By the time I figured out what was going on, Slavick had packed up and disappeared. We've been looking for him ever since."

"So you knew right away Slavick was involved in Carol Cranmore's abduction because of the boot prints I found."

"Yes, I told you that."

"But you didn't tell me Slavick's DNA profile was loaded into CODIS. You didn't tell me it was classified. That way, when a match was found, the FBI would know, and then you guys could come in and clean up your mess quietly. You didn't want anyone to know that the man making all these women disappear was a former FBI informant. The remains we found in the woods, she was one of Slavick's victims, wasn't she?"

"Congratulations," Evan said in a cold tone. "You've connected all the dots."

"One last question," Darby said. "How did you find out where Traveler—excuse me, Earl Slavick—was hiding?"

Evan didn't answer.

"Let me guess," Darby said. "It was the map I found. The URL was printed on the bottom. You tracked Slavick through his IP address, didn't you?"

"We've traded information. Now it's your turn."

"We found a shed in the back of a house equipped with the same prison cells we saw in the pictures with Carol Cranmore. The house belongs to Daniel Boyle. I'm willing to bet he set up Slavick to take the fall."

Evan didn't answer.

"Sounds like you guys are going to have a real PR disaster on your hands," Darby said. "I hope it doesn't make the news. They'll drag the story out all year, don't you think? No, probably not. You guys will find a way to bury it. When it comes to hiding the truth, nobody does it better than the federal government."

"Where's Boyle?"

"He's dead."

"You killed him?"

"Banville did." She gave Evan the address. "Don't forget to bring the chopper."

Darby hung up. She closed her eyes and pressed the ice pack against her face. The skin was cold and numb.

CHAPTER 65

The Black Hawk made two runs over the woods and failed to find a heat signature. Either Boyle had killed Carol several days ago or her body was buried too deep.

The search for the graves would resume tomorrow morning at eight, when the New Hampshire state police showed up with cadaver-sniffing dogs. It was their case now.

Forensic technicians from the state lab had arrived shortly before midnight and divided themselves into two teams—one to process the house, and the other to work the crime scene in the woods.

Evan wasn't allowed access to either the woods or the house. He spent most of his time on the phone, pacing near the far end of the lawn, under the oak trees. Darby spent her time going over her statement with two of Holloway's detectives.

Banville trotted out of the woods, looking drained. "Holloway found Boyle's wallet, phone and keys—lots of keys," he said. "How much you want to bet one of those keys belongs to Slavick's house?"

"I doubt the feds will let us anywhere near it until we allow them access to Boyle's house."

"What's Manning been up to?"

"He's been working the phone. I'm sure Zimmerman and his band of merry elves will be here any moment trying to weasel their way in. They've got to be real nervous now that they know they killed the wrong man."

"Boyle had one of those BlackBerry phones in his pocket," Banville said. "Holloway took a look at it. He didn't find any email, but the phone keeps a log of all incoming and outgoing calls. Boyle called someone at nine-eighteen tonight."

"Who was he calling?"

"Don't know yet. The call lasted roughly forty-six seconds. Holloway said it's a Massachusetts area code. He's tracking down the number now. Have you talked with Manning?"

"No. He hasn't said anything to me."

"Good. Keep it that way. Let the asshole sweat for a change."

Banville's phone rang. His face changed.

"Dianne Cranmore," he said. "I've got to take this. Then I'll see if I can get someone to drive you home—don't fight me on this, Darby. I don't want you here when the feds arrive. I'll take the heat for this. If anyone asks, I ordered you to come along."

Darby was watching two men from the coroner's office carrying out a body bag on a stretcher when Evan stepped up next to her.

"The swelling on your face still looks pretty bad. You should put some more ice on it."

"I'll grab some on the way home."

"Are you heading out?"

"As soon as Banville finds me a ride," Darby said.

"I can drive you."

"You're not sticking around?"

"I'm not too popular right now."

"I can't imagine why."

"How about we call a truce and you let me drive you home? Better yet, why don't you let me drive you to a hospital?"

"I don't need to go to the hospital."

"Then I'll take you home."

Darby glanced at her watch. It was well after midnight. If Banville couldn't get someone here to give her a ride, she'd have to call Coop or wait for one of Banville's men to come up here. Either way, she wouldn't be back in Belham until at least three a.m. But if she left now, with Evan, she could get home at a reasonable hour, get some sleep and arrive here well rested for tomorrow morning's search.

"Let me tell Banville," Darby said.

Inside the car, Darby watched the passenger's side rearview mirror and stared at the blinking pulse of blue and white lights grow smaller and dimmer. Some part of her felt as though she were abandoning Carol.

When the glow of lights finally disappeared, the road in front of her dark except for the headlights, Darby found it difficult to breathe. The inside of the car felt too close. She needed air. She needed to move.

"Stop the car."

"What's wrong?"

"Just stop the car."

Evan pulled over. Darby threw the door open and stumbled out onto the dirt road. Dark woods surrounded her; all she could see was Carol locked inside that cold, gray prison cell, alone and scared, away from her mother.

Darby knew that kind of fear. She had felt it when she was hiding under the bed, when she was locked inside her mother's room and later, when Melanie was downstairs crying out for help.

The car's engine shut off. A door opened and shut behind her.

A moment later, Darby heard Evan's footsteps crunching over the gravel.

"You've done everything you could to help find her," he said in a gentle voice.

Darby didn't answer. She kept staring at the dark woods. Carol was buried somewhere out there.

Darby turned her attention to the tiny throb of blue and white lights blinking in the distance. She thought about Boyle standing up in one of the bedroom windows, watching as the surveillance van pulled into his driveway and then—

"He made a phone call," Darby said out loud.

"Excuse me?"

"Boyle made a phone call *after* we pulled into his driveway—there was a record of it on his BlackBerry. Boyle called someone at nine-eighteen. We pulled into his driveway a little after nine—I remember seeing the time on the surveillance monitor."

Darby saw it clearly in her mind's eye—Boyle standing behind the window and seeing the telephone repair van pulling into his driveway. How did he know the police were in there? He didn't. Banville was standing in the driveway. Had Boyle spotted him? Maybe.

So let's assume Boyle spotted Banville. Boyle grabs the shotgun, and before he heads downstairs, he makes a phone call. Who was he calling? Who could possibly help—

"Oh Jesus." Darby grabbed the back of her neck. "Boyle made that phone call because he had someone working with him. Traveler wasn't one person—it was two. Boyle was calling to warn his partner."

Darby turned around. Evan looked off in the distance, his eyes filmed with thought.

"Think about it," Darby said. "Boyle orchestrated three bomb-

ings—the bomb in the van, the bomb he planted inside a mannequin stuffed inside a FedEx box, and the last one, the fertilizer
bomb that took down the hospital."

"I know where you're heading. Boyle could have dropped off
the van the night before, left it there and headed out the next
morning with the FedEx truck."

"The listening devices turned on at a specific time. The only
way Boyle could have done that was if he was watching us. But he
couldn't have been watching us and driving the FedEx truck at the
same time."

"It's not a bad theory," Evan said. "Maybe Slavick was his partner. We found plenty of evidence inside his house."

"Slavick wasn't the partner—he was the fall guy."

"Maybe Slavick turned on Boyle, and Boyle decided to let
Slavick take the fall. With Slavick dead, Boyle can pack up and
leave. He was getting ready to leave, wasn't he?"

"You told me you searched every inch of Slavick's house and
didn't find any prison cells."

"Correct. But you found them at Boyle's house."

"They were holding pens."

"I'm not following."

"There were only two prison cells at Boyle's house," Darby
said. "Rachel told me about the other women who were with
her—Paula and Marci. That's three women—no, four. There were
four other people with Rachel. Paula, Marci, and Rachel's
boyfriend, Chad. So besides Rachel, there were three other people
being kept where she was. Boyle must have kept them all someplace else."

"Maybe Chad was with Rachel first. After he was gone, maybe
Boyle brought this Marci woman in first, and after she died,
Boyle—or Boyle and Slavick—brought in Marci."

"No. They were all there at the same time."

"You don't know that for sure," Evan said. "Rachel Swanson was delusional. When she was in the hospital, she thought she was still inside her prison cell."

"You heard the tape. Rachel told me there wasn't any way out, only places to hide. The cells at Boyle's house were small. There wasn't any place for Rachel *to* hide. And she wrote those directions on her arm. They were directions out of somewhere. Rachel said, 'It doesn't matter if you go right or left or straight, they all lead to dead ends.' Rachel and the other women were kept someplace else, I'm sure of it."

"I know how much you want to find Carol, but I think you—"

Darby brushed past Evan.

"Where are you going?"

"Back to Boyle's house," Darby said. "I need to talk to Banville."

Evan shoved his hands in his pockets. "Have you considered the possibility that Boyle brought Rachel and the other women to his basement? Maybe he chased Rachel and the other women down there. There are plenty of rooms, lots of places to hide."

"How do you know so much about Boyle's basement?"

"Because that's where I killed Melanie," Evan said, and pressed the chloroform-soaked rag against her face.

CHAPTER 66

Darby came awake to a hazy layer of thoughts. She was lying on her stomach—not on a bed, no, it was too hard. Her good eye, the one that wasn't swollen shut, fluttered open to pitch-black darkness. She turned onto her back and sat up.

For a brief moment she thought she might have been blinded in some terrible accident. Then she remembered.

Evan had pressed a rag against her face. The man who had tried to comfort her that day on the beach when he told her about Victor Grady and the fate of the missing woman was the same man who had pressed a chloroform-soaked rag against her face and said he killed Melanie—*Evan* was Boyle's partner. Evan planted evidence while Boyle abducted women and brought them here.

Darby stood, dizzy in the dark. She tried to breathe it away as she patted down her body. Her jacket was gone, but she was still wearing her clothes and boots. Her pockets had been emptied. She wasn't bleeding and she didn't seem hurt, but her legs wouldn't stop shaking.

The dizziness passed. Now she had to get her bearings.

Hands reaching out through the cool darkness, Darby inched forward, stopping when her fingertips bumped up against a flat, rough surface—a concrete wall. She moved to her left, counting her steps, one, two, three—her leg bumped up against something hard. She reached down, felt the shape with her hands. A cot. Five steps and the wall ended. Turn. Six steps, another bump against her leg. Here was a toilet. She was in a prison cell similar to the one that she had seen at Boyle's house, the one that had held Carol.

A buzzer sounded, loud and angry like the ringing of a school bell.

The door was opening, *clank-clank-clank,* a thin skin of light parting the darkness of her prison cell.

She needed to defend herself. She needed a weapon. Search the cell. Everything was bolted down. There was nothing in here she could use.

The door had opened to a corridor of very dim light.

Music started playing—Frank Sinatra's "I Get a Kick Out of You."

Evan didn't come in.

The dizziness was gone, lost in the adrenaline. Think.

Was Evan waiting for her to come out?

Only one way out, Darby inched closer to the strange corridor, straining to listen for any sound behind the music. Watch for sudden movement. If he came at her, she'd go straight for the eyes. The son of a bitch couldn't hurt her if he couldn't see.

Darby stood with her back against the cell wall. Okay. Get ready to run. Her heart was racing faster, faster . . . Okay, do it *now.* She turned and stepped into a long corridor holding six doors made of wood.

All of the doors were shut. Some had doorknobs. Two of them were padlocked.

Across from the doors were four opened prison cells. Darby checked the other three rooms. Empty. She checked them for something to use a weapon. Nothing. Everything was bolted down.

In the last cell she detected an intense body odor that immediately reminded her of Rachel Swanson. This was where Rachel Swanson had been kept. This was where Rachel Swanson had lived all those years.

The alarm bell sounded again. The steel doors clanked shut and locked into place.

A new sound coming from somewhere far ahead of her—doors opening and slamming shut, opening and slamming shut.

Evan. He was coming for her.

She had to move, had to think about moving, but get moving to where? Pick a door.

Darby tried the one directly in front of her. It was locked. The door next to it was unlocked. She opened it and stepped into the kind of maze that haunted her dreams.

Facing her was a narrow corridor with no lights. She could make out the shape of four doors, two on each side—no, five, there was a fifth door at the end of the corridor. The walls were made of nailed-up sheets of plywood. Some of the wood had been split open. She looked through a small hole and peered into another room similar to this one.

And then it hit her, the numbers and letters Rachel Swanson had written on her arm and on the map—they were directions for this maze. Rachel had figured out a way through each of the doors.

Darby scrambled to recall the combinations of numbers and letters as doors opened and slammed shut all around her—someone else was in here besides Evan. Was Carol here? Was she alive? How many women were down here and why were they running? What was Evan going to do to them? To her?

No time to think, Darby moved into another room, this one with two doors to choose from, only one unlocked. There were holes in the wall. Bullet holes. Evan had his gun. If he had a gun, oh Jesus, what would she do—what *could* she do? She couldn't do anything. She had to keep moving and find a way to sneak up on him and hurt him. First, she needed to find something to use as a weapon, had to find it quick.

Darby froze. Someone was moving closer.

The next room was bigger, with four doors. One of them was padlocked. She slipped inside and tried one door, and when it opened, she headed into another room, closing the door softly behind her, not wanting to give away her location.

This room had a corridor so narrow she had to go down it sideways. Some of the doors, she noticed, could be locked from the inside. Some had no doorknobs at all. Some rooms had no doors, just doorways. Why the variations?

They hunt their victims down here. They hunt them through this maze and let them try to find places to hide to make the hunt more exciting.

Moving deeper into the maze of changing rooms, her eyes adjusting to the darkness, pieces of her conversation with Rachel came back to her: *There's no way out of here, there are only places to hide . . . doesn't matter if you go right or left or straight, they all lead to dead ends, remember? . . . There's no way out of here. I tried.*

There *had* to be a way out of here. Rachel Swanson had survived down here for years; there *was* a way out, or at least a place to hide—

A piercing scream made Darby jump.

THUMP and the woman screamed again—she was close, somewhere behind this thin wall. More doors opened and shut. *How many women were down here?*

"HEEEEEEEEEEELP."

Not Carol's voice. Darby didn't know who the woman was, but she was close. Call out and let her know she wasn't alone? *No, don't give away your location.* Darby crept deeper into the maze, quickly taking in each room's markings as she searched the floors, hoping to find a piece of wood to use as a club, anything.

Here was a room with splintered wood on the concrete floor. Black liquid was leaking from beneath one the doors. Darby knew what it was even before she knelt down. Blood. She could smell it. The door facing her wasn't locked. She eased it open. *Please God, don't let Evan be in there.*

A woman lay facedown on the floor, blood pooling beneath her. Seeing how she had been butchered caused a scream to rise in Darby's throat.

Darby stifled it back, her whole body shaking, her mind reeling as she looked around—bloody footprints were on the floor. The footprints moved down the corridor and disappeared. Evan was gone.

Faint movement coming from the wall behind her. No door here, but near the bottom of the floor was a rectangular-sized hole large enough for her to move through. Was Evan in there?

Darby had to look, didn't want to look. She got on her knees and peeked through the hole, looking up into the room at Carol Cranmore's small, trembling frame.

CHAPTER 67

"Carol," Darby whispered. "Carol, down here."

Carol Cranmore, crouching down on the floor, stared at Darby through the hole.

"I'm with the police," Darby said. "Are you hurt?"

Carol shook her head, her eyes wide and terrified.

"I think there's enough room for you to wiggle through," Darby said. "Come on, I'll help you."

Carol shimmied through the hole of jagged wood and got stuck. Darby grabbed Carol's hands and pulled her through, the ragged ends of the split wood scratching her legs. Carol was barefoot. Her feet and ankles were scraped, bleeding in spots. She was dressed only in her underwear and bra and she was trembling.

"He's holding an axe, I saw him—"

"I know who he is," Darby said. "I need to know *where* he is. Have you seen him?"

Carol shook her head.

"How many people are down here with us? Do you know?"

"I've heard some people—some women—but I've only seen one. She was bleeding. I was trying to wake her up when he came for me and I ran away and saw a skeleton." Carol's face collapsed. "Please, I don't want to die—"

Darby gripped the teenager by the shoulders. "Listen to me. I know you're scared, but you can't cry or scream. You can't do that, understand? I don't want him to find us. We've got to find a way out of here, and I need you to be strong for me. I need you to be brave. Can you do that?"

A woman screamed—too close, the sound coming from directly in front of them.

Darby clamped a hand over Carol's mouth and pressed her up against the wall as a door slammed shut. The woman screamed again, coming from the room Carol was just in.

The woman started begging for her life. "Please . . . I'll do anything you want, just don't hurt me, please."

Carol sobbed beneath Darby's hand, her tears spilling over Darby's fingers.

THUMP and Carol jumped as the woman screamed in horror.

CRACK and the woman's scream turned to a gurgling rasp, Frank Sinatra singing "Fly Me to the Moon."

THUMP, CRACK, THUMP, and then there was nothing but the sound of Evan's heavy breathing. He was in the next room. Evan had killed one of the women and now he was tapping the axe against the wall, *thump-thump-thump,* trying to get Carol to scream, to find out where she was hiding.

The thumping sound stopped. Darby stared down at the hole. *Come on, put your head through and take a look.* All she needed was one good kick and she could break his nose. If he poked his head through and looked the other way, she could kick him hard in the back of the head and kick him unconscious.

Frank Sinatra started singing "My Way."

Evan didn't look through the hole.

Had he left?

Darby waited. Waited some more. Risk it, take a look.

Darby whispered in Carol's ear: "I'm going to look through the hole. Stay here, and whatever you do, don't move or scream, okay?"

Carol nodded. Darby knelt on the floor.

Past the dead woman's hands, Darby saw black boots standing by an opened door. Evan was still in there, waiting. She saw the bloody axe hovering near his ankle.

Evan headed into another room, slamming the door behind him. Another door slammed shut, Frank Sinatra singing "The Way You Look Tonight."

Darby had an idea. *Oh God, please let this work.*

"Carol, this skeleton you saw, do you remember where it is?"

"It's back through there," Carol said, pointing at the hole.

"I need you to show me."

"Don't leave me here."

"I'm not going to leave you."

"You promise?"

"I promise." Darby took off her shirt and handed it to Carol. "I'm going to go through the hole first. Once I get in there, I'm going to tell you to close your eyes and then I'm going to help pull you through again. Just give me a moment."

Darby wiggled her way through the hole, the blood soaking through her T-shirt. After Carol came through, her eyes closed, Darby held her hand and led her away from the mangled body on the floor.

"You can open your eyes now," Darby said. "Now show me where you saw the skeleton."

"It's through that door."

Darby eased it open. The hallway was empty. She closed the door softly behind them. Carol led Darby through two rooms, then a third, Darby staying out front and checking the blind spots while committing each room to memory.

Now they were standing in a corridor with a concrete wall. *We must be at one end of the maze. But which end?*

Carol pointed to the pitch-black end of the corridor. Lying on the floor was a torn shirt.

"It's down there."

Breathing hard, Darby led the way through the dark, holding Carol's hand.

At the dead end of the corridor was a scattering of bones small and large—the fractured end of a femur, a tibia and a cracked skull. Darby wondered if Evan and Boyle had left the bones here to scare the other women.

Wait, back to the femur. It was spiked at the end. Sharp. Use that.

Bone clutched in her hand, Darby ran to the opposite end of the corridor with Carol. Only one door down here. Darby eased the door open and came face-to-face with the man from the woods.

CHAPTER 68

Evan's head was covered by the same mask of dirty Ace bandages she had seen over two decades ago, the eyes and mouth covered with the same strips of black cloth. Blood was splashed against his blue coveralls and carpenter's belt, which had been modified to accommodate several knives and a gun holster.

Carol screamed as Evan swung the axe. Darby slammed the door shut and threw her weight against it. This door didn't have a push-button lock like some of the others. Carol helped her try to hold the door in place.

THUMP as the axe split the wood, the blade sinking deep into Darby's cheek.

Darby screamed but kept her weight against the door. Had to run, where could they run? *THUMP* as the axe came down again. Think, they had to hide, think—the hole in the room with the dead body. Evan couldn't fit through it. Go that way. They'd have to run fast to make it.

A gunshot blew away the wood next to Darby's head. She gripped Carol's hand and ran fast through the dark rooms and corridors. *Please God, please don't let either of us trip.* Darby threw doors shut behind her as she ran, Evan chasing after them, his footsteps growing closer . . . closer . . . too close.

Another gunshot hit the wall behind her. Carol screamed and Darby pushed her into the room with the dead body. Darby turned and saw Evan raising the gun. She swung the door shut as he fired, blowing a chunk out of the door. It had a push-button lock, oh thank you God. Darby pounded it shut with her fist.

Carol was staring at the dead woman. Darby gripped Carol by the shoulders, turned her around and moved her to the hole. Evan tried to open the door but couldn't. He was locked out.

"Go through," Darby said.

Carol wiggled her way through the jagged opening and got stuck. Darby pushed her through as Evan kicked the door, *THUMP-THUMP-THUMP.*

Darby got down on her knees again, whispering to Carol kneeling on the other side: "Bang the doors like we're running away—bang them as loud as you can, okay? I'll join you in a minute."

"You promised you wouldn't leave me—"

A gunshot blew another hole through the door.

"Run, Carol. Run."

Darby stood, almost slipping in the blood. The room was dark, but she could see Evan's black-gloved hand reaching through the hole. Carol slammed doors open and shut. Darby pressed her back against the wall. She felt blood sliding down her neck. She touched her cheek, felt the deep gash and the bone. The eye above it was swollen shut.

Evan found the doorknob, turned it and opened the door.

He came through holding the gun. Darby gripped the bone with both hands and sunk the jagged end deep into Evan's stomach.

Beneath the mask a scream of pain, and Darby tore the bone free and stabbed him again in the stomach. Evan tried to bring the gun around and she stabbed him again. He fired the gun next to her ear, the sound deafening, and when he grabbed her hair she brought up the bone's jagged end and sunk it deep into Evan's throat.

He dropped the gun as he grabbed the bone with both hands. Darby pushed him back into the other room. His gun was lying on the floor—a nine-millimeter Glock, his FBI-issued sidearm. She picked it up, swung the door shut and locked it.

"Carol, stay where you are," Darby said. Then, louder: "I'm with the police. If there's anyone else in here, stay where you are until I tell you to come out."

Darby threw the door open and raised the Glock.

Evan was staggering around the small room, the spiked end of the femur sticking out of his neck. He was trying to control the blood pouring out of his stomach. He was bleeding out. Let him bleed.

Evan saw her and went to pick up the axe.

"Don't do it."

He brought the axe up over his head. Darby fired and blew a hole through his stomach.

Evan slumped back against the wall. She kicked the axe away. He tried to get up, fell, kept trying until his arms went limp.

Behind the mask came a wet, sick, wheezing sound. He managed to say one word:

"Melanie."

Darby ripped off the mask.

"Buried . . . She's buried . . ." Evan started choking on his blood.

"Where? Where is Mel buried?"

"Ask . . . your . . . mother."

Darby felt the skin stretch tight across her face.

Evan smiled, and that was all.

Darby removed Evan's belt and unzipped his coveralls. She patted down the pockets and found a set of keys. She didn't find a cell phone, but she did find a small digital camera stuffed inside one of the pouches on the carpenter's belt. She slid the camera in her back pocket.

Hands slick with blood, she tried each key until she found the one that unlocked the padlocks on the doors. Darby drew in a breath and looked up at the dark ceiling.

"He's dead. He can't hurt you. Is there anyone else in here?"

No answer. The music kept playing.

"I have his keys. I can come help you. If you're there, call out to me."

No answer. The music kept playing.

Darby went back for Carol. The teenager was hunkered against a dark corner in the hallway, rocking back and forth, in shock.

"It's over, Carol. Everything's okay. Here, take my hand. That's it, hold on tight, I'm going to pull you through . . . No, don't look at the floor, look at me. I'm going to take you out of here, but I want you to close your eyes until I tell you to open them, okay? Good. That's it, keep them closed. Only a few more steps. That's it. Don't look down. We're almost there. We're almost home."

CHAPTER 69

It seemed to take forever to find their way out of the maze.

Darby stood on the opposite end of the dungeon, in a corridor with four identical cages. She knew she was on the other side because this corridor had an extra steel door armed with four padlocks. She used the keys. It was the only time Carol let go of her hand.

A ladder bolted against the wall led up to a basement illuminated with soft light coming from an opened door on the far left, across from the stairs. Darby approached the door, Carol's hand gripped fiercely in her own.

Six video monitors were set up on top of an old desk. Each screen showed a prison cell in dark green color—night vision. Evan and Boyle had installed surveillance cameras equipped with night vision so they could watch their prisoners. All the cells were empty.

Evan's clothes were neatly folded on top of a table. His cell phone was lying on top of his wallet, along with his car keys.

Darby was about to head into the room with Carol when she spotted the various costumes draped over mannequins. The heads were covered in Halloween masks—some store bought, some homemade. Behind the mannequins was a Peg-Board-covered wall holding various weapons—knives, machetes, axes and spears.

"I want you to stand outside here for just a moment," Darby said. "Stand right here, okay? I'll be right back."

Darby picked up the cell phone and keys and saw a locked door. One of the keys opened it. Inside she found a locked filing cabinet and a wall crammed full of pictures of the women who had been brought here. She tried the keys on the cabinet. None of them worked.

In some of the pictures, the women were smiling. In others, they were frightened. Mixed among them were horrible snapshots showing how they had been killed. Darby imagined Boyle and Evan standing in here, staring at the pictures as they put on their costumes, getting ready for the hunt.

Darby stared at all the faces until she couldn't bear to look at them anymore. She grabbed Carol's hand, grateful for its warmth, and headed up the basement steps into the first floor of the old house. The lights worked. No furniture, just cold and empty rooms full of decay. Several of the windows had been boarded up.

Darby opened the front door, hoping to find a street sign. There were no street lights out here, just darkness and a cold wind blowing across rolling, empty fields. The rundown farmhouse behind them was the only home out here.

Evan's car, she remembered, had a GPS unit. She found his car parked behind the farmhouse. Darby started the car and cranked up the heat.

Their location was on the GPS screen. Darby gave the 911 operator the address and requested more than one ambulance. She didn't know if any of the other women in the basement were still alive.

"Carol, do you know the phone number for your next-door

neighbors who live across your driveway? The white house with the green shutters?"

"The Lombardos. I know their number. I babysit for their kids sometimes."

Darby dialed the number. A woman answered the phone, her voice thick with sleep.

"Mrs. Lombardo, my name is Darby McCormick. I'm with the Boston Police Lab. Is Dianne Cranmore there? I need to speak with her immediately."

Carol's mother came to the phone.

"I have someone here who would like to speak to you," Darby said, and handed the phone to Carol.

CHAPTER 70

According to the GPS unit, the abandoned farmhouse was twenty-six miles away from Boyle's house. Darby called Mathew Banville and told him what happened and what she had found.

The four ambulances arrived first. While Carol was being examined, Darby told the EMTs what was waiting for them in the basement maze. She showed them which key opened the padlocks and which one opened the locked doors. She sat in the back of the ambulance with Carol until the sedative kicked in. Darby allowed the EMT to look her over but refused a sedative herself.

The EMT was stitching up her face when Banville arrived with the local police. He stayed with Darby while Holloway and his men headed inside the farmhouse.

"Did you bring Boyle's keys?" Darby asked.

"Holloway has them."

"There's a locked filing cabinet in the room with the pictures. I'd like to see if there's anything on Melanie Cruz in there."

"The state's forensic crew should be here any moment," Banville said. "It's their case now. We'll let them process the crime scene. How are you holding up?"

Darby didn't have an answer. She gave him Evan's camera.

"There are some pictures on there showing what he did to the women."

"Holloway said you could give your statement tomorrow, after you've had some sleep. One of his officers is going to drive you home."

"I already called Coop. He's on his way."

Darby told Banville about Melanie Cruz and the other missing women. When she finished, she wrote a phone number on the back of his business card.

"That's my mother's home number. If you find out anything about Melanie, I don't care what time it is, give me a call."

Banville slipped the card in his back pocket. "I called Dianne Cranmore right after I hung up with you," he said. "I told her that if it wasn't for you, we wouldn't have found her daughter. I wanted her to know that."

"We found her together."

"What you did . . ." Banville looked at Evan's car and stared at it for what seemed like a long time. "If you hadn't pushed me, if I had turned my back on you, this would have turned out differently."

"But it didn't. Thank you."

Banville nodded. He didn't seem to know what to do with his hands.

Darby put out her hand. Banville shook it.

By the time Coop pulled up in his Mustang, the road in front of the farmhouse was crowded with police cars and forensic vehicles. The local media was here, too. Darby spotted a couple of TV cameras set up behind the barricades. A photographer was trying to take her picture.

Coop took off his jacket and wrapped it around her shoulders. He hugged her tight against him for a long time.

"Where can I take you?"

"Home," Darby said.

Coop drove down the dark, bumpy roads in silence. Her clothes smelled of blood and gunpowder. She rolled down the window, closed her eyes and let the wind blow across her face.

When the car pulled over, she opened her eyes and saw that they were parked in a breakdown lane on a highway. Coop reached into the backseat and came back with a small cooler. Inside, packed on top of ice, were two glasses and a bottle of Bushmills Irish whiskey.

"I thought you could use it," Coop said.

Darby filled the glasses with ice and poured the whiskey. She had nearly drained her second drink by the time they reached the state border.

"Much better," Darby said.

"I was tempted to call Leland, but I thought you might want to tell him yourself, in person."

"You would be correct."

"I'd like to tag along with my camera. I want to capture the moment on film."

"There's something I want to tell you," Darby said, and told Coop about Melanie and Stacey. It was the second time she told the story. This time, she wanted to tell it slowly. She wanted to tell Coop all the things she had felt.

"I told Mel I didn't want to be friends with Stacey, and Mel just couldn't let it go," Darby said. "She had to keep pushing. She wanted everything to go back to the way it was. She had to be the peacemaker. When I saw her downstairs, I wanted—" Darby caught herself.

Coop didn't push. Darby felt the sting of tears and tried to breathe it back.

Then it welled up inside her, ugly and razor sharp, the truth she had been dragging around all these years. When the tears came, Darby didn't fight it, was tired of fighting.

"Mel was screaming. Grady had a knife, and he was using it on Mel and she was screaming for him to stop. She begged me to come back down and help her. I didn't . . . I didn't ask Mel to come over or to bring Stacey—Mel made that decision. *She* was the one who made the decision to come over, not me, and a part of me . . . Every time I saw Mel's mother, the way she looked at me as though I was the one who made Mel disappear, I wanted to tell her the truth. I wanted to scream it at her until I knocked that god-damn look out of her eyes."

"Why didn't you tell her?"

Darby didn't have an answer. How could she explain how a part of her hated Mel for coming over that night—and for bringing Stacey? How could she explain the guilt she felt for not only what had happened but for how she felt afterward, forced to carry not only the guilt but the anger?

She closed her eyes, wanting to go back in time to that moment at the school lockers when Mel asked if they could go back to being friends. Darby wondered what would have happened if she had said yes. Would she still be alive? Or would she be buried out in the woods where no one would ever find her?

Coop wrapped his big arm around her shoulder. Darby leaned against him.

"Darby?"

"Yeah?"

"Leaving Melanie . . . It was the right thing to do."

Darby didn't speak again until they were on Route 1. She could see the tall buildings in Boston lit up in the distance.

"I keep thinking about that day Evan came to the beach and

told me about Victor Grady and Melanie Cruz. That was over
twenty years ago. Twenty *years*. It hasn't fully sunk in yet."

"But at some point it will."

"Oh yes."

"Whenever you need to talk about it, I'm here," Coop said.
"You know that, right?"

"I do."

"Good." Coop kissed the top of her head. He didn't let go. She
didn't want him to let go.

Dawn was breaking by the time they arrived in Belham. Darby
showed Coop to the guest bedroom and then headed to the
shower.

Dressed in a clean pair of clothes and fresh bandages, she went
to check on her mother. Sheila was fast asleep.

Tell me where you buried Melanie.

Ask . . . your . . . mother.

Darby crawled into bed and pressed herself up against her
mother's back, hugging her close. She had a memory of her parents sitting in the front seat of the old Buick station wagon with
the wood paneling, Big Red tapping his thumbs against the steer-
ing wheel to a Frank Sinatra song and Sheila sitting next to him,
smiling, the two of them still young, strong and healthy. Darby listened to her mother's soft breathing rise and fall, rise and fall,
wanting it to last forever.

III

—

LITTLE GIRL FOUND

CHAPTER 71

Darby's eyes blinked open to bright lines of sunlight glowing around the drawn shades.

Her mother wasn't in the room. Seeing the empty side of the bed caused a flutter of panic. Darby threw back the sheets, dressed quickly and headed downstairs. It was three in the afternoon.

Coop was sitting at the island counter, drinking coffee and watching the small TV. He caught the expression on her face and knew at once what she was thinking.

"Your mother wanted some fresh air, so the nurse put her in the wheelchair and took her around the block," Coop said. "Can I get you something to eat? I make a mean bowl of cereal."

"I'll just stick to coffee, thanks. What are they saying on the news?"

"NECN is about to do another report after the commercials. Grab a seat and I'll get you some coffee."

The Boston media had jumped on the story hard and fast. During the ten hours she had slept, reporters had uncovered the connection between Daniel Boyle and Special Agent Evan Manning.

Evan Manning's real name was Richard Fowler. In 1953, Janice Fowler, suffering from what would nowadays be called a severe case of postpartum depression, hanged herself while in the care of a state-run psychiatric facility. Hospital records indicated she had been committed shortly after her husband, Trenton Fowler, caught her trying to drown their only son in the bathtub. Janice told her husband she had woken up from her afternoon nap and found Richard standing next to her bed, holding a large kitchen knife. Richard Fowler was five years old.

Seven years later, when Richard was twelve, his father was running his combine through his corn crop when the auger got clogged. Trenton Fowler had left the machine running. He stood on the platform above the auger, trying to clear away the obstruction when he slipped on the fine, silky blanket of corn dust on the platform and fell into the auger. Richard told police he didn't know how to shut off the combine.

Richard's aunt, Ophelia Boyle, took in the young, bright orphan and moved him to her daughter's newly built home in Glen, New Hampshire. Ophelia's daughter, Cassandra, was expecting her first child. Cassandra was twenty-three and unmarried. She had refused to give the baby up for adoption.

In 1963, single, unwed mothers were scandalous affairs that could ruin a family's reputation—especially in the affluent social and business circles in which Ophelia and her husband, Augustus, frequently traveled. They moved Cassandra, their only child, to Glen, New Hampshire, far away from Belham, and provided her with a sizable monthly allowance to raise her child, a boy she named Daniel. The boy's father, Cassandra told friends and neighbors, had died in a car accident.

Interviews with former neighbors, many of whom were still living in the area, described Daniel as the classic loner—moody and withdrawn. They had a difficult time understanding the close relationship between Daniel and his good-looking, charismatic older cousin, Richard.

Alicia Cross lived less than two miles away from the Boyle home. She was twelve years old when she vanished during the summer of 1978. By this time, Richard Fowler had changed his name to Evan Manning to start a new life. It seemed the only person who knew Richard had changed his name was his cousin, Daniel Boyle.

Evan, a recent graduate of Harvard Law School, was living in Virginia when Alicia Cross disappeared. He had been accepted into the FBI's training program. Daniel Boyle was fifteen and living at home. The girl's body was never found, and police never caught her killer.

Two years later, after graduating from an exclusive military school in Vermont, Daniel Boyle joined the army and became a trained marksman. His goal was to become a Green Beret. He was discharged from the army, at age twenty-two, for aggravated assault. A local society woman claimed Boyle had tried to strangle her.

When Boyle left the army, there was no reason for him to work. He had access to his sizable trust fund. He wandered around the country for a year, doing odd jobs as a carpenter, and then finally returned home in the summer of 1983 to find that his mother's closets had been cleaned out. Daniel called his grandmother and asked about his mother's whereabouts. Ophelia Boyle didn't know. She filed a missing person's report, but it was later dismissed when police discovered Cassandra Boyle's passport was missing. The family never heard from Cassandra again.

Ophelia paid for Evan's private schooling and later, college and Harvard Law School. Ophelia had even purchased the farm and kept it running profitably until her own death, in the winter of 1991, when she and her husband were shot to death during a home invasion. Police thought it might be an inside job and went to question Daniel Boyle. Boyle wasn't home that weekend. He was in Virginia visiting his cousin, who was now working in the FBI's newly formed Behavioral Science Unit. Evan Manning had corroborated Boyle's alibi.

With his grandparents dead and his mother missing, Daniel Boyle became the sole beneficiary of an estate worth more than ten million dollars.

Early this morning, police had unlocked a filing cabinet in Boyle's basement and discovered pictures of the women who had disappeared in Massachusetts during the summer of 1984, the time period the local media called the Summer of Fear. The pictures indicated that Boyle had kept them in the basement of his home.

Not much was known about the time after Belham, when Boyle traveled the country. At some point, he returned east and, in the basement of his cousin's farmhouse, constructed a maze of locked rooms that one investigator described as "the most horrific thing I have ever seen in my thirty years in law enforcement." A specialized unit made up of forensic archeologists had been called in to search for unmarked graves in the extensive woods behind Boyle's home.

Carol Cranmore was being treated at an undisclosed facility. In a taped interview, Dianne Cranmore discussed her daughter's condition: "Carol's still in shock right now. She's got a long road ahead of her, but we're going to get through this together. My baby girl's alive, and that's what matters. She wouldn't be alive if it wasn't for Darby McCormick of the Boston Crime Lab. She didn't give up hope."

The news reporter mentioned that the mothers of the majority of victims weren't so lucky. Next they played an interview with Helena Cruz.

"I've been wondering what happened to Melanie my whole life," Helena Cruz said. "I've carried all these questions about what happened to my daughter and now, more than twenty years later, I've come to find out that the man responsible for killing her wasn't Victor Grady but a federal agent. The FBI won't answer my questions. Someone there knows what happened to my daughter, I'm sure of it."

Darby was staring at Helena Cruz's face when the house phone rang. It was Banville.

"Have you seen the news?" he asked.

"I'm watching NECN right now. They're talking about the connection between Evan and Boyle."

"It gets even better. The mother, Cassandra Boyle? Turns out she was Boyle's *sister.*"

"Jesus." That certainly explained why the family had shipped her all the way up to the boondocks of New Hampshire. "Did Boyle know?"

"I have no idea. As for the mother packing up and running off, everything I've seen so far looks legit, but who knows? I also pulled the case file on the grandparents' deaths. No suspects or witnesses. Someone came in, shot them while they were sleeping and cleaned them out."

"And Manning provided the alibi," Darby said.

"Yes. I also got a look at Manning's BlackBerry. There were several text messages on it that confirm that he helped Boyle with the bombing. And that number Boyle called? It belongs to Manning. Boyle must have been calling to warn him."

"What's the status on Boyle's laptop? You have any luck breaking the passwords?"

"We did. He did all his banking online. We can't access a lot of the information—he has a private bank in the Caymans—but what we did manage to find were the pictures. Boyle stored the pictures of his most recent victims on his computer. We also found some maps of his burial locations. They span the country."

"What about Melanie Cruz? Did you find anything out about her or the other women who disappeared in eighty-four?"

"We haven't found a map for Belham. But I know Melanie Cruz is dead. We found Polaroids in Boyle's filing cabinet. If you want to see them, swing by the station. I'll be here all day."

"What's in the pictures?"

"It's best if I show them to you in person."

CHAPTER 72

Banville was talking on the phone when Darby showed up with Coop. Banville saw them standing outside his doorway, motioned them to come in and pointed to the two chairs set up against the wall, near the coat rack.

Fifteen minutes later, Banville hung up. He rubbed the fatigue out of his face. "That was the state's forensic anthropologist. I sent Carter out to the woods early this morning to take a poke around the area where the feds found the set of remains. There's nothing else buried out there."

"I'm surprised the feds allowed him access to the site," Coop said.

"Oh, they put up a fuss. Problem is the cat's already out of the bag. Manning's all over the news. The feds pounced on his Back Bay apartment. I know this is going to come as a total surprise to the two of you, but our good friends from Fart, Barf and Itch aren't sharing any information on Manning or that white supremacist asshole they killed. These guys have a *huge* public relations nightmare on their hands." Banville looked to Darby. "Get ready for your close-up. The media is going to be all over this story for weeks."

"Carter found a full set of remains?"

"A full set," Banville said. "Definitely a female, buried out there between ten and fifteen years, maybe longer. He wants to carbon-date the bones to establish a timeline."

Banville leaned back in his chair. "I told Carter about the women who disappeared around here during the summer of eighty-four. The remains may belong to one of those women, but, given the height and some bone characteristics, it's definitely not Melanie Cruz."

"I'd like to see the pictures."

Banville handed her an envelope.

It was difficult to look at the harsh color photographs of Melanie bound and gagged in the wine cellar in Boyle's basement. The camera had captured the terror in her face. In each photo, Melanie was alone. In each photo, she was crying.

That could have been me.

"Do we have any idea how she died?"

Banville shook his head. "If we find her remains, we might have a shot. You think Manning or Boyle buried her out in the woods?"

Ask . . . your . . . mother.

Darby shifted in her chair. "I don't know what to think any-more."

"Carter said that unless we come across some specific piece of information or evidence which can pinpoint where Melanie Cruz is buried, then we'll probably never find her."

Darby tucked the photos back in the envelope. *Melanie fumbled with the charms on her bracelet as she listened to Stacey crying behind the Dumpster.* "*Why can't we go back to being friends?" Mel asked later, at school.*

If only I had said yes, Darby thought.

It took her a moment to find her voice. "What about the other women? Do you know anything?"

"Boyle brought them all to the basement and did different . . . things to them." Banville handed her a larger envelope. Inside were bundles of Polaroids bound together by rubber bands.

Darby immediately recognized some of the faces—Tara Hardy, Samantha Kent, and the faces of the women who disappeared after them. At the bottom of the envelope were pictures of a woman with a thin face and long blond hair. Like Rachel Swanson, she appeared to have been starved.

Darby held up one of Samantha Kent's photos. "This is the woman I saw in the woods," she said. "Do we know what happened to her?"

"We have no idea what happened to her, or where her remains are," Banville said. "Did Manning tell you anything?"

"Just that she was missing." Darby didn't want to hold the pictures anymore. She placed the envelopes on the corner of the desk and wiped her palms on her jeans.

"Do you want to hear the rest of it?"

Darby nodded. She took in a deep breath and held it.

"The basement you were in was wired with cameras," Banville said. "Boyle stored the videos on his computer. They go back about eight years, roughly around the time he returned east. In the beginning, Boyle and Manning hunted one victim at a time, then two, then three . . . Then Boyle built more of those cells and changed the rules of the game. He released his victims into the maze, and if they made it to the other side, the cell doors would be open and food would be waiting for them, and they'd be allowed to live."

"That's how Rachel Swanson had survived for so long," Darby said. "She had figured out a way through each door."

"If I had to guess, I'd say Boyle did the kidnapping while Evan worked on planting the evidence based upon whatever case he was working on—Victor Grady, Miles Hamilton, Earl Slavick. I'm sure there are others we don't know about."

Coop said, "How long have they been doing this? Do we have any idea?"

Banville stood. "I'll show you what we've found."

CHAPTER 73

Darby followed him through tight corridors humming with conversations and ringing with phone and fax machines.

Banville brought them into the large conference room where he had outlined the details of the trap to catch Traveler. The chairs had been stacked together and pushed to one corner to make space for presentation-style corkboards mounted on wheels. There were about a dozen boards in here, and each one held 8 x 10 pictures of several women.

"Someone from the computer division came out this morning and broke the security on Boyle's laptop," Banville said. "All these pictures you're looking at were stored on there. We transferred the pictures to CDs and printed them out here. Fortunately for us, Boyle had the pictures organized in folders named after the states he visited. We think Boyle started here after he left Belham."

Banville stopped in front of a board marked "Chicago." The top picture was of a pretty blond woman with a bright and inviting smile. Her name was Tabitha O'Hare. She had been missing since 10/3/85.

Underneath Tabitha O'Hare's picture was another 8 x 10: Catherine Desouza, missing since 10/5/85.

Next: Janice Bickeny, missing since 10/28/85.

Four more women were listed, but they didn't have any names or dates, just pictures. Seven women, all missing.

"We called Missing Persons in Chicago and had them email all their cases from eighty-five and matched the pictures to the ones stored on Boyle's computer," Banville said. "So far we've identified three of the seven missing women."

"Where are they buried?" Coop asked.

"Don't know," Banville said. "We haven't found a map."

Darby looked to the next board, "Atlanta." Thirteen missing women, all prostitutes, according to the information posted beside their pictures.

Boyle's next stop was Texas. Twenty-two women went missing from Houston over a two-year period. After Texas, Boyle moved on to Montana and then Florida. Darby counted the pictures on the two boards. Twenty-six missing women. No names, no dates to indicate how long they were missing, just pictures.

"We just started contacting police agencies across the country," Banville said. "They're going to fax or email their missing persons cases. It's going to be a massive effort. It will take weeks—months, probably."

Darby found the board marked "Colorado." Kimberly Sanchez's picture was up at the top; eight more women were tacked underneath her.

"What I can't figure out is the story Manning told us about being attacked," Banville said. "You think it was Boyle who attacked him?"

"Yes," Darby said.

"He was already planting evidence to pin it all on Slavick. Why go through the trouble to stage that?"

"By attacking Manning, Boyle made Manning an eyewitness

who could turn around and pin it all on Slavick, when the time came."

"And Boyle needed to keep Manning close to control the investigation," Coop said. "I'm thinking that's why they bombed the lab and the hospital. They could label it as a terrorist attack, allowing the feds to step in and take over the investigation."

"Allowing Manning to pull the strings," Banville added.

Darby nodded. "Of course, we could be wrong. Unfortunately, the only two people who can answer any of these questions are dead."

A cop poked his head into the room. "Mat, you've got a phone call. Detective Paul Wagner from Montana. Says it's urgent."

"Tell him to hold, I'll be right there." Banville turned back to Darby. "They did Boyle's and Manning's autopsies this morning. Manning was the one who entered your house. They found a hairline fracture on his left arm. I thought you'd want to know."

Banville left them standing in the room full of missing women. Darby looked off at a board marked "Seattle," more pictures of missing women, more boards running down the long wall, each one crammed with pictures of missing women, some identified, some blank.

"Take a look at this one," Coop said.

This board held the smiling faces of six missing women. There wasn't a state listed at the top. None of the women had names.

"Judging by the hairstyles and clothes, I'm guessing these pictures were taken in the eighties," Coop said.

The woman with the pale skin and blond hair looked familiar for some reason. Something about the woman's face, Darby felt as though she knew her—

Darby remembered. The picture of the blond woman on the board was the same picture the nurse had given her—the one the nurse had found inside the clothes Sheila had donated. Darby had shown the picture to her mother. *"That's Cindy Greenleaf's daughter, Regina,"* Sheila had told her. *"You two played together when you were kids. Cindy sent it to me one year in a Christmas card."*

Darby took the picture down from the board. "I want to make a copy of this," she said. "I'll be right back."

CHAPTER 74

As Darby walked back through the corridors, searching for a color copier, she saw a patrolman escorting an older woman toward Banville's office.

No question the woman holding on to the patrolman's forearm was Helena Cruz. Mel and her mother both shared the same prominent cheekbones and the small ears that always got red when it was cold.

"Darby," Helena Cruz said in a dry whisper. "Darby McCormick."

"Hello, Mrs. Cruz."

"It's Miss Cruz, actually. Ted and I divorced a long time ago." Melanie's mother swallowed, fighting hard to keep the painful memories from reaching her face. "Your name was on the news. You work with the crime lab."

"Yes."

"Can you tell me what happened to Mel?"

Darby didn't answer.

"Please, if you know something—" Helena Cruz's voice broke. She quickly regained her composure. "I need to know. Please. I can't live with not knowing anymore."

"Detective Banville can tell you. He's in his office. I'll take you there."

"You know what happened, don't you? It's written all over your face."

"I'm sorry." *I wish I could tell you how sorry I am.*

Helena Cruz stared down at the tops of her shoes. "This morning, when I arrived in Belham, I went by my old house. I hadn't been there in years. A woman was outside raking leaves, and her daughter was playing in the sandbox—it's still there, in the same corner of the yard where you and Mel used to play. The two of you used to sit there for hours when you were little. Melanie liked to make sandcastles, and you used to smash them. Only Melanie never got mad when you did it. She never got mad at anything."

Darby listened to Mrs. Cruz's voice strip away time, taking her back to late-night sleepovers with Melanie, back to weeklong summer vacations in Cape Cod. The woman speaking to her right now was the same woman who made sure Darby always wore enough sunscreen because of her pale skin.

Only that woman was gone. The woman standing in front of her was nothing more than a husk. The kindness had been sucked from her eyes. The look on her face was the same one Darby had seen in countless victims—filled with the pain and confusion about how the people you loved so fiercely could at any moment be ripped away from you through no fault of your own.

"I brought Mel up to be too trusting. To always look for the good in people. I blame myself for that. You try and do the right thing by your children, and sometimes you just . . . Sometimes it just doesn't matter. Sometimes God has his own plan for you, and you'll never understand it, no matter how much you try to, no matter how much you pray for an answer. I keep telling myself it doesn't matter because nothing can ever take away this kind of hurt."

Darby had imagined this moment happening hundreds of times, had mentally rehearsed what words she would stay and how Helena Cruz would react. Seeing the pain in her face, hearing the pleading desperation in her voice, brought back all those letters Darby had written when she was younger, that guilty part of her secretly believing that if she could take every awful thing she was feeling and put it into the right combination of words, she could somehow build a bridge across their mutually shared grief and, at the very least, come to a place of understanding.

She had ripped up each of those letters. The only thing Helena Cruz wanted was her daughter back. And now, after twenty-four years of waiting, she wasn't any closer to bringing her home.

"I don't know where Melanie is," Darby said. "If I did, I would tell you."

"Tell me she didn't suffer. At least give me that."

Darby tried to think of an appropriate answer. It didn't matter. Helena Cruz turned and walked away.

CHAPTER 75

Coop dropped Darby off and headed home. She entered the kitchen, looking for her mother. The nurse said Sheila was out in the backyard.

Sheila was sitting near her old flower garden. The early evening air was cool and crisp as Darby trotted across the grass with one of the deck chairs. Sheila wore Big Red's Red Sox baseball cap and his blue down vest over a polar fleece jacket. A heavy wool blanket covered her lap and much of the wheelchair. She looked so incredibly frail.

Darby placed the chair next to her mother, in a patch of dimming sunlight. Spread across Sheila's lap was a photo album full of baby pictures. Darby saw a picture of herself as a newly born infant swaddled in a pink blanket and matching cap.

Her mother's eyes were bloodshot. She had been crying.

"I saw the news. Coop told me the rest." Sheila's voice was quiet as she stared at the bandages on the side of Darby's face. "How bad is it?"

"It will heal. I'm fine. Honest."

Sheila grabbed Darby's wrist, squeezed it. Darby held her mother's hand and looked out across the backyard, at her mother's white bedsheets flapping in the early evening breeze. The clothesline was planted a few feet away from the basement door where Evan Manning—not Victor Grady—had entered over two decades ago.

Darby thought back to the day she found Evan waiting in the driveway. He was there to see how much she knew about what she had seen in the woods. Was Evan the one who had found the spare key? Or had Boyle cased the house earlier?

"Where have you been?" Sheila asked.

"I went down to the police station with Coop. Banville—he's the detective running the case—he called and said he found some pictures." Darby turned back to her mother. "The pictures were of Melanie."

Sheila looked out across the yard. The breeze picked up, shaking the branches overhead and blowing the leaves across the yard.

"Helena Cruz was there," Darby said. "She wanted to know where Mel is buried."

"Do you know?"

"No. We'll ever know unless someone comes forward with new information."

"But you know what happened to Mel."

"Yes."

"What happened?"

"Boyle kept Mel in the basement of his house and tortured her over a period of days, maybe even weeks." Darby shoved her hands deep in her coat pockets. "That's all I know."

Sheila traced a finger along a picture of Darby sleeping in a crib.

"I keep thinking about these pictures—about the memories behind them," her mother said. "I keep wondering if you take these memories with you, or if they just vanish when you die."

Darby's chest was fluttering. She knew what she had to ask.

"Mom, when I was in the basement with Manning, he said

something about where Mel was buried." It seemed to take a long time to get the words out. "When I asked him where she was, what had happened to her, Manning told me to ask you."

Sheila looked as though she'd been slapped.

"Do you know something?" Darby said.

"No. No, of course not."

Darby squeezed her hands into fists. She felt light-headed.

She removed the folded piece of paper—the color copy of the picture of the woman from the bulletin board. She placed it on top of the photo album.

"What's this?" Sheila asked.

"Open it."

Sheila did. Her face changed, and then Darby knew.

"Am I supposed to know this person?" Sheila asked.

"Remember the picture the nurse found in the clothes you donated? I showed it to you, and you said it was a picture of Cindy Greenleaf's daughter, Regina."

"My memory is very foggy from the morphine. Can you take me back inside? I'm very tired, and I'd like to lie down."

"That picture is posted on a bulletin board down at the station. This woman was one of Boyle and Manning's victims. We don't know who she is."

"Please take me inside," Sheila said.

Darby didn't move. She hated this. She had to do it.

"After Boyle left Belham, he headed out to Chicago. Nine women disappeared and then Boyle moved on to Atlanta. Eight women vanished there. Twenty-two women disappeared in Houston. Boyle kept moving from state to state while Manning set up people to take the fall. We're talking close to a hundred missing women, probably more. Some of them, we don't even know their names. Like the woman in this picture."

"Leave this alone, Darby. Please."

"These missing women had families. There are mothers out there just like Helena Cruz who are wondering what happened to their daughters. I know there's something you're keeping from me. What is it, Mom?"

Sheila's gaze was lingering over a picture of Darby, her two front teeth missing, standing in the upstairs bathtub.

"You need to tell me, Mom. Please."

"You don't know what it's like," her mother started.

Darby waited, heart quickening.

"I don't know what, Mom?"

Sheila's face was pale. Darby could see the tiny blue veins in her mother's egg-white skin.

"When you hold your baby for the first time, when you hold it in your arms and nurse it and watch it grow, you'll do anything in this world to protect your child. Anything. The kind of love you feel . . . It's like what Dianne Cranmore told you. It's more love than your heart can ever hold."

"What happened?"

"He had your clothes," Sheila said.

"Who had my clothes?"

"The detective, Riggers, he told me he had found clothes belonging to some of the missing women inside Grady's house. And there were pictures. He had pictures of you and he had taken some of your clothes."

"He didn't take any clothes that night."

"Riggers told me Grady must have come inside the house at some point and took some of your clothes. He didn't say why. It didn't matter. None of it mattered because Riggers botched the search—it was an illegal search, and all the evidence they found was worthless because these men, these so-called professionals, they blew it, and Grady was going to walk."

"Riggers told you this?"

"No, Buster did. Your father's friend. Remember, he used to take you to the movies and—"

"I know who he is. What did he tell you?"

"Buster told me how Riggers had botched the case, about how they were watching Grady's every move, seeing if they could find something before Grady packed up and moved away."

Sheila's voice was trembling. "That . . . monster came into *my* house, for *my* daughter, and the police were just going to let him go."

Darby knew what was coming, felt it speeding toward her like a train.

"Your father . . . He had an extra gun—a throwaway piece, he called it. He kept it downstairs in his workbench. I knew how to use it. I knew it couldn't be traced. When Grady left for work, I went to his house. It was raining out. The back door underneath his porch was unlocked. I went inside. He had been packing. There were boxes everywhere."

Darby felt cold beneath her clothes.

"I was hiding inside his bedroom closet when he came home," her mother said. "I waited for him to come upstairs and go to sleep. The TV was on, I could hear it. I figured he must have fallen asleep in front of the TV, so I went downstairs. He was passed out in a chair. He had been drinking. There was a bottle on the floor. I turned up the TV and walked over to the chair. He didn't move or wake up, even when I pressed the gun against his forehead."

CHAPTER 76

In her mind's eye Darby saw Victor Grady's house, the one from her nightmares—the squalid rooms full of hand-me-down furniture and garbage overflowing with beer bottles and fast food. She imagined him coming home from work and ripping clothes from bureau drawers, stuffing them into boxes, garbage bags, whatever he could find. He had to get out of town and get moving because the police were trying to frame him for this business of these missing women.

And here came Sheila creeping down the stairs. Sheila moving quickly across the carpet to where Victor Grady lay passed out in a chair. Her mother, bargain hunter and coupon clipper, pressed the muzzle of the .22 to his forehead and pulled the trigger.

"The gunshot didn't make a lot of noise," Sheila said. "I was putting the gun in Grady's hands when I heard footsteps racing up the basement steps. It was that man, Daniel Boyle. I thought he was with the police, and I was right. He had a badge. It said he was a federal agent."

Darby could see the way it unfolded—the gunshot muffled by the rain and the TV, but Boyle had heard it because he was inside the house, in the basement, planting the evidence. He ran up the stairs thinking Grady had killed himself and found Sheila standing over the body.

"When I saw that badge, I broke down," Sheila said. "All I could think about was you—what would happen to you if I went to jail. I begged him to let me go. He didn't say anything. He just stood there, staring at me. He didn't seem upset or surprised, just . . . blank."

Darby wondered why he hadn't killed her mother or, worse, abducted her. No, abducting her would look too suspicious; so would killing her. Boyle was there to plant evidence to frame Grady and now Grady was dead. Boyle had to think of something. Quick.

Then Darby remembered what Evan had told her about how he had been watching Grady's house. Evan knew Boyle was inside the house, planting evidence. Evan had seen the fire.

"He told me to go home and wait for him to call," her mother said. "He said if I told anyone, I would go to jail. He told me to go through the basement door. I didn't know about the fire until the next morning.

"He called me two days later and told me that he had taken care of Grady. But the fire had burned away most of the evidence. He said he had an idea, something that would keep me out of jail. He said he found evidence, but I had to get it because he was busy working the case. The evidence was buried out in the woods. He gave me directions and told me to get it and bring it home. Then he was going to come by and get it. He wouldn't say what it was. He kept saying not to worry. He understood why I had killed Grady.

"I went out early the next morning with my gardening gloves and a hand trowel. I found a brown paper bag full of clothes— women's clothes—and a picture."

"The one I just showed you."

Shelia nodded. Her lips were pressed together.

"Do you know her name?" Darby asked.

"He never told me."

"What else did you find?"

There was something lurking behind her mother's eyes that made Darby want to run away.

"Was it—" Darby's voice cracked around the words. She swallowed. "Did you find Melanie?"

"Yes."

Darby felt a hot knife slice its way through her stomach.

"I saw her face," Sheila said, the words coming out raw, as if wrapped in barbed wire. "The bag had been buried over Mel's face."

Darby opened her mouth but no words came out.

Sheila broke down. "I didn't know what to do, so I put the dirt back in the hole and went home. He called me early the next morning and I immediately told him about Melanie. He said he knew and told me to go out to the mailbox. There was a videotape in there and a sealed envelope. He told me to play the videotape and tell him what was on it. It was me. Digging out in the woods."

Darby's head was spinning, everything around her a blur of colors.

"The pictures inside the envelope—they were pictures of you at your aunt and uncle's house. He said if I told anyone what happened, if I told anyone what I found out in the woods, he said he'd mail the videotape to the FBI. And then, after I was in jail, he said he would kill you. And I believed him. He had already tried to take you away from me once, I couldn't . . . I wasn't going to risk that."

Sheila pressed a fist against her mouth. "He kept sending pictures to remind me—pictures of you at school, pictures of you playing with your friends. He even put them in Christmas cards. And then he started sending me clothes."

"Clothes? My clothes?"

"No, they were . . . they belonged to other people. Other women. They came in these packages, along with pictures, like this one." Sheila gripped the sheet of paper in her fist. "I didn't know what to do."

"Mom, these clothes, where are they?"

"I thought maybe, just maybe, I could do something with them. Maybe mail them anonymously to the police. I don't know. I don't know what I was thinking, but I hung on to them for a long time."

"Did you tell anyone? Maybe a lawyer?"

Sheila shook her head, cheeks wet from the tears. "I kept thinking what would happened if I came forward. What if I told the police what I did? About how I kept the clothes of all these missing women and said nothing? If I did that, people would have thought you helped me hide the evidence. It didn't matter if it wasn't true. People would think you had something to do with it—look what happened to you when you worked on that rapist case. Your partner planted the evidence, and they thought you helped him. If I came forward, it would have ruined your career."

It took a great effort for Darby to speak. "What did you do with the clothes?"

"They were in the boxes you donated to the church."

"And the pictures?"

"I threw them away."

Darby buried her face in her hands. She saw the pictures of all the missing women, dozens and dozens of them lined up on the bulletin boards at the police station. If her mother had only come forward, then those women would be alive. That knowledge was inside her now, planted like a seed, its roots sinking deeper and deeper.

"I didn't know what to do," Sheila said. "I couldn't change what I did. I thought about going to the police hundreds of times, but all I could think about was you—what he would do to you if I went away. You were more important."

"This place where you found Mel," Darby said.

"I don't know."

"Think about it."

"I've been thinking about it all day, ever since I saw that man's face on TV. I don't remember. It was over twenty years ago."

"Do you remember where you parked the car that morning? How far you went in?"

"No."

"What about the directions Boyle gave you? Did you save them?"

"I threw them away." Sheila was sobbing, the words sounding as though they were being ripped out of her. "Don't hate me. I can't die knowing you hate me."

Darby thought about Mel lying somewhere in the woods, buried beneath the ground, alone, where no one would ever find her.

"Can you forgive me?" Sheila said. "Can you at least do that?"

Darby didn't answer. She was thinking about Mel—Mel standing by the locker, asking Darby to forgive Stacey so they could go back to being friends. Darby wished she had said yes. She wished she had forgiven Stacey. Maybe Mel and Stacey would have stayed home that night. Maybe they would be alive right now. Maybe all those women would.

"Mom . . . oh Jesus . . ."

Darby grabbed her mother's hands—the same hands that had

hugged her were the same hands that had killed Grady and pushed
the dirt back over Melanie. Darby felt the strength in her mother's
grip; it was still there but not for much longer. Soon her mother
would be gone, and Darby would bury her. And one day Darby
would be gone too, buried alone, forgotten. Someday, if there was
such a place as heaven, she hoped she could find Melanie and tell
her how sorry she was. Maybe Mel would forgive her. Maybe
Stacey would, too. Darby wished for that more than anything.

ACKNOWLEDGMENTS

This book could not have been written without the support and insight of criminalist Susan Flaherty. Susan was not only kind enough to take me through her job at the Boston Crime Lab, she patiently answered all of my technical questions. All mistakes are mine.

Thanks to Gene Farrell, who was extremely helpful with police procedural questions, as was Gina Gallo. George Dazkevich helped me understand a lot of the technical information regarding computers without laughing too hard.

Special thanks to Dennis Lehane, for his many words of encouragement over the years, his advice and friendship.

Big thanks go to fellow writers and good friends John Connolly and Gregg Hurwitz, who patiently read through many drafts of this book and offered their advice and insights.

And last but not least, thanks to my publicist and friend, Maggie Griffin, for everything. You're the best, Mags.

Writing—at least my own—is more painful than it is pleasant. *The Missing* was especially difficult, and the following people deserve a special round of thanks for their input and for putting up with me: Jen, Randy Scott, Mark Alves, Ron and Barbara Gondek, Richard Marek, Robert Pépin and Pam Bernstein. Mel Berger helped get me through the rough patches and patiently read through every incarnation of this book. My editor, Emily Bestler, once again gave me insights that made the book better. Thanks, Emily, for your astounding patience.

Thanks are also due to Stephen King's excellent book *On Writing* and the songs of U2, most notably the album *How to Dismantle an Atomic Bomb*, which kept me going through the long months of rewriting.

What you have in your hands is a work of fiction. That means, like James Frey, I made everything up.